The yellowbacks... classics of popular fiction

The yellowjackets or yellowbacks were a great series of bestselling adventure and crime thrillers that had its origins in the mid to late 19th century following on from the 'penny dreadfuls'. They virtually began the mass market revolution of the early 20th century with a clear standard format and imprint/series livery (what would today be called branding). Hodder & Stoughton published the yellow jackets in two main series with series run dates of: 1923-1939 and later 1949-1957.

As the tagline ('where thrillers really began') on the back cover implies, the imprint and series focused on thrillers that were the bestsellers of their time. This current reissue or retro revival if you will, brings back many of these masterpieces, now classics in their own way and extends it further by including key titles from that period that were either great crime or thriller or even general commercial fiction (including sub-genres of noir, horror, gothic, romance, westerns etc) influences of their time. There are some perennial favourites and many rarities either lost or not easily available being revived in the current series. Writers and characters ranged from adventure heroes like Bulldog Drummond, Allan Quatermain, Richard Hannay or the Saint through thriller grandmasters Edgar Wallace and E. Phillips Oppenheim, crime and mystery maestros like Patricia Wentworth, GK Chesterton, Agatha Christie and the Detection club, to western and swashbucklers like Zane Grey, Max Brand, Captain Blood and even romance or general fiction classics like Hermina Black, Denise Robins, Marie Corelli or Stella Morton. These were books that had storytelling at their heart and always entertained.

The yellowbacks had both hardback (with varying design elements) and paperback (which built the series look) versions with the latter still carrying the imprint 'yellowjacket'. The current reissues pay tribute to both and use an amalgam of elements from both editions while retaining the complete yellow (or 'mustard-plaster') livery with the author's name in blue beveled type with a 'simulated emboss' effect and a white outer 'outline', and the book title in black. These reissues retain the distinctive size of the original mass market paperback and follow the three main category variations—the thrillers (crime, westerns, mystery, adventure) had blue lettering for the author's name, while Romance and 'softer general fiction had red; and other categories like humour had green.

For more detail and a full list of titles visit https://www.hachetteindia.com/home/yellowbacks

IN RE: SHERLOCK HOLMES

The Adventures of Solar Pons

IN RE: SHERLOCK HOLMES – THE ADVENTURES OF SOLAR PONS

August William Derleth (February 24, 1909 – July 4, 1971) was an American writer and anthologist. Though best remembered as the first book publisher of the writings of H. P. Lovecraft, and for his own contributions to the Cthulhu Mythos and the cosmic horror genre, as well as his founding of the publisher Arkham House (which did much to bring supernatural fiction into print in hardcover in the US that had only been readily available in the UK), Derleth was a leading American regional writer of his day, as well as prolific in several other genres, including historical fiction, poetry, detective fiction, science fiction, and biography. Derleth wrote more than 150 short stories and more than 100 books during his lifetime.

IN RE: SHERLOCK HOLMES

The Adventures of Solar Pons

August Derleth

HODDER AND STOUGHTON
YELLOW JACKET

hachette
INDIA

(Registered Name: Hachette Book Publishing India Pvt. Ltd.)
An Hachette UK Company www.hachetteindia.com

1

The texts in these editions in most cases have been reprinted as is, with minimal editorial changes and by and large no bowdlerizing for political correctness; though in some editions, a few words and phrases considered archaic, or those considered offensive now, along with archaic punctuation may have been modified in places to make the text more accessible to today's readers. The narratives, language, beliefs, social mores and/or cultural depictions, in these volumes are a reflection of their times and must be viewed as such. They may also contain certain cultural, racial and gender prejudices and stereotypes that may be outdated or clearly wrong then and wrong today; but their removal would be tantamount to claiming these prejudices never existed. The Publisher does not endorse or support those depictions or stereotypes; and these books have been made available for a discerning audience that will read it for entertainment value and a chronicle/record of popular fiction of past times.

Cover design by Priya Singh adapted from the original classic yellowjacket by Hodder & Stoughton.

Cover illustration by Ishan Trivedi.

Series note: Some of the books in the series (unless otherwise credited) may have cover or inside illustrations from the original yellowbacks or early editions, and while full restoration has been attempted, some images may be grainy or faded due to the condition of the original material. The end notes or bonus material or blurb details may have been sourced from the public domain or free use publications such as Wikipedia and attribution is hereby made also allowing similar free use reproduction from here. Sources requiring further specific attribution may write in and further detailing and/or corrections shall be made in subsequent printings/editions.

Reprint specifications may be subject to change including but not limited to finishes, paper, colour sections.

ISBN: 978-93-5731-184-7

Hachette Book Publishing India Pvt. Ltd.
4th & 5th Floors, Corporate Centre,
Plot No. 94, Sector 44, Gurugram - 122 003, India

Typeset in Electra LT STD 10/12.5 pt by Manipal Technologies Limited

Printed and bound in India by Manipal Technologies Limited

MIX
Paper from responsible sources
FSC www.fsc.org FSC™ C043100

CONTENTS

Foreword

In Re: Sherlock Holmes

AUGUST DERLETH
"IN RE: Sherlock Holmes"
With a foreword by VINCENT STARRETT

Foreword

REGARDING SHERLOCK HOLMES BY DAVID MARCUM

In 1928, a college student in Wisconsin named August Derleth (1909-1971) wrote to Sir Arthur Conan Doyle, asking if there would be any more Sherlock Holmes stories. The response was *No*. Then, Derleth ambitiously countered: Could *he* write some? The reply? Another *No*.

Derleth, unsatisfied with that answer, resolved to write Sherlockian-style stories of his own. Flipping ahead on his calendar, he wrote on an upcoming date, *In Re: Sherlock Holmes*. When that date arrived, he duly sat down and recorded "The Adventure of the Black Narcissus".

As Derleth related in "The Beginnings of Solar Pons", contained in *A Praed Street Dossier* (1968), he wrote several Pons stories in quick succession, selling them to pulp magazines and using the profits to buy long-coveted books for his personal library. The Great Depression quickly put an end to his aspirations as the market for Pons stories dried up, and after 1930, it would be years before another Pons story appeared.

In 1944, Ellery Queen's *The Misadventures of Sherlock Holmes* was published, and one of Derleth's Pons stories, "The Adventure of the Norcross Riddle", was included. He was encouraged by such great Sherlockians as Frederic Dannay and Vincent Starrett to make up a full volume of Pons stories. He did so, but – unable to find a publisher – he formed his own imprint, Mycroft & Moran, which continued to publish his own Pons tales, even after his death in 1971.

This first Pons book was called *In Re: Sherlock Holmes – The Adventures of Solar Pons.* The title was taken from that fateful day recorded on his calendar when Derleth had decided to write his own Holmes pastiche. Only three-thousand copies of the handsome little volume were originally published, and it's now an expensive collector's item. If Derleth had been a weaker man, it might have ended there.

In those days, Sir Arthur's sons, Denis Conan Doyle and Adrian Conan Doyle, were attempting to control all aspects of Sherlock Holmes. They were able to force the suppression of *The Misadventures of Sherlock Holmes*, making copies of it a Sherlockian treasure, and one of the reasons that Derleth was unable to find a publisher was because they were all afraid of the Conan Doyle contingent. Derleth was contacted by the Conan Doyle Estate soon after publication of *In Re: Sherlock Holmes* and told to withdraw his Pons book, but he ignored the threats, and the matter withered. Through Derleth's efforts, it became apparent that others besides Sir Arthur could provide – without hindrance – new adventures regarding Sherlock Holmes – and also the Sherlock Holmes of Praed Street, *Solar Pons*.

The stories in this volume are a wonderful introduction to Solar Pons. The narratives cover the period from 1919 when Pons and Parker meet, as related in the introductory "A Word from Dr. Lyndon Parker", to "The Lost Holiday", set in 1931. Also included is "The Black Narcissus", the initial tale recorded by Derleth while still in college, and "The Purloined Periapt", which Derleth himself acknowledged as Pons's most Holmes-like adventure.

For those meeting him for the first time, Pons is very much like Holmes. He solves crimes by using ratiocination and deduction. He plays the violin, smokes pipes, and lounges around his rooms in dressing gowns, as well as occasionally conducting chemical experiments there. His brother, Bancroft Pons, is an important fixture in the British Government, rather like Sherlock Holmes's brother, Mycroft. His landlady is Mrs. Johnson, and his closest contact at Scotland Yard is Inspector Jamison. And his friend and biographer, in the mold of Dr. John H. Watson, is Dr. Lyndon Parker.

While most of Holmes's Canonically-recorded adventures stretch from the 1870's until his retirement to Sussex in 1903, Pons operates in the post-World War I era, with his cases extending from when he and Dr. Parker meet in 1919, after Parker has returned to England following his war service, to 1939, just before the beginning of World War II. Pons had also served in the War, in cryptography, and when the two meet, Parker is disillusioned at the England to which he has returned. However, this is quickly subsumed as the doctor's interest in his new flat-mate and friend grows when he joins Pons on a series of cases that he later records.

For too long, the Solar Pons adventures have been too difficult to obtain. Fortunately, these new editions will change that. Here's how that came about.

In the late 1970's, I had been a Sherlockian for just a few years, having found Mr. Holmes in 1975. Those were the early days of the Sherlockian Golden Age that began with the publication of Nicholas Meyer's *The Seven-Per-Cent Solution* in 1974, and has continued to the present. Meyer reminded people that there were *other* manuscripts by Dr. Watson out there, still waiting to be found – hidden in attics, filed away in libraries, or suppressed by paranoid individuals for a plethora of reasons. These began to be discovered, one by one. Meyer himself subsequently published the amazing *The West End Horror* (1976), along with an explanation as to how the appearance of the first book had led to the second. Other Sherlockian adventures continued to surface – *Hellbirds* by Austin Mitchelson and Nicholas Utechin (1976), *Sherlock Holmes and the Golden Bird* by Frank Thomas (1979), and *Enter the Lion* by Sean Hodel and Michael Wright (1979), to name just a very few. The Great Sherlockian Tapestry, after consisting of mainly just sixty main fibers for so long, was about to get much heavier.

And around that time, someone with great wisdom realized that Solar Pons should be a part of that.

Pinnacle Books began reprinting the Pons adventures in late 1974, just months after the July publication date of *The Seven-Per-Cent Solution.* In the world of book publication, at least in those days when things took forever, Pinnacle certainly didn't jump on the bandwagon at the last minute to get the books immediately into print, after seeing how popular both *The Seven-Per-Cent Solution* and Sherlock Holmes were. Rather, the re-publication of the Pons books must have been planned for quite a while, and it was just their great good luck that their Pons editions appeared right around the same time as Meyer's *The Seven-Per-Cent Solution.* Planning and setup would have required a great deal of effort, as would designing the distinctive "Solar Pons" logo that they would use on both their Pons books, and later on Sherlock Holmes books by Frank Thomas. And most of all, they would have needed time to solicit the wonderful cover paintings of Solar Pons and Dr. Parker.

It was these paintings that drew me into the World of Solar Pons.

Living in a small town in eastern Tennessee, finding things related to Sherlock Holmes in the latter 1970's was difficult. My hometown had both a new and used bookstore, and I regularly scoured them looking for new titles. Strangely, several of my most treasured Sherlockian books from these years were found – not in the bookstores – but on rotating paperback racks at a local drugstore. However, it was at the new bookstore, a few weeks before my fourteenth birthday, that I happened to notice seven books lined up in a row, all featuring a man wearing an Inverness and a deerstalker.

I grabbed them, thinking I'd found a Holmesian motherlode. Instead, I saw that they were about... *Solar Pons?*

I had a limited amount of Sherlockian research material then, and I don't recall if I found anything about Mr. Pons to explain why he dressed like Sherlock Holmes. (I had quite forgotten then, although it came back to me later, that I'd first read a Pons story back in 1973 – before I'd ever truly encountered Sherlock Holmes. That story, "The Grice-Paterson Curse", was contained in an Alfred Hitchcock children's mystery anthology, and I credit how much I enjoyed it then with shaping my brain to be so appreciative when I first read about Holmes a couple of years later, in 1975. That one is still my favorite Pons story to this day.)

Those seven books haunted me, and I somehow managed to hint strongly enough to my parents about it that they ended up being birthday gifts a few weeks later – along with some other cool Holmes books. And so I started reading the Pontine Canon, as it's called – the first of countless times that I've been through it. (It's strange what the brain records. I vividly remember reading and re-reading those books frequently in an Algebra class throughout that year – particularly one story on one certain day, "The Man With the Broken Face". I was lost and behind for a lot of that year in that class, and instead of trying to catch up, I'd pull out a Pons book, which felt much more comfortable. The teacher, who later went on to be beloved and award-winning for some reason that escapes me, knew what I was doing and did nothing to pull me back. Pfui on her! But I did like reading about Pons.)

As time went on, I discovered additional Pinnacle paperbacks, featuring new Pons stories by British horror author

Basil Copper. It was great to have more Pons adventures, but his weren't quite the same. Around the time I started college, I discovered that Copper had edited a complete *Omnibus* of the original Pons stories, and it was the first grown-up purchase that I made with my first real paycheck. (Many thanks to Otto Penzler and The Mysterious Bookshop!) I was thrilled to see that the stories had been arranged in chronological order, which appealed to me. (That kind of thing still does.) Little did I realize then that Copper's editing had been so controversial within the Pons community.

For it turned out that Copper had taken it upon himself to make a number of unjustified changes. For instance, he altered a lot of Derleth's spellings in the *Omnibus* edition from American to British, causing some people to become rather upset. I wasn't too vexed by that, however, as I was there for the stories.

Copper continued to write new Pons stories of his own, published in various editions. I snapped those up, too, very happy to have new visits to 7B Praed Street. Over the years, I noted with some curiosity that Copper's books came to take on a certain implied and vague aspect – just a whiff, just a tinge – that Pons was *his* and not Derleth's.

Meanwhile, the Battered Silicon Dispatch Box published several "lost" Pons items, and also a new and massive set of the complete stories, *The Original Text Solar Pons* (2000), restoring Derleth's original intentions. It was in this book that I read Peter Ruber's extensive essay explaining Copper's changes in greater depth, and the reaction to them within the Ponsian community. However, Ruber didn't mention what I found to be Copper's even more egregious sin. But first a little background...

Over the years, there have been various editions of the Pons books – the originals published by Derleth's Mycroft & Moran imprint, the Pinnacle paperbacks, the Copper *Omnibus*, and the Battered Silicon Dispatch Box *Original Text Omnibus*. (There has also been an incomplete set of a few titles from British publisher Robson Books, Ltd.) Only a few thousand of the original Mycroft & Moran books were ever printed, and for decades, Pons was only known to a loyal group of Sherlockian enthusiasts by way of these very limited volumes. The Pinnacle books made Pons available to a whole generation of 1970's Sherlockians – such as me – that would have never had a chance to meet him otherwise if he'd only remained in the hard-to-find original editions.

As time has passed, however, even these Pinnacle books have become rare and quite expensive. For modern readers who have heard of Pons and are interested in learning more about him, or for those of us who are Pons enthusiasts who wish to introduce him to the larger world, it's been quite difficult, as all editions of his adventures are now quite rare and expensive, unless one is stumbled upon by accident. The Mycroft & Moran books can be purchased online, usually for a substantial investment of money, and the Copper and Battered Silicon Dispatch Box *Omnibi* were always expensive and hard to come by, and now it's only worse. Finally, with these new publications, the Solar Pons books will be available for everyone in easily found and affordable editions. With this, it's hoped that a new wave of Pons interest will spread, particularly within the Sherlockian community which will so appreciate him.

In 2014, my friend and Pons Scholar Bob Byrne floated the idea of having an issue of his online journal, *The Solar Pons Gazette*, contain new Pons stories. Having already written some Sherlock Holmes adventures, I was intrigued, and sat down and wrote a Pons tale – possibly almost as fast as Derleth had written his first Pons story in 1928. It was so much fun that I quickly wrote two more. After that, I pestered Bob for a while, saying that he should explore having the stories published in a real book. (I choose real books every time – none of those ephemeral e-blip books that can disappear in a blink for me!) When that didn't happen, I became more ambitious. Bob put me in touch with Tracy Heron of The August Derleth Society, and he in turn told me how to reach Danielle Hackett, August Derleth's granddaughter. I made my case to be allowed to write a new collection of Pons stories, as authorized by the Estate, and amazingly, I received permission. I introduced Danielle (in this modern email way of meeting people) to Derick Belanger of Belanger Books, and then set about writing some more stories, enough to make a whole book. Amazingly, the first new authorized Pons book in decades, *The Papers of Solar Pons*, was published in 2017.

But that started me thinking...

Realizing that this new book had the possibility to reawaken interest in Pons, or spread the word to those who didn't know about him, I wondered if the original volumes could be reprinted. After all, interest in Sherlock Holmes around the world is at an all-time high, getting the word out by way of the internet has never been easier, and shifts in the publishing paradigm mean that the old ways of grinding through the process for several years before a book appears no longer apply.

The Derleth Estate was very happy with the plan. Now came the hard part.

Being fully aware of the controversy surrounding Copper's *Omnibus* edition, it was evident that that new editions had to be from Derleth's original Mycroft & Moran volumes – for after all, he had edited and approved those himself. Thankfully, modern technology allows for these books to be converted to electronic files with only a moderate amount of pain and toil.

I had several friends, upon hearing of this project, who very graciously offered to help me to "re-type" the original books. I can assure you that, if these books had needed to be re-typed from scratch, there would have been no new editions – at least not as provided by me. Instead, I took a copy of each of the original Mycroft & Moran Pons books, of which I am a very happy and proud owner, and scanned them, converting them all into electronic files. So far so good – that only took several hours of standing at a copy machine, flipping the pages of the books one at a time, and hitting the green button. (And sometimes re-doing it if a scanned page had a gremlin or two.)

After that, I used a text conversion software to turn the scans into a Word document. That raw text then had to be converted into another, more easily fixed, Word document. Then came the actual fixing. Early on, it was decided to try and make the new editions look as much like the originals as possible. Therefore, many inconsistent things that niggled me as an editor-type remain in the finished product, because they were that way in the originals. For instance, Derleth's punctuation improved quite a bit from his early books to the latter – but it was very tempting to start fixing his punctuation in the earlier books. If you see something that looks not-quite-right, chances are it was that way in the original books.

There were times that a letter or a note, as quoted in a story, would be indented, while on other occasions it would simply be a part of the paragraph. I wanted to set up all of those letters and notes in a consistent way throughout the various books, but instead I kept them as they had appeared in the original editions, no matter how much the style varied from story to story. Finally, some of the racial stereotyping from those stories would not be written that way today. However, these are historical documents of sorts, and as such, they are presented as written, with the understanding that times have changed, and hopefully we have a greater awareness now than before.

Since the early 1980's, whenever I've re-read the Pons stories – and I've done so many times – it's been by way of the Copper

Omnibus editions. I enjoyed having them all in one place in two matching handsome and heavy books, and I was very pleased that they were rearranged for reading in chronological order. The fixing of British-versus-American spelling didn't bother me a bit. This time, as part of the process to prepare the converted-to-text files, I was reading the stories as they had originally appeared, in the order that they had been published in the original volumes. I hadn't done it that way for years. The conversion process captures everything, and that means some items do have to be corrected. For instance, when setting up for printing, original books from the old days often *split* words at the end of a line with hyphens, whereas modern computer programs *wrap* the text, allowing for hyphens to be ignored. When converting the text of the original books, the program picked up every one of those end-of-line hyphens and split words, and they all had to be found and removed. Likewise, the text-conversion program ignores words that are italicized in the original, and these each have to be relocated and re-italicized. (However, in some cases, Derleth himself was inconsistent, italicizing a word, such as a book title or the name of a ship, at one point in a story, and not at a later point. That had to be verified too.)

I have long been a chronologicist, organizing all of the thousands of traditional Sherlock Holmes stories that I've collected and read into a massive Holmes Chronology, breaking various adventures (book, story, chapter, and paragraph) down into year, month, day, and even hour to form a *complete* life of Holmes, from birth to death, covering both the Holmes Canon and traditional pastiches. It was inevitable that I would do the same with Pons. For several decades, I've had a satisfying Pons Chronology as well, based on research by various individuals, and largely on Copper's arrangement of the stories within his *Omnibus* – with a few disagreements. By re-reading the original stories in their original form, for the first time in years, I realized that, in addition to changing spelling, Copper had committed – as referred to earlier – a far bigger sin.

I discovered as I re-read the original stories for this project that a number of them weren't matching up with my long-established Pons Chronology, based a great deal upon Copper's arrangement in his *Omnibus*. Some of the stories from the originals would give a specific date that would be a whole decade different from where I had placed the story in my own chronology. A quick check against Copper's *Omnibus* revealed that he had actually changed these dates in his revisions, sometimes shifting from the 1920's to the 1930's, a whole decade, in order to place the story where he thought that it ought to go. Worse, he sometimes eliminated a whole sentence from an original story if it contradicted his placement of that story within his *Omnibus*.

As a chronologist, I was horrified and sickened. This affront wasn't mentioned in Ruber's 2000 essay explaining why Ponsians were irritated with Copper. I can't believe that this wasn't noticed before.

There has always been ample material for the chronologist with the Pons books, even without these changes. Granted, the original versions, as written, open up a lot of problems and contradictions about when various stories occur that Copper smoothed out – apparently without anyone noticing. For this reason, and many others, I'm very glad and proud that the original Solar Pons adventures, as originally published by Derleth, are being presented here in these new volumes for a new generation.

David Marcum
"The Obrisset Snuffbox", PSI
(excerpted from the Belanger edition reissues)

In Re: Sherlock Holmes

The Adventures of Solar Pons

IN RE: SHERLOCK HOLMES - BY VINCENT STARRETT

As a boy August Derleth couldn't get enough Sherlock Holmes stories; there were not enough of them in the world to satisfy his craving for the society of the fascinating disentangler of Upper Baker Street. When he had read them all, many times over, and being then nineteen years of age, he wrote to Sir Arthur Conan Doyle setting forth his reasonable complaint. Are you or are you not, he courteously asked the great storyteller, going to write any more stories about Sherlock Holmes?

Sir Arthur made no promises in his good-humored reply; so there and then young Mr. Derleth determined to carry on the tradition himself. A desk calendar stood at his elbow; he stabbed a finger into its pages at random and scribbled a note to himself: "*In re – Sherlock Holmes*." On that day, when it should have arrived, he told himself, he would write a story in imitation of the Master.

The precise date of this impatient episode is lost to literary chronicle with the memorandum; but Derleth was attending the University of Wisconsin at the time, and when the day came he did actually sit down and write *The Adventure of the Black Narcissus*, which you will find in this book. I don't know how he hit on the name Solar Pons – probably he considered a lot of names before he found one that pleased him. The story was sold immediately, however, to Harold Hersey, and published in the Dragnet Magazine, a development that inspired the youthful author to new feats of imitation. There followed in rapid succession the adventures of *The Missing Tenants*, *The Broken Chessman*, *The Late Mr. Faversham*, *The Limping Man*, and *The Black Cardinal*. On one red-letter day, a day of gilt and glory, the young man dashed off three Solar Pons adventures at a sitting and two of them survive in this collection, *The Norcross Riddle* and *The Three Red Dwarfs*.

That is the true story of the birth of Solar Pons; he was – as it were – an ectoplasmic emanation of his great prototype, and his adventures are pure pastiche. As such we acknowledge them gratefully. By we, I mean those frantic and incurable Sherlockians who, with August Derleth, deplore the paucity of canonical entertainments and view without alarm the mounting uproar of our hero's triumph, which already has called forth so garrulous a stream of apocryphal recollections. It is impossible not to wonder about those many untold tales half-promised by the exasperating Watson; and it is the obvious duty of writers with information concerning them, or with other adventures to relate, to give them to the world. No doubt we should rather have more of the great originals, but we accept the imitations, *faute de mieux*, to satisfy a normal appetite. And we accept them with enthusiasm. They are the work of affectionate minds and hands. There is no intention to deceive. These stories, and others in their field, are intended only to please. They are nostalgic reminders of vanished days and nights in Baker Street.

The scheme of Derleth's "sequels" is more than just a little reminiscent; it is frankly borrowed. Dr. Lyndon Parker returns to London just in time for this book to become possible. Solar Pons, the "Sherlock Holmes of Praed Street," is even then looking about him for some amiable fellow to act as his Watson; he loses no time in persuading the doctor to share the Pontine lodgings. Their meeting is right out of *A Study in Scarlet*:

"Fine color," says Pons crisply, coming to a stand beside the doctor's restaurant table. "Not long back from Africa, I see.

"Two days."

"Your scarab pin suggests Egypt and, if I am not mistaken, the envelope on which you have been writing is one of Shepheard's."

He is not mistaken, you may be sure; and almost immediately the game is afoot. One comes upon the rest of the cast, from time to time, without surprise. Mrs. Johnson is their estimable and "long-suffering" landlady, and Baron Ennesfred Kroll, that "arch-criminal" whose hand Pons does not fail to recognize in several adventures, makes an admirable Professor Moriarty. The "Baker Street Irregulars," too, are in at least one of the tales (not the Morleian conversation club, but the original gamins), and so is the collection of scrapbooks, whose indexing still goes forward. One is happily moved by some of the reminiscent story-openings; for example, this one:

"When I look over my notes on the cases that engaged Solar Pons' attention during the decade begun in 1919, I find many amazing adventures whose details ought to be placed before the public."

And there is some use of Watson's effective and annoying trick of mentioning "other cases" unrecorded in the volume at hand. These include "the perplexing affair of the Mumbles, known to the public for many months as the Swansea Mystery," and "that unbelievable conspiracy which threatened to undermine the Papacy and overthrow half the governments of Europe." Perhaps Derleth intends to tell us more about these little matters some other time – although that "unbelievable conspiracy" sounds a bit like what the war correspondents have been telling us for a number of months.

One likes the author's trick of using the exact words and phrases of the original saga, when it suits his purpose, and greets with a smile of pleasure such familiar lines as:

"Dark waters, Parker, dark waters!"

"Come, Parker! The game is afoot."

"'Elementary,' I said." (A nice touch that, to hand the familiar word to Parker.)

As to the stories Derleth has imagined, some are better than others, which was true also, I seem to recall, of the stories written by Sir Arthur Conan Doyle. My own favorite is *The Adventure of the Late Mr. Faversham*, largely, I think, because it is a satisfying telling of one of the tales Watson once promised to tell and never told. I had often wondered profoundly about the incredible mystery of "Mr. James Phillimore, who, stepping back into his own house to get his umbrella, was never more seen in this world," one of Watson's most provocative hints. Ellery Queen had a go at this problem, too, as readers of *The Misadventures of Sherlock Holmes* are aware; so now we have two versions of the incident, and I hope everybody is happy. The "deduction" involved in this episode in the career of Mr. Solar Pons seems to me in the best tradition; but, indeed, there is a lot of quite plausible deduction in all these tales. Note particularly that in the first part of *The Adventure of the Norcross Riddle*.

Although these stories by August Derleth are frankly and seriously intentioned pastiches, I wonder if I am right in thinking I find in them a hint – just a mild flavor – of burlesque. Or is something of the sort inevitable in any imitation? Just the faintest suggestion of a tongue in the auctorial cheek is all I am supposing, and perhaps I am imagining it. But I hope not, and I don't think so, for it seems to me the best pastiches must have just that remote savor of affectionate spoofing.

Solar Pons is not a caricature of Sherlock Holmes. He is, rather, a clever impersonator, with a twinkle in his eye, which tells us that he knows he is not Sherlock Holmes, and knows that we know it, but that he hopes we will like him anyway for what he symbolizes.

VINCENT STARRETT

A WORD FROM - DR. LYNDON PARKER

The way in which I first made the acquaintance of Mr. Solar Pons, who was destined to introduce me to many interesting adventures in crime detection, was exceedingly prosaic. Yet it was not without those elements suggestive of what was to come. Though it took place almost thirty years ago, the memory of that meeting is as clear in mind as if it had taken place yesterday.

I had been sitting for some time in a pub not far from Paddington Station, ruefully reflecting that the London to which I had returned after the first World War was not the city I had left, when a tall, thin gentleman wearing an Inverness cape and a rakish cap with a visor on it, strode casually into the place. I was struck at once by his appearance: the thin, almost feral face; the sharp, keen dark eyes with their heavy, but not bushy brows; the thin lips and the leanness of the face in general – all these things interested me both from a personal and a medical standpoint, and I looked up from the envelope upon which I had been writing to follow the fellow with my eyes across the floor to the bar.

A waiter, who was wiping tables next to me, noticed my interest and came over. "Sherlock Holmes," he said. "That's who he is. 'The Sherlock Holmes of Praed Street,' is what the papers call him. His real name's Solar Pons. Ain't much choice between the two, eh?"

Pons had had a few words with the man behind the bar and now turned to look idly over the room. I looked away as

I saw that his glance was about to fall on me, and I felt him examining me from head to toe. I felt, rather than saw, that he was walking over toward my table, and in a few moments he came to stand beside my bag on the floor next to my chair.

"Fine color," he said crisply. "Not long back from Africa, I see.

"Two days."

"Your scarab pin suggests Egypt and, if I'm not mistaken, the envelope on which you have been writing is one of Shepheard's. From Cairo, then."

"On the ship *Ishtar*."

"At the East India Docks."

I looked up and he smiled genially.

"But, really, you know, my dear fellow – London is not as bad as all that."

"I should not like to think so," I answered him, without at once realizing that I had given him no clue to my thoughts.

"Obviously you have been walking considerably. In search of lodgings, no doubt."

"Yes."

"And you are disappointed. But it is not so much London that has changed, as it is the tempo of living here, and the time. You are needlessly morose. Besides, we have a need for good medical men. I observe your peacetime profession by the bag you are carrying – which is clearly a discarded medical kit."

By this time Mr. Solar Pons had, I confess, captivated me completely. I introduced myself and invited him to sit down. "No, it is you who must be my guest," said he.

He went on to say that he had recently been contemplating sharing his own lodgings, and, one thing leading to another, before long I was on my way at his side to Number 7, Praed Street, which was to remain my home and office for many years.

I soon learned that I had taken up my abode with a private detective of no mean ability, a man who, openly espousing the old-fashioned methods of ratiocination and deduction, had already established for himself a reputation for skill and intelligent sleuthing for which he was held in high regard by many persons connected with Scotland Yard and His Majesty's Government.

It was not long, too, before I became fascinated by the number and variety of Solar Pons' adventures, quite apart from his equally varied interests, which included occult lore and scientific treatises on the nature of evidence, as well as chess and an addiction to good music of all kinds, whether primitive or classic, romantic or modern. And within a few months I had begun to take notes on Pons' cases, at first for my own edification, the better to observe his methods, and then ultimately because I felt that some day these curious adventures might quite conceivably be of interest to a larger public, if presented in some more readable fashion.

I have accordingly at last brought myself to select at random twelve of Solar Pons' adventures, and I present them herewith, in the hope that readers may enjoy these accounts as much as I enjoyed taking part in the cases about which they are written.

London, 1944

LYNDON PARKER, *M.D.*

I

THE ADVENTURE OF THE FRIGHTENED BARONET

From the chess problem in which he had been absorbed, Solar Pons slowly raised his head, cocked a little, and smiled. His fingers relinquished their hold upon the knight; he leaned back.

"Yes, yes, as I thought," he murmured, "we are about to have company."

London was lost in fog, a heavy autumnal curtain shutting the city away from our lodgings in Praed Street, and at first there was only the distant hum of diminished traffic that was the pulse of the city, and the several small noises of water dropping; then I heard the curiously muffled sound of hoofbeats, traveling a short distance, stopping, then coming forward again.

"Surely he is looking for Number 7," observed Pons with satisfaction, for time had been pressing heavily on his hands since the bizarre adventure of the Octagon House. "To whom else would he address himself at this hour of the night? Nor is it amiss to surmise that he has come up from the country not far from London; horse-drawn carriages are uncommon indeed within the city. Clearly now," he went on, listening intently, "he has got down just a few doors away; he has gone up to the door, flashed his light on the number. No, that is not number seven; yet, number seven cannot be far away. Hear him! He returns to his carriage – but he does not get in; no, he is too close to the desired address for that – he leads his horse down the street a few doors, and here he is.

I looked toward the night bell, back to Pons' expectant features, marking his keen eyes, his aquiline nose, his firm, thin-lipped mouth, touched still by his smile, and once more at the bell. On the instant it jangled. Pons stepped to the speaking tube and invited our visitor to come up, and in a few moments there was a tap on the door giving to our lodgings. I strode across the room and opened it.

Across the threshold stepped a short, stout, sturdily built gentleman of approximately sixty years of age, swarthy of skin, heavily bearded, and still dark haired; he fixed his small glittering eyes on Pons, bowed curtly, and handed him an envelope. It was unsealed.

I crowded up to Pons and looked over his shoulder at the card he took from the envelope. *Alexander Taber Rowan, K.C.B. Chiltern Manor*. Pons turned the card over. In a shaky script someone had scrawled thereon: *"For God's sake, come! I can't stand it much longer."* I flashed a glance of inquiry at Pons, and saw that his eyes had lit up with the excitement of the chase.

"Late of His Majesty's Service, attached to the staff of the Viceroy of India," said Pons, returning the card to the envelope and dropping both to the table. He looked across the lamplight to where Sir Alexander's man stood, fingering his cap.

"I am Kennerly, sir."

"What is it?" asked Pons.

"It's the curse of the stone, Mr. Pons."

His voice was gruff but not discourteous. What he said apparently conveyed something to Pons, though it meant nothing to me, and I saw that at the moment at least Pons had no intention of enlightening me. He nodded.

"You were sent to bring us?"

"If possible."

"Good. We'll be with you in a few moments."

While Pons got into his rainproof, I saw him scrutinizing Kennerly with marked interest.

"A veteran of India yourself, I see," he said presently.

"Yes, sir."

"Of great personal service to the Maharajah of Indore."

"I saved his life, sir."

"Very likely in the encounter in which you lost your foot."

"Yes, sir."

By this time Pons was ready; he turned to me, his eyes twinkling at the sight of my obvious efforts to observe the bases for his deductions and seeing only the telltale smoothness of the shoe which betrayed the lack of a foot. "Coming, Parker?"

We descended the stairs after leaving a message for Mrs. Johnson, our landlady, and passed into the thick fog which lent to Pons and Kennerly a shadowy, almost intangible being. The carriage loomed abruptly out of the night. We entered it. Kennerly mounted before us; and soon we were traveling westward through London in the direction of the Chiltern Hills. Our pace was necessarily slow, but the horse seemed to proceed with an uncanny instinct and, as far as I could determine, no errors in direction were made.

Pons sat deep in thought, his visored cap low over his face, and I hesitated to disturb him; yet I rankled within at my own inability to follow his deductions, and finally I could contain myself no longer.

"Doubtless it is a most elementary matter, but how in the devil did you know this fellow is a veteran of India?"

"Come, come, Parker – it should be obvious. For one thing, his military bearing; for another, he is the trusted servant of the baronet. What more likely than that he was his orderly in service? But, primarily, he wears a ring he could have got only in India."

"I can follow the observation about the lost foot easily enough, but what about his service to the Maharajah of Indore?"

"The ring he wears bears the crest of the Maharajah. Such rings are not for sale. It follows therefore that he must have been given it by the Maharajah himself. Since such a ring is not given simply as a gift, for it is too personal, but rather as a mark of esteem, it is not at all a shot in the dark to assume that our visitor did the Maharajah a personal service of such vital importance that nothing short of the crested ring would satisfy the Maharajah's sense of gratitude."

"And the card?" I asked, determined that nothing should escape me. "What did you make of that?"

"Only that our client is badly frightened, that his sending for me is done with the knowledge of no one else in the household save this man, that the matter is one in which he hesitates to seek police protection, very probably because of the attendant publicity, and that he has been drinking to keep up his nerve. From what his man has said, I take it that something has come up to remind him that the Eye of Siva which he acquired some thirty years ago during a campaign in the hill country of India was, after all, cursed, and that the fruits of this curse are now being visited upon him."

I took a deep breath and considered. "The script and what he writes betray some fright," I ventured.

"Capital! Though obvious."

"But the other matters – ?"

"He comes to us in preference to the police, and he comes at an hour which indicates secrecy; since he himself has nothing to fear from us, clearly he believes his family will disapprove of his sending for us. He therefore summons us at a time when he can present us to his household in fact, as a *fait accompli*. It is, further, not ill-advised to assume that there are troubled waters there. Finally, there was the distinct odor of rum about his card."

It was in the early hours of the morning that we arrived at Chiltern Manor in the low rolling country immediately adjacent to the hills which gave the house its name. We had ridden out of the fog not far from the environs of London and a waning moon shone down, shedding its pale light upon the wooded country and fields through which we now rode. The estate lay behind a high old stone wall, almost totally concealed by a heavy growth of vines, and surrounded by many trees and bushes. Rowan's man drove through a gate in the side-wall and directly around to the carriage sheds, where he left horse and carriage standing to lead us into the house, which rose up from among trees, an old stone building not without Victorian magnificence, at this early morning hour dark and sombre save for a faint glimmer of yellow light from a window on the second floor.

I could not help observing that we entered the house by a side entrance, and that Kennerly's movements were marked by a singular care, thus confirming Pons' surmise that Rowan had sent for us in secret; moreover, the entrance gave almost at once upon a narrow staircase, which clearly led up between the wall and a room below, almost a part of the wall as it were, for we were forced to proceed in single file by the small light of a pocket flash which Kennerly used to illumine the stairs.

Pons' client waited in his own rooms. The pale light shed by the single lamp burning there presently disclosed him, an elderly man, deep in an upholstered chair, and wrapped in a steamer rug, as if for warmth. His chin rested upon his chest, and his sunken eyes looked at us from over his pince-nez. A thin moustache and beard, both white, in singular contrast to Kennerly's black growth, and a fringe of white hair seen from under the black skull-cap he wore, ornamented his thin, ascetic face, white within the darkness of his immediate environment.

"Ah, Mr. Pons!" he said in a cultured, well-modulated voice. "I had hoped Kennerly could bring you." He glanced interrogatively at me, and Pons introduced me as his assistant. "I am afraid my message may have seemed somewhat incoherent to you."

"Not at all," responded Pons. "In fact, it is perfectly clear that something has happened to make you believe there may after all be something more than legend to the curse on the Eye of Siva."

A wan smile touched the baronet's lips. "I am reassured. I made no mistake in sending for you."

"Let us hope that we may be able to justify your confidence," said Pons quietly. "However, if I remember rightly, the stone is now in the British Museum."

"It has been there for twenty-five years." He shrugged. "But apparently this has made no difference. I will not attempt to deny that I am badly frightened, Mr. Pons. Approximately two months ago the first of these mysterious events took place. I thought initially that I was the subject of a practical joke in the worst possible taste. The occasion was the Naval Conference; since Chiltern Manor is not too far from London, friends of mine in the diplomatic service in Britain for the Conference called on me. At the end of one of those days, I found a card in the tray. It read, *Puranas Mahadeva*. I regret that at the moment the significance of this did not occur to me; I assumed that it had been left by some minor official whom I had met at Delhi and forgotten.

"That night, Mr. Pons," he went on after a short pause, his eyes glittering strangely now, and his breath coming a little faster, testifying to his excitement at the memory of the incident he was about to relate, "that night, as I was preparing to retire, I was summoned from my work by a tap on my door and I stepped into the hall. No one was there. Now, sir, since I am as familiar with this house by night as by day, I did not turn up the light. I stepped out into the hallway, and had begun to walk down towards the stairs when my attention was attracted to what appeared to be a spot of illumination low on the floor along the wall; at second glance, I saw that it was moving steadily before me. And then, sir, I observed that it was not a light at all – but a kind of spectral image. Mr. Pons, *it was the image of Siva, the Destroyer!* Perfect in every detail, a miniature spectre! I was startled. I was not immediately disturbed; I felt I had experienced an illusion of some kind, and quickly turned on the lights. There was nothing in sight, nothing whatever. I examined the wall, the floor – nothing. I returned to my rooms somewhat shaken, thinking naturally of that old curse; an article not long before in the feature section of an American newspaper had brought all those old painful memories back; and it was then that it struck me with the force of a thunderclap what those words on the calling card stood for: *Puranas* is the title of Hindu scriptures; and *Mahadeva* is a less-widely known name for Siva! I took out the card at once – or perhaps I had better say, sir, that I took out the one I thought was the card I wanted. Mr. Pons – there was nothing whatever on it; it was perfectly blank; there was nothing to show that a single letter of printing had ever been on it!"

"Ah," murmured Pons delightedly.

"That was the beginning of a series of events which I am unable to explain save as the malign evidence of the workings of that ancient curse! The pattern has been repeated endlessly; the tap on the door, the strange apparition – nor has this been all; I have seen the spectre with increasing frequency on the top of the estate wall on the north and in other places where I would not have expected to come upon it. Moreover, within the past few nights, events have taken a more serious turn; I have awakened to the sound of voices warning me to prepare for death; I have also heard the strange whistles the Sepoys used to give; I am ashamed to confess that I have had recourse to rum to steady my nerves. It is the firm conviction of the family that I am losing my mind, for no one else has seen any of these apparitions, and they have held out against me in summoning help from outside, no doubt for fear of any publicity which might attend having you here. But last night the mastiff which guards the north gate vanished without a sound; I have no speculation as to what may have happened to him. And now I am convinced that at last the curse on the stone has become active again."

"Why?"

"You know the story of the stone, Mr. Pons. How the priests in that temple opposed the Maharajah – indeed, they made their temple a base of operations. We destroyed the temple, and the Eye of Siva was a prize of war; it is true that in the melee attendant upon the destruction of the temple, one of the guardian priests was slain. The newspapers will have it that it was this man who put a curse upon the stone, but the fact is that the only curse connected with it was a general and ancient curse upon anyone who desecrated the temple; it is really not attached to the stone at all. However, as you know, the Maharajah died shortly thereafter, three of the soldiers accompanying me into the temple died within a year, and four months ago – the *raison d'être* for that American newspaper article – Sir James McLeen, who commanded my right wing in that engagement, fell to his death under mysterious circumstances. These events, looked upon in the light of that ancient curse, naturally point to but one conclusion – to which I did not come until after I had begun to witness these manifestations; only then did the other events fall into their place in the pattern."

"You suggest that the design is to retrieve the Eye of Siva?"

"Not alone that, but to punish those responsible for the destruction of that temple." He touched his lips with his tongue, nervously. "But I feel that you do not put much credence in the curse, Mr. Pons."

Pons smiled drily. "Let us say rather that I am at the moment concerned only with the problem of which aspect of the matter is cause, and which is effect. I take it you own more than one dog."

"Yes, of course."

"You have said you have witnessed the apparition of Siva on the estate wall. Was its appearance accompanied by any demonstration from the dogs?"

"None."

"Does this suggest nothing to you?"

"Only that whatever is out there is meant for me alone. The Hindus have many very strange beliefs, Mr. Pons, and stranger things than this have happened in India, without any explanation."

"I have some acquaintance with the lore and legends of India," replied Pons absently. "Have you ever seen the spectre of Siva in someone else's company?"

"Yes, on one occasion my brother Ransom was with me. On another, my daughter's fiancé, Geoffrey Saring. Neither of them was able to see anything. Yet the thing was as plain to me as you are, sitting there."

"Your man Kennerly has never seen it?"

"No."

Pons sat for a few moments with his eyes closed, touching the lobe of his left ear thoughtfully with his thumb and forefinger. Presently he gazed at the apprehensive baronet once more. "I wish you would instruct Kennerly to answer any questions I put to him."

"It shall be done."

"Further, I would like to have you show me approximately the space in the hallway covered by the apparition at such times as you have seen it."

Without a word the old man got up. Pulling his steamer rug around him, he walked a little unsteadily over to the door, threw it open, and stepped hesitantly into the hall. He turned up the light and pointed to the base board along the farther wall.

"Beginning there, Mr. Pons – and going for a distance of twenty to thirty feet – I cannot be sure, which, but in any case it varies."

"At which end?"

"It is usually at this end."

"Who occupies this floor besides yourself?"

"My daughter's rooms are across the hall. Down the hall – Geoffrey Saring, next to him my brother Ransom, then my sister Megan's room; and then across, a guest room of some dimensions; Kennerly has got it ready for you and Dr. Parker."

Pons stood in the hall, hands clasped behind him, his cap back on his head, gazing thoughtfully along the wall where it joined the floor, which, for a distance of approximately a foot from the wall, was not covered by carpet. He stood thus for perhaps three or four minutes; then he turned abruptly, as if dismissing the hall, and said that except for one thing, there was nothing further he could do tonight. And that one? inquired the baronet.

"I want to have a talk with Kennerly, if you will send him to our room."

"Certainly." The baronet hesitated briefly; then a look of great anxiety crept into his eyes; he put one trembling hand on Pons' shoulder, and said, "I hope you will be able to explain this strange mystery, sir. I am close to the edge."

"We shall see," said Pons imperturbably.

We entered our room and found everything laid out for us with the skill and comprehension possessed only by someone who had served in the capacity of an orderly for many years. Pons threw himself into a chair without pausing to remove anything but his rainproof and his cap; he looked quizzically over at me, but his mouth was grim.

"This is devil's work, Parker."

"You attach no importance to the curse, then?"

"I attach every importance to it, on the contrary; it is the most important single factor in the matter."

"Indeed! You did not let Sir Alexander think so."

"There is time for that, Parker."

I was about to say more when Pons cautioned me to be silent, rising from his chair and moving with cat-like quiet towards the door.

"Kennerly," I whispered.

"Kennerly's slight limp is distinctive in his walk," replied Pons in an equally low voice. "It is not Kennerly."

There was a quick, rustling tap on our door. Pons threw it open.

A young woman stood there, her ash-blonde hair wild, one hand almost protectively in the pocket of her dressing *saque*, the other holding it close about her neck. Her dark eyes darted from one to the other of us before she stepped into the room, closed the door, and stood with her back against it, her mouth working a little, a frown heavy on her brow.

"It *is* Mr. Solar Pons, isn't it?" she said, looking at Pons.

"At your service," replied Pons.

"I have seen your picture in the papers often enough," she said bitterly. "Oh, Mr. Pons – surely you are not going to make my poor father's madness the subject of scandal? I beg you to go away, to say nothing..."

"I am not in the habit of announcing myself to the press, Miss Rowan."

"I'm sorry. But it is a painful thing to witness the decay of a man like my father – quite apart from his being, after all, my father."

"You are convinced his mind is going?"

"I wish I were not. But there is no other explanation. He has seen things neither Uncle Ransom nor Geoffrey saw when he was with them; it isn't the mere hallucinations alone, but the added fact that they prey upon his mind and fill him with fear. He has for some years suffered from a heart weakened by coronary trouble, and now that his mind has given way, the end is only a matter of time."

"Perhaps I may be able to relieve him," said Pons.

"If only you could!" she said earnestly. "But I'm afraid it is too late. I feel only that your being here will give him a false hope which, when it is destroyed, will affect him all the more adversely."

"I understand that he suggested calling in outside help and that the members of his household opposed this."

"Yes, I did. So did my brother, who was visiting us at that time. So did my aunt. Only Geoffrey and Uncle Ransom seemed to think it a good idea, and I could see that my uncle was none too keen, for all that."

"Well, then, I promise you I shall not be here long." Thus assured, Miss Rowan left us. Pons glanced at me curiously.

"Would you say she was sincere, Parker?"

"Undoubtedly."

"So I thought."

"Perhaps, after all..."

Pons smiled. "Did Sir Alexander strike you as a man who was mentally deranged?"

"Oh, you cannot make such generalizations, Pons. He is certainly under great mental stress. But many madmen are perfectly normal to all but the experienced eye; my eye is hardly experienced to such a degree."

"Let us just ask Kennerly what he thinks," suggested Pons.

The sound of Kennerly's footsteps paused, he knocked on the door, and, in response to Pons' invitation, came in. Like Miss Rowan, he stood with his back against the door until bidden to come forward and sit down.

"I was told to answer some questions, sir," he said in a voice that was courteous without being servile, and toneless without being colorless.

"Why, Dr. Parker has a question to put to you first of all, Kennerly."

Pons turned to me, and thus prodded, I put the question: did Kennerly think that Sir Alexander was losing his mind?

Kennerly favored me with a hostile, stony stare. "I do not think so," he said coldly.

Pons said nothing to this. "Now, then, Kennerly – to what extent does Ransom Rowan live on his brother's bounty?" Kennerly was clearly taken aback by the personal nature of Pons' question, but in a moment, reflecting that he had been instructed to answer any questions Pons asked, he rallied. He spoke cautiously. "Sir Alexander does give Ransom money from time to time."

"How does he spend it?"

Kennerly looked squarely at Pons. "He gambles."

"Ransom is constantly in need, then. What about Miss Rowan?"

"She adores her father sir, and he is very fond of her. But not so fond as to be blinded by her."

"Intimating that he stands in her way occasionally. How?"

"He has not yet given his consent to her marriage."

"She hardly needs his consent, does she?"

"Not necessarily. But Miss Winifred is that kind of girl, she will not do anything against her father's wish."

"He does not trust Mr. Saring?"

"Sir Alexander is a hard man to please."

"And his son?"

"Philip is wilful and determined to have his own way. Sir Alexander is difficult to get along with in many ways, though I have always managed to do my best for him, and have no reason whatever to complain."

"Philip wishes his own way about what?"

"His inheritance, sir. He has devised some way of obtaining it before his father's death so that he will not have to pay so much tax to the Crown."

"And Sir Alexander's sister?"

"Miss Megan is a very strong-willed woman."

"They do not get along?"

"I think they get along as well as any sister and brother do, sir."

"You have seen none of these phenomena reported by Sir Alexander?" inquired Pons then.

"Nothing whatever. But the dog is missing."

"Yes, the dog is missing. Sir Alexander says he did not make a sound."

"Aye. So he thinks. But he did call once – it wasn't pretty, sir."

"Yes, it is plain that he was lured off by someone whom he had no reason to fear, and killed. He cried out when he was slain. That is what you want to say, is it not, Kennerly?"

"It might be."

"Come, come, Kennerly. We are both working towards the same end. But enough – you may go."

I could not help observing after he had gone, that Kennerly was not only reluctant to speak but singularly uncommunicative.

"Say rather he is very loyal," replied Pons. "He has managed to say enough. Sir Alexander is no martinet, but he is difficult. On the other hand, his brother Ransom is a wastrel, his son Philip is none too honorable, his sister has aspects of the termagent. Sir Alexander is crochety, distrustful, neurotic: so much is plain. Only for Winifred does Kennerly have the same kind of respect and devotion he has for the old man."

I observed that Kennerly had said nothing whatever about Kennerly.

"There was no need to. I had already seen all that I needed to see about him; and he was well aware of that. Now then," he went on, "let us just step out into the hall for a moment."

"The light switch is up the hall a way," I said, remembering its place.

"If it were light I wanted, we could well wait until after dawn," said Pons cryptically.

Accordingly, we went out into the darkness of the hall; there we stood for a few moments until our eyes grew accustomed to the darkness. Then Pons walked up toward Sir Alexander's rooms, got down on his knees, and began to scrutinize the baseboard of the wall with great preoccupation.

"What in the world can you hope to see without a light?" I demanded in a whisper.

"I can see very well," replied Pons imperturbably.

I came down on my knees beside him. "What is it?"

Here and there the wall-board and the floor showed obvious color changes which, observed at this proximity, were curious and startling, for the effect of these strange streaks and marks was as if a faint illumination were given off into the darkness.

"Elementary, my dear Parker," said Pons, rising and walking slowly down the hall, only to sink to his knees again to crawl from one of the doors to another opening off the hall there.

I was nettled, but it was not until we had returned to our room that I asked Pons what he made of it.

"You know my methods, Parker. The whole problem is as plain as a pikestaff, and it only remains for us to obtain sufficient evidence to convince Sir Alexander. I fancy that our presence will bring matters to a climax rapidly enough."

"You have seen something that has escaped me!" I cried.

Pons chuckled. "Perhaps you have not pursued the facts to their obvious conclusion. Or, even more likely, you have started out on a wrong premise. We shall see in good time. Now let us get a little sleep, for I daresay we have a busy day ahead of us."

Our day began before breakfast, when Pons woke me and suggested that we might walk out upon the gorse and bracken-grown rolling country surrounding the estate of Sir Alexander. Clouds loured in the heavens, but the way was pleasant enough despite the absence of the sun. It was soon clear, however, that Pons was not idling away time. We slipped out of the house and left the estate behind us by way of the north gate, from which point Pons began what initially appeared to be an aimless angling away, but proved ultimately to be only one of a series of concentric circles which he described with the utmost casualness, while he sought diligently for broken ground, so that it soon became obvious to me that he was on the track of the missing dog.

The country away from the north gate was fairly open, apart from the gorse and bracken which covered it, and a kind of heather with which I was unfamiliar in these latitudes, and it was not long before our peregrinations ended at the edge of an abandoned quarry in the foothills.

Gazing down into the dark water which filled a large part of the quarry, Pons said, "I have no doubt that the mastiff lies down there. In the absence of any place which might serve as a burial ground for the dog, and presuming the need to be rid of him as quickly as possible, this is the likeliest place; we may therefore assume with ample justification that this is the spot to which the dog was lured and slain. In all likelihood, too, the body was weighted, so that it will not rise."

We had hardly taken our leave from this spot when we were suddenly confronted by a burly individual dressed in hunting clothes and carrying a gun; he stepped out from behind a small gnarled tree down the slope (having also partly been hidden by a projecting wall of rock), and appeared before us with a decidedly menacing air, his eyes narrowed, his mouth turned down so that his face had a surly expression. Nevertheless, his resemblance to Sir Alexander was so marked, that his identity was no mystery.

"What are you doing here?" he demanded gruffly.

"That is a question I should be more inclined to put to you than to answer, Mr. Ransom Rowan."

Rowan looked closely at Pons. "Mr. Solar Pons, is it! So Alec sent for you after all!"

"Against your advice?"

Rowan shrugged and stood off to one side. "No difference to me what he does," he said curtly.

He eyed us sullenly and with unmistakable apprehension, but said nothing further to us as we walked past him.

"So that is the gambler," I said when we had passed out of earshot. "He looks like a man caught in the middle of his game and uncertain of the way the numbers are coming up."

"Yes, doesn't he?" agreed Pons noncommittally.

At the north gate we had yet another encounter. This time we came upon a young man on his knees beside the gate, who got up, abashed, and stood grinning before us – a husky young fellow of close upon thirty years of age, whose blue eyes regarded us with some chagrin. He introduced himself as Geoffrey Saring.

"Looking for footprints and such," he explained nonchalantly. "Don't believe myself the dog would simply have walked off."

"Surely it is a little too long after the event," observed Pons.

"Well, perhaps. I didn't think of it until now, after Winifred told me you were here."

"If you discover anything, you might just let me know," said Pons drily. "I understand that you were with Sir Alexander on the occasion of one of his – shall we say, 'visions?' – and saw nothing."

"Yes, Mr. Pons. A rather painful few moments, I must admit. I hope they will not be repeated. It was one evening about a month ago. I had just come downstairs to rejoin Winifred, when I heard him shout; I ran back up immediately. He stood there in the hall pointing to the floor along the wall and demanded of me whether I saw 'it.' There was nothing whatever there. Apparently, whatever it was vanished, for he said, 'There – the infernal thing's gone.' Then he turned to me and asked whether

I had seen anyone, or *anything* in the hall or on the stairs; I had not, and said so. He said someone had rapped on his door only a few moments before. That was all there was to it. He seemed gravely upset when I could not see whatever it was he saw."

"Do you remember where Sir Alexander's brother was at that time?"

"I believe he was in his room, but I do not know. He had a similar experience – except that he was in Sir Alexander's room at the time, and Sir Alexander thought he saw something moving along the estate wall. Ransom didn't see anything, either."

Pons' next question was disconcerting. "Have you been long away from the stage, Mr. Saring?"

Saring laughed pleasantly. "Surely it's not that obvious, Mr. Pons?"

"Your clothes are by Du Beune, who caters to the profession. Your hands give no evidence of manual or clerical work. It might be either the stage or the cinema."

"Bit parts, Mr. Pons. I've been off the stage for about a year. I met Winifred as a result of my stage work, and since it was, I believe, the basis for her father's disapproval of me, I abandoned it."

Pons smiled, wished him good hunting in his search for clues about the dog's disappearance, and went on into the house, only to be met just beyond the entrance by Miss Winifred Rowan, who gave us a glance of mute appeal. Behind her, Miss Megan Rowan, Sir Alexander's testy sister, looked upon us with poorly-concealed disdain and made it clear and emphatic in her entire manner that she thought us intruders who had taken advantage of a man who was mentally sick. Moreover, her replies to Pons' cursory questions left us in no doubt; she shared her niece's conviction that Sir Alexander was losing his mind.

Sir Alexander himself, seen in the light of mid-morning, was not a heartening spectacle. His face was lined and haggard, not alone with age and sleeplessness, but with manifest fear. His hands trembled a little, but this morning the slight odor of rum which had permeated his rooms on the previous night was absent; this fortification, however, would not have been amiss. I paid him the closest attention during the conversation Pons and he carried on, and was struck by the curious way in which he looked over his shoulder every little while, as if he feared an attack from behind, and by the troubled manner in which his eyes wandered; so that I did not find it difficult to understand how his sister and his daughter could believe in his derangement.

After luncheon the sun came out, and Pons again expressed a desire to walk about the countryside. After all, he pointed out, we were too seldom away from London, and we ought to take the fullest possible advantage of a day in the country.

"A day," I cried. "There is no evidence that we won't be here a week."

"My dear Parker, how you belittle my poor talents! I fancy another twenty-four hours or so will see an end of this business."

"You have clearly seen more than I have," I said.

"On the contrary, everything presented to me has been presented to you also. But while you, and Sir Alexander as well, have proceeded along the obvious lines, I have chosen to follow a different course. Either Sir Alexander is the victim of a mental breakdown, or he is not. You have sought every evidence to prove that his is a mental case; I had on the contrary only to look about me to discover every evidence that it is quite the contrary – he is a victim not of his own mind, but of someone else's."

"You speak as if you knew him."

"The identity of the culprit is so elementary that it is needless to discuss it. The *modus operandi* is the moot point. I fancy we shall soon witness a change of method. We are dealing with a clever, unscrupulous rogue, who does not lack for a tremendous egotism."

"You speak with such confidence that I am almost reluctant to point out that Sir Alexander does betray very definite signs of mental derangement."

"Undoubtedly."

"Are you changing your mind, then?"

"Certainly not. Sir Alexander was meant to betray such signs."

"Do you doubt the sincerity of Miss Winifred?"

"Not in the slightest. She is honestly concerned, and honestly convinced that her father's mind is failing. It was meant that she should be. It was meant that all of them in that house should be."

"What then is the motive for these events?"

"Why, surely it can be but one of two: either it is hoped that Sir Alexander's heart will give out as a result of fright, or that he will be adjudged mentally incompetent and the management of his affairs pass to someone else."

"His son!"

"I have not had the honor of reading Sir Alexander's will. You have a disappointingly professional mind, Parker. I would caution you to observe that there are other ends which may be as immediate as money."

"But in that case – what does the removal of the mastiff signify?"

"Come, come, Parker – surely it is evident that the mastiff had to be removed for two reasons: primarily because it was quite possible that, even though the dog knew the miscreant who was bringing about the 'vision' Sir Alexander saw on the north wall – recall that he emphasized last night that he saw the thing especially on the north wall – he might disturb the family sufficiently to attract attention to him; secondarily, because the strange absence of the dog could contribute still more to Sir

Alexander's fright. It is all of a piece, and you, who know my methods, ought properly to have applied them, have mistaken the point of beginning," he said soberly.

"Yes, the newspaper article was the point of beginning – or perhaps even the coincidental death of Sir James McLeen four months ago. The curious events which have frightened Sir Alexander are not the effects of the curse by any means, nor is the curse their reason for being; no, the curse is simply being used, no more. Sir James McLeen's death, followed by the lurid newspaper article, gave rise to the diabolical plot of which Sir Alexander was picked to be the victim. With any luck, we may be able to forestall the projected ending of this little melodrama."

Pons would say no more, but directly upon our return to the house, now shadowed by the late afternoon sun, he went up to Sir Alexander's rooms. The baronet looked up anxiously at our entrance; he had been with Kennerly, who got to his feet and would had Pons not signalled to him to remain.

"I have only two more questions to ask Sir Alexander," said Pons.

"Yes?" asked the old man.

"On the occasions of your seeing this spectral miniature of Siva, was it ever still?"

"No, not that I recall. It always seemed to move, to float away from me."

Pons nodded with satisfaction. "Now then, try to think back, Sir Alexander. Can you remember ever hearing anything whatever on the occasion of your sight of this spectral image?" The baronet slowly shook his head, his eyes puzzled. "Nothing? Think, man; it is of the utmost importance."

Here Kennerly interjected himself. "Begging your pardon, sir, but you did say that one night – you said – "

"Yes, that's right, Kennerly," said the baronet with more animation than he had shown at any time previously. "I did once or twice hear a sound I thought was like – well, like a clock being wound, only steadily, a kind of whirring sound."

"Capital!" exclaimed Pons. "Well, sir, I think we may say that we shall soon have this ghost laid for you."

"I am not going mad then? I have actually seen things?"

"You have seen things you were meant to see, Sir Alexander. You will hear from me again before you retire tonight."

I was awakened from a doze into which I had fallen in the room's only easy chair by Pons' hand on my shoulder, and his whispered, "Come, Parker. The game is afoot." I started awake. Save for a small lamp beside our bed, the room was in darkness.

"What time is it?"

"Close to midnight. The house has settled down. Come."

He led the way silently into the hall, and in darkness we went down to the door of Sir Alexander's room, upon which Pons rapped quietly and called out in a low voice to identify himself. In a few moments the bolt was drawn, the door opened cautiously, then swung wide as Sir Alexander recognized us. Pons and I slipped into the room.

"What is it?" asked the old man uncertainly.

"We are effecting a change of rooms, Sir Alexander," said Pons composedly. "If I may, I want to borrow your dressing-robe, your steamer rug, your skullcap. And that leaded cane I see over there; I daresay I may have a use for it. Thank you."

Pons offered no explanation; Sir Alexander asked for none. He took Pons' decision like a military man responding to orders, and within a few moments we had completed the exchange; Sir Alexander was ensconced in our old room, and we were in his.

"Do you now conceal yourself, Parker, behind that chest of drawers near the door," said Pons, while he took up Sir Alexander's position in the old man's chair; in the half-light, there was a remarkable resemblance between them, and a casual glimpse would not have detected the difference.

"What in the devil are we doing here?" I asked.

"Waiting for the ghost of Siva. Unless I am badly mistaken, I think a major attempt will be made tonight to bring matters to a head. My talents may be modest, but there is no need of daring them too much – is that not the way a criminal might reason? Or a scoundrel at least, eh? Now, then, let us be still."

The midnight hour struck, and the minute hand crept slowly around towards one. The old house was quiet, and the only sounds to invade the room were the soft, keening voices of a pair of owls, and the harsh booming of night-jars coasting down the sky. It was not yet one o'clock when I felt rather than heard Pons stir, and at once I became more alert, anxious to miss nothing. Was it a rustle I heard? Was it someone in the hall? In my eagerness I almost gave the show away by calling to ascertain if Pons had heard, but I caught myself in time.

A furtive tapping sounded on the door. I looked over at Pons, who shook his head silently. Once again the tap sounded, a little more peremptorily this time.

In a hoarse, quavering voice, Pons called out, "Who is it?"

Then he got up and shuffled over to the door, not, however, forgetting to carry with him, concealed in the folds of his dressing-robe, the leaded cane which he had elected to use as a weapon.

The place where I stood offered me a view of the threshold; and I turned to face the doorway as Pons threw open the door. I do not know what I expected to see there, I do not know what Pons anticipated, but the reality was most unnerving and almost demoralizing; what would have happened to Sir Alexander if he had been confronted in this fashion by the spectacle that met our eyes, is difficult to guess. For what stood on the threshold and seemed to lean into the room, whistling eerily, was nothing less than a great glowing image of Siva, a terrifying vision filling the doorway. Only for a moment did it stand there; then it seemed to rise up and tower above Pons, who cringed before it as no doubt Sir Alexander might have cringed. A solitary threatening movement caused Pons to fall back; then the thing would have retreated, but Pons' backward movement was a falling away designed only to permit him to grasp and swing the leaded cane he carried.

Before the creature in the doorway could dodge, the cane swung around and crashed down against the side of its head with a horrible tearing sound, which I realized almost at once was the crushing and ripping of papier-mache. The creature lunged for Pons, but at the same time that I leapt forward in response to Pons' call, the cane landed once more, and this time reached its objective, for the thing slumped grotesquely and collapsed on the floor.

"Lights, Parker," said Pons, breathing fast as he stepped back.

I turned up the lights and saw that from beneath the cleverly-wrought likeness of Siva projected a pair of very human legs. Under the light, the glow had disappeared, and the papier-mache of the costume seemed almost drab. But on the instant I understood the secret of that horrifying glow.

"Phosphorus!" I exclaimed, looking over at Pons, who was matter-of-factly removing Sir Alexander's dressing-robe and skull-cap; the steamer rug had fallen from his shoulders when he had delivered the first blow.

"Yes, yes, of course," replied Pons impatiently. "Surely that was patent? You saw it yourself in the hall last night, though I have no way of knowing how you interpreted it. Now then, come along, before the others get here."

Already there were sounds of movement in the rooms adjoining the hall.

"Aren't you stopping to see... ?" I said to Pons' retreating back.

"What need? My dear fellow, it is only too obvious that it is young Saring. Come along. We have yet to verify one aspect of the matter."

He darted from the room, down and across the hall, and into Saring's room, the door of which stood partly open. Here he stood for a moment in soundless concentration; then he went to the closet and began to examine Saring's luggage, where he quickly found what he sought – the tiny, phosphorescent image of Siva, the thin thread which had drawn it along the hall and the garden wall, and the electric contrivance and reel which served to draw the spectral miniature along the hall floor and into the room through the slightly open door, giving the illusion of having disappeared.

When we emerged from the room, Sir Alexander was coming down the hall, Miss Winifred stood on her threshold, looking with horror across to her father's room, and Miss Megan had appeared.

"We have caught the scoundrel, Sir Alexander," said Pons gravely, and, taking the baronet's arm, he drew him into his rooms and closed the door behind him, admonishing me to give my attention to Miss Winifred, who had plainly recognized the clothing and legs projecting from beneath the elaborate costume worn by Geoffrey Saring in the furtherance of his diabolical scheme.

What took place behind the closed door of Sir Alexander's rooms, I did not know; but shortly after Pons emerged from the room, Kennerly appeared to drive us back to our lodgings in London. Pons said no word until we were on our way into the city, driving under that same moon, smaller still, which had spilled its wan light upon the earth only the previous night.

"You are silent, Parker; did Saring's unmasking surprise you?"

I admitted that it had astonished me.

"You had fixed upon Ransom, of course. Ransom was not without guilt, but he had nothing to do with it. The matter really turned upon the character of our client. The most reliable witnesses for him were his daughter and Kennerly. Kennerly admitted that Sir Alexander was 'difficult,' but, clearly enough for anyone to see, he intimated that the old man had his reasons. These were manifest. And obviously his distrust of Geoffry Saring was not ill-founded, however slender may have been its reasons for existing.

"Furthermore, the entire matter rested upon one fundamental decision: either Sir Alexander saw the things he described, or he did not. Everyone was quite willing to believe that he had not seen them, most particularly since both Ransom and Saring had reluctantly admitted they had seen nothing. I had no alternative but to act upon the assumption that Sir Alexander saw precisely what he described. Once I had formed this conviction, I had only to look for evidence. There was no lack of it. For one thing, the mysterious calling card was doubtless abstracted and replaced with a blank card in the interval between its receipt and its re-examination. For another, I detected despite some manifest attempt to eradicate it, evidence of phosphorus along the wall of the hall at the baseboard. Phosphorus had immediately suggested itself in the course of Sir Alexander's narrative. Finally, the phosphorus led to Saring's threshold and there stopped. While this was not conclusive in itself, taken in connection with two other inescapable factors, it was.

"The first of these quite clearly was the fact that both Ransom and Saring lied in denying they had seen anything. Both had seen the image quite well; each had his own reasons for denying sight of it. One because he was its author, the other because he saw no reason why he should spoil a game which would benefit him also. The second of these factors was the motive: this seemed quite manifestly to be an attempt to have Sir Alexander declared mentally incompetent, and only secondarily to bring about his death. Now, Ransom would not particularly benefit by having his brother declared mentally incompetent; he would benefit only by his death. It was he who gambled on Saring's game. It was Saring who would benefit – an actor without a stage, a young man without an occupation, a fortune-hunter, in short, whose marriage was being opposed with what must have seemed to him particularly galling baselessness; for once the old man's mind was suspect, his opposition to his daughter's marriage would be suspect, too. A diabolical plan, Parker, but it might have worked. Its mechanics were well wrought, but simple, too.

"For instance, you did not suspect Saring primarily because his manner was engaging, and because he told us so disarmingly about the way in which he had been called back upstairs by our client to witness the spectral image moving down the hall. It did not occur to you that it was quite within the bounds of possibility for Saring to have tripped his machine, tapped on Sir Alexander's door as he passed, and hurried downstairs before the baronet got to the door to open it. The plan was so simple that you would have rejected it even if I had suggested it. And you were deceived by his by-play at the gate, where instead of looking for clues to the dog's disappearance, he was examing the ground lest he had left anything for me to discover."

"Yet he was one of the most firm in suggesting that Sir Alexander call you in," I objected.

"His scheme called for as much self-confidence as my investigations." He laughed. "We have had a good day and a long day of it, Parker. An interesting matter but one which might well have been fatal. Fortunately for Sir Alexander's frightened determination, it was not. What a pity young Saring did not keep his special talents for the stage!"

II

THE ADVENTURE OF THE LATE MR. FAVERSHAM

When I look over my notes on the cases that engaged Solar Pons' attention during the decade begun in 1919, I find many amazing adventures whose details ought to be placed before the public. There were in that time, for instance, the perplexing affair of the Mumbles, known to the public for many months as the Swansea Mystery; the curious interlude of the Sotheby Salesman, who was found dead in an empty house; the adventure of the Black Cardinal, that unbelievable conspiracy which threatened to undermine the Papacy and overthrow half the governments of Europe. But few of the problems of that decade so fascinated me as the affair of the late Mr. Faversham.

The facts of the case were utterly baffling when Pons first read of it in the *News of the World*, where it appeared under the head: "Amazing Mystery in Strand." I saw his eyes gleam, and I observed that he read the account twice before he turned to me.

"Now here's a pretty mystery, Parker," he chuckled. "Professor F. V. Faversham of Merk College, has walked into his house and disappeared."

"Of course there's some mistake in the report."

Pons shook his head thoughtfully. "That seems hardly likely at first glance. The word *into* is especially black-faced, and while the matter is treated rather lightly, the fact remains that Faversham's disappearance into his house is unmistakably emphasized."

"No doubt there are any number of ways he might have got out."

"It does not seem so. Observe: the house was boarded up during the extent of the professor's six months' leave; his front door, the only entrance not so treated, was under observation. Faversham had returned to London from Scotland and was to spend a five-day interval in London before completing his vacation in Germany."

"Aha!" I laughed. "Secret passages!"

Pons smiled. "Perhaps we shall walk over in that direction this evening."

"It will certainly do no harm. But I daresay the matter is much more simple than the papers would have it."

"That is quite possible, Parker," returned Pons. "But at least this gentleman, Mr. Faversham, has done us a favor in so radically departing from precedent as to walk *into* his house and vanish. So many persons walk out of their houses and are never seen again; the occurrence is so common that it seldom attracts my attention, unless, of course, its salient features are so strange that I cannot help feeling drawn toward the matter."

"His name is familiar to me," I said presently. "It occurs to me that I have seen it in connection with Lincoln's Inn Fields – a barrister, I believe."

"So? Then doubtless he holds classes in law at Merk College."

He said nothing more, and apparently the matter of the lost Mr. Faversham was relegated to the past, for Pons did not again touch upon his suggestion of walking to the house on Slade Street that evening.

But our attention was shortly recalled to the case of Mr. Faversham, for an hour afterward, there was a sharp ring at the bell, and in a few moments Mrs. Johnson ushered two elderly gentlemen into the room. I recognized one of them immediately as Dr. Joseph Dunnel, President of Merk College. He took precedence over his companion and bowed to Pons, introducing himself, and then his companion, Dr. Hanley Fessenden, likewise of Merk College.

"Be seated, Gentlemen," said Pons.

"Thank you," replied Dr. Dunnel gravely, nervously fingering his sideburns. "We've come to consult you professionally about a matter deeply concerning our college – a very delicate matter, Mr. Pons."

"Indeed?" Correctly interpreting their glance in my direction, he introduced me, and almost instantly diverted their attention from me by observing that if they insisted upon walking, they might better have come up Southampton Road and crossed to our lodgings on Praed Street than to have come up Kingsway and along Oxford Street and Edgware Road, which were considerably more dusty than the more direct route. The dust on their trousers clearly indicated the basis for Pons' deduction, which served his purpose in bringing their attention back to him. Pons leaned back, bringing his fingertips together, and waited, suggestively.

Dr. Dunnel coughed. "You may have seen the account of the disappearance of Professor Faversham, of our faculty?"

"Walked into his house and vanished," said Pons, reaching again for the paper he had only a little while before put to one side.

Dr. Dunnel nodded. "Then you know the primary facts of the matter. Professor Faversham has always been a man of the most upright character, Mr. Pons; he is highly respected at the college, with a reputation for extraordinary wit and a very pleasant personality. His life has always been very regular, and therefore his strange disappearance is all the more amazing. We cannot help but suspect foul play."

"You have someone in mind, perhaps, Gentlemen?"

"No one," answered Dunnel.

"Then obviously you have some specific reason for believing that someone has made away with Professor Faversham. May I know it?"

"Certainly, Mr. Pons. It is this. Professor Faversham is our treasurer; for the last year he has had complete charge of ten thousand pounds of our money. Five days ago Professor Faversham returned to London from a three months' vacation in Scotland; he is on a six months' leave at present. On his return, he saw fit to draw our money from the bank. We did not question his motive, confident that his action would be to our ultimate benefit."

"When was the money drawn out?"

"Yesterday morning, Mr. Pons. It was to have been returned today, for Professor Faversham was to leave for Berlin tomorrow morning to complete his leave of absence."

"He notified you that he was drawing out the money?"

"Certainly. Everything was done in the proper order."

"How many people knew of the transaction?" asked Pons, after a momentary hesitation.

"I fear you will gain nothing in that direction, Mr. Pons. I admit that we were rather indiscreet about the matter, and it came out; virtually all the tutors and lecturers in the college knew of it. And then there are, of course, the bank officials."

Pons contemplated his pipe thoughtfully. "You asked no questions of Professor Faversham?"

"None. We suggested as a matter of course that he give us some clue to his intention, but he did not do so."

"Surely that is an unusual, not to say irregular, procedure?"

"Oh, most irregular, Mr. Pons, admittedly. But we have done it before, and we have never lost anything through any of Professor Faversham's transactions. He has a good eye for investments, and in every case previous to this time, his investment has proved a very good thing."

"As a barrister, Mr. Faversham may have known prominent people in other fields – brokers, perhaps. Is there any possibility that he might have invested your money in stocks?"

Dr. Dunnel looked uneasy, his austere features colored a little. He glanced at his companion before he admitted at last that it had been suggested that Professor Faversham might have dabbled in the market.

His statement was reserved almost to coolness. Pons said nothing for a moment, but a keen look came into his eyes. "Did Professor Faversham spend his London interlude at his home on Slade Street, or at an hotel?"

"That we cannot say. He spent a part of each day at his home; but it is equally certain that he did not spend his nights there."

"Do you know whether he at any time entertained visitors at his home?"

"We know of one man, Mr. Pons, of whom he spoke to us. Dr. Hans von Ruda, a professor retired from the University of Bonn."

"You saw them together?"

"We saw von Ruda enter Faversham's home. My own home is just across the street from number 27."

Pons sat for a few moments, his eyes contemplative. "I take it you want me to find Professor Faversham and the ten thousand pounds," he said presently.

"Quite so, Mr. Pons. We would not like the members of the college board to know that we had been in the practice of following so irregular a procedure in regard to our funds. Dr. Fessenden and I are making this our personal concern, and you will have *carte blanche* – we will cover all your expenses in addition to your fee."

"Very well, Gentlemen, I will take the matter up."

Pons had hardly bowed the two professors from our lodgings before we were on the street ourselves. He hailed a cab at once, and in a few moments we passed our recent visitors walking slowly in the direction of the college. We drove rapidly along Edgware Road, but were halted for a short time at the Marble Arch by the increasing traffic along Bayswater Road and Oxford Street. In considerably less than half an hour, however, we drew up before number 27 Slade Street, from the steps of which came a young constable whom I recognized as Mecker, with whom Pons had previously worked. He came down the path to meet us as we crossed from the curb.

"Common sort of house, isn't it, Mecker?" observed Pons in greeting, looking at the ordinary, one-storey stuccoed house that faced us.

"Like most of the others on this street, Mr. Pons. This one was built by Faversham about three years ago."

"All boarded up, just as the papers had it."

"Yes, for the length of Faversham's leave. A good job, too. He couldn't possibly have got out by any passage but this front door." His intelligent young face clouded in perplexity.

"And he's not in the house?"

"Certainly not, Mr. Pons. We searched it from top to bottom. No tunnels, no secret passages, nothing. We did look, on the theory that we can't afford to neglect any openings, no matter how improbable."

"Dear me!" said Pons with a thin smile. "If Faversham isn't in the house, and couldn't have got out any other way than this front door – then he must have come out the front."

"And that's just what he did not do."

"No?"

"No! Professor von Ruda swears that the door was not lost to his sight for a moment. Not only that, but from the time he gave up Faversham as lost, I was here at the door."

"That is most singular. How did it come about?"

"Von Ruda had been visiting Faversham. When he got ready to leave; Faversham kindly offered to walk to the Strand with him, and to wait there with him until an omnibus came. The two men came out on the stoop. It was a frightfully foggy and wet night, and Faversham went back into the house to get his waterproof. Von Ruda remained standing on the stoop, waiting for Faversham to return. When he tired at last, he went into the house and directly down the short hall to the alcove where he knew Faversham kept his waterproof.

"The coat was there, but the professor was not. All this time he had the front door in sight. When von Ruda could not find the professor, he called him and finally came back to the stoop. I was passing and, hearing his calls, I came up the walk where von Ruda discovered me and related the incident. I instructed him to wait, which he did, and called Inspector Jamison. The door was therefore not out of our sight for so much as a moment."

Pons gazed reflectively at Mecker, taking out his pipe now and filling it. "You admit that the fellow simply couldn't have vanished into air?"

"Certainly, Mr. Pons. But where did he go? We've ransacked the house even to the extent of digging up the basement floor."

"Well, one of two solutions presents itself. Faversham either went out of this door, or he did not."

"I give you my word that he did not go out of it," said Mecker.

"Then you may take my word that he never went in." Mecker looked sharply at Pons. "But von Ruda insists that he did. He saw him."

"What about von Ruda?"

"Retired from Bonn in 1921. As far as we know, he has a perfect record. He lectured in philosophy, with part time in law and logic; he has a string of degrees that would put the alphabet to shame. We wired the university immediately."

"Von Ruda is being held, I take it?"

"Jamison insisted on it. He's in a temper by this time, to my way of thinking. He's booked to sail tomorrow, and as it looks now, he won't get away until we find some clue to Faversham's disappearance."

Pons chuckled. "Count one for Jamison; he has had the good sense to see that there is a serious flaw somewhere in this fabrication, and he's taking no chance of allowing his star witness to escape!"

Mecker threw open the front door, and we found ourselves gazing down a short hall, at the far end of which was the alcove where a waterproof coat hung in plain sight. Pons stood briefly on the threshold; then he strode rapidly down to the alcove, where he turned and looked speculatively at us.

"He certainly could not miss seeing the door, could he?" he remarked drily. "Did von Ruda explain why he didn't go through the house?"

"Faversham was using only his library, where he had put up a cot for the nights he meant to be in London, since he didn't want to open a bedroom. The door immediately to the right of this front entrance leads directly into his library, and Faversham was not there when von Ruda looked into it as he came back to the stoop."

"And the other doors? What about them?"

"All locked, Mr. Pons. I tried them at once before I called Jamison."

Pons nodded and came briskly toward the library door. "Well, then, let us just have a look at the library."

The library was a low, dimly-lit room. Mecker turned up the lights as we entered, and revealed that every wall, to the jambs of the doors and the one window, was lined with high shelves, and every shelf filled with books. In the center of the room stood an old-fashioned desk-table. On it were a few scattered papers and two books – one closed, with a projecting slip of paper to mark a place, the other turned face down at a point to which Faversham must have got when von Ruda came to visit him. Against the shelves to the left of the table was a cot, which gave evidence of having recently been slept in, for the sheets were partly thrown back and rumpled.

Pons went directly to the bed and came to his knees the better to examine it. He pulled back the sheets gingerly, and spent some moments scrutinizing the impression in the bed. That he had discovered something when he rose, I saw at a glance, but I forebore to question him, knowing that if his discovery should utimately fit into the pattern of his solution, he would reveal it in good time. Then he went to the library table and proceeded to examine the books and papers on it. One paper he passed over to Mecker; it was Professor Faversham's passport, dated for the following day.

Pons next gave his attention to the books on the shelves, passing from one shelf to another and drawing books from their places to leaf through them. He crossed and re-crossed the room, and finally returned to his starting point. Contrary to our expectations, he did not stop his examination of the books, but started all over, taking each book as he came to it, skipping only those he remembered having looked into before.

"You might take Parker over the house, Mecker," he said, turning to the constable. "It will take me some time to finish here."

Mecker agreed reluctantly.

When we returned to the library, we found Pons engrossed in a volume of German prose written, as the printing on its cover gave evidence, by Dr. Hans von Ruda. He looked up at our entrance.

"Will you want to look over the rest of the house, Mr. Pons?" asked Mecker.

"I think not. My little examination has been most valuable, and I doubt whether anything found in the other rooms could contribute much more. I'm taking this book with me, by the way. It's a text on philosophy by Dr. von Ruda, a presentation copy from the author to Faversham – a gift, I take it, since the inscription is Christmas, 1921.

"Was it on the shelves?"

"No – in one of the drawers of the desk."

We left the house, Mecker walking down the path with us. At the walk, Mecker asked, "Have you any suggestion that might help us, Mr. Pons?"

"I might suggest only that you examine the books in the library. It may lead you to something. Then, you might look into the drawers, if you have not already done so. By the way, you've looked up the hotel at which Dr. von Ruda stayed?"

"Of course. It is the Adelphi."

"Indeed! Well, I may call them." Pons half turned, then hesitated. "And, Mecker, you might give that bed a closer scrutiny. You'll find, I think, that it's been slept in only once; it looks rather as if it had been used with the intention of giving that impression. Faversham, however, has been in London five days. Dr. Dunnel, who lives just across the street in that white, railed-in house, informs me that Faversham did not spend his nights here."

"What do you make of it?"

"I think it would be wise to discover where Faversham spent his nights, eh, Mecker?"

"Yes, it might be," agreed Mecker, now deeply puzzled. "When are you relieved here?"

"At seven-thirty this evening. Then I report to the Yard before being released for the night."

"Well, if it is not too inconvenient, try to get over to 7 Praed Street before midnight. I may have something for you."

It was already dark when we ascended to our lodgings in Praed Street. Under the green-shaded table lamp in our study, Pons took the German book from his pocket and handed it to me.

"Take a look at it, Parker. It's rather interesting."

I took the book and began to examine it, while he occupied himself on the telephone. The book was bound in black cloth, and the printing on its cover was large. The gold-leaf lettering of the title read, *Die Philosophie*. It was a ponderous volume of some, nine hundred pages. The title page was inscribed: *Mit Freundlichen Gruss, Hans von Ruda – Weinachten, 1921*. The text was printed in large type and easy to read, though the pages were uncommonly thin. I turned the book over and over in my hands, and leafed through it in the hope of discovering what Pons seemed to have found. But when he turned from the telephone at last I knew no more than when he had handed me the book.

"Well, what do you make of it?" asked Pons.

"At first glance, I'd say the book was little used," I ventured.

"Elementary – but still of some significance in view of the fact that von Ruda and Faversham are warm friends, and since Faversham has had the book since 1921, with ample time to go through it. Yet several pages are still uncut. You noticed nothing else?"

"Nothing. Why?"

"No matter. I'll come back to the book later." He put the book away. "You went through the house, Parker. What did you see?"

"Enough to assure me that Faversham couldn't have got out of any window or either back or side door; everything is securely boarded up, and no one could go through without leaving telltale marks. There are none. Moreover, Mecker systematically tapped the walls. There just isn't room in the small proportions of the the building for anything in the nature of a secret passage – but that would impute a criminal motive to Faversham himself, rather than to some outsider."

Pons shrugged. "Not necessarily. But I hardly expected to discover any secret passages."

"Well, there's certainly a flaw somewhere – the professor simply didn't walk into his house and vanish."

"Well, that is the story, Parker," said Pons, chuckling. "But perhaps the flaw is not in the story. We shall see. I have just called the Yard and asked to have Professor von Ruda sent up with Mecker when he comes. Until then, let us forget about the matter."

We had not long to wait, for in something like two hours the bell rang. The ringing of the bell was followed by Mecker, who trailed in his wake a shabby, bent old man, who bore all the obvious ear-marks of a professor. He was not thin, yet his features gave the impression of being wizened and drawn. His eyes were hidden behind old-fashioned green spectacles. On his scant hair he wore an equally old-fashioned beaver hat, and a long black cape-coat reached below his knees. To cap this almost ridiculous outfit, the German professor carried firmly in one hand a bulging umbrella of indeterminate age.

"Well, sir," he addressed Pons in a high, shrill voice, "I hope you have found what has become of my esteemed colleague; it is certainly not to my liking to be detained much longer."

"Especially since your boat leaves tomorrow, eh, Doctor?" asked Pons quietly.

"Exactly. I don't want to miss it. But come, sir, tell us – you've discovered something?"

"Yes, I may say I have," replied Pons in that unfailingly calm manner in which he was accustomed to make the most important announcements. "I look forward to producing the lost Mr. Faversham before the night is over."

Surprise stilled the room, following Pons' statement. Mecker flashed a glance of perplexity at me; I returned it. Only von Ruda remained unmoved; he did not ask, as I expected him to, whether Faversham would be found alive or dead, but only said that he hoped Pons was right, and that he would then be able to sail after all.

"To begin with," said Pons, "I should like to hear your story, Doctor."

"Again?" snapped the professor curtly. He shrugged. "I suppose I must go through with it. Must you have all of it?"

"All."

Von Ruda shrugged his shapeless shoulders again and began. "As you no doubt know, I have been visiting in London; I was in Paris and had arranged to meet my good friend and colleague, Professor Faversham, at his home directly on his return from Scotland. That was five days ago. I came to London, registered at the Adelphi, and that evening went to Faversham's home. He had just got in, and we spent some hours together. It was late when I returned to the hotel, as perhaps the clerks will tell you, if you care to inquire."

"Quite so. I have already done so. I am informed also that you left the hotel regularly each day some time before dawn. I take it you spent every day with Professor Faversham?"

"Yes. We were working together. That is, up to last night. I spent yesterday with Faversham. When I rose to go close to midnight, he volunteered to walk with me to the thoroughfare – the Strand, I believe it is called – where I could take a conveyance. We came out together to the front stoop. There Faversham left me to get his waterproof coat, which was not far down the hall from the front door. I stood on the stoop to wait for him."

"How long did you wait?"

"I should say not quite ten minutes. Then I entered the house and looked for him. I had the open front door within sight at all times. He was not in the alcove, his waterproof coat had not been taken from its hook, he was not in the library, and finally, he was not on the stoop when I returned there. I called him, and my calls attracted the attention of the constable who brought me here tonight. Doubtless you already know his story."

"You say you glanced into the library. Could Dr. Faversham have been hiding in that room?"

"That is impossible, sir. If you have seen the room you will realize that the walls present even expanses of book-lined shelves. The only object at all large enough to conceal someone is the desk, and that is so placed that from the door fully three sides of it are visible."

Pons nodded. "There is a door leading from the library into an inner room. Could Professor Faversham have passed through this?"

A mirthless smile crossed the German professor's face. "No, no, my dear sir," he replied in an irritated voice. "That door was securely locked. Had you taken the trouble to investigate further, you would have seen that it leads into a narrow closet."

Pons paid no attention to von Ruda's caustic reply. "Of course, my dear Doctor, you realize that there is a flaw of some magnitude in the problem as it is being presented to us?"

"Indeed, Mr. Pons? Perhaps you would like to suggest that I myself made some magic to bring about my friend's disappearance without trace?"

"Nothing so crude, my dear Doctor, nothing so crude," replied Pons, chuckling. "But consider the logic of your statements. You say you had the door in sight every moment; this door is the only available mode of exit from the house. Yet, after having seen Professor Faversham enter the house, and having kept the only usable entrance under observation, you continue to hold that Faversham did not leave this house, in the face of the fact that Faversham is not now in it."

"Overlooking your rambling way of putting it, that is what I maintain."

"Did you look behind the waterproof?" asked Pons suddenly.

"Yes, I did."

"Suppose we wish to assume that Faversham had a reason to disappear. Suppose he were hiding behind the library door when you walked down to the alcove. If this were true, could he have stepped from the house at the moment when you looked behind the waterproof?"

The professor's features underwent an almost ludicrous change. "If – I say, *if* that were true, yes, he could."

"Good! Very good!" exclaimed Pons. "We seem to be getting somewhere." He reached over now and picked up *Die Philosophie*. "Do you recognize this volume, Professor?"

"I do. I gave the book to Dr. Faversham as a Christmas gift in 1921."

"I gathered as much from the inscription." As he replaced the book, Pons asked, "At about what date did you dispatch this gift to Faversham?"

"I think it was sometime in the first week of December, 1921."

Nodding, Pons rose from his chair. "I think that is all, Professor von Ruda."

"And Professor Faversham?" queried the German in his sharp, shrill voice.

"I am ready to produce him," said Pons tranquilly.

With these words he leaned forward easily and with one movement snatched the green spectacles from the face of the German scholar at the same time that he brought away most of the skillfully drawn lines on one side of the face. The fellow was up at a bound, and upon Pons, but Mecker collared him from behind.

"Professor Faversham – at our service," said Pons. To Mecker he added, "You may arrest him on the charge of attempting the embezzlement of ten thousand pounds of the funds of Merk College."

Faversham said nothing, but his eyes were steady in their intentness upon Pons. Pons sat down and drew out his pipe as casually as if he had done nothing unusual.

"My good Faversham," said Pons, "your scheme was too perfect. Your mind worked two paces ahead of the plan. You made your first mistake in this book –" he tapped *Die Philosophic* – "when you dated a second edition printed in April, 1922, as of Christmas, 1921. Your second error was in the matter of your books. When a man's library is stripped of all books possessing any intrinsic personal value – gift books, books with other pleasant association such as a professor is in a position to receive – it is a safe guess to assume that all such books have been permanently shipped away. Certainly a professor on his leave would not take them along. Where, then, were they, and why were they gone?

"The answer is fairly obvious. You entrenched yourself in the trust of the authorities of the college to such an extent that even now it will be difficult for them to believe in your duplicity. You hoped to vanish completely under suspicion of being the victim of foul play, so that you would not be sought, and then later you could turn up somewhere on the Continent as a respectable middle-aged man – at that place to which you doubtless shipped your books before you went to Scotland.

"On your return then, you registered at the Adelphi as Dr. Hans von Ruda, whom you knew to have been retired from the University of Bonn in 1921, and who would therefore be difficult to locate at short notice. You knew also that inquiry might be made at Bonn, and you were quite safe there. Then, in order to substantiate your friendship, you obtained a copy of von Ruda's book and inadvertently dated the edition five months before it was printed. This you left for us to see – a kind of circumstantial evidence of a friendship which did not exist.

"As von Ruda you spent your nights at the Adelphi, but before dawn you left the hotel and spent your days as Professor Faversham, allowing yourself to be seen frequently by Dr. Dunnel, a dependable witness who lived across the street, and who was permitted to see von Ruda also, so that he could testify to von Ruda's presence, if necessary. You even went to the extent of getting two passports, one for yourself and one for von Ruda. Your own you left on your library table to help give the impression of an unpremeditated departure.

"You failed to realize that you might be held as a material witness. Up to that point, you were relatively safe. Had you simply decamped with the money, you would have been hounded for the rest of your life; with Faversham given up for dead, you would be free to live your own life. And then when you saw that there were suspicions, you seized upon the first suggestion I made to alter your story – that perhaps Faversham had got out of the door while you were peering about in the alcove: this in the face of your emphatic denial of any such suggestion.

"Incidentally, your little maneuver of sleeping once on your cot was rather amusing. There is a great difference between sleeping once and five times in a bed, as the sheets and the impressions will quickly reveal to a careful observer. The single impression is consistently clear, the outlines usually quite plain, the sheets rumpled only in the place where you lie; but a number of impressions will produce a blurred and broadened rumpling and outline."

"Is that all?" asked the professor calmly.

"I fancy it will be quite enough, Dr. Faversham."

"Well, it has been an amusing hour, Mr. Pons," said the professor in a relieved voice. "But I fear we shall have to bid you good night."

He left the room, shepherded by Mecker, whose delight shone in his grateful eyes, as if he had not a care in the world. Pons strode to the window to watch them enter a cab.

"I fancy," he said over his shoulder, "Faversham might have been a really great criminal. The potentialities were there." His tone was almost regretful.

III

THE ADVENTURE OF THE BLACK NARCISSUS

It has often been said that truth is stranger than fiction, and I know of no better evidence in support of that statement than the facts attending the adventure of the Black Narcissus, as the crime is listed in my notes. There was little real deduction in Solar Pons' typical vein connected with the case; that is to say, the discovery of the murderer was in itself a comparatively simple problem, but the clue that presented itself was so curiously different that Pons was struck by it at once.

At five-thirty o'clock on a rainy May evening, Mr. Jackson Deming, a stock broker, was found slain in his offices in Paternoster Row. Pons and I had been comparatively inactive that day; we read and wrote; I had little business, for my practice had not at that time taken on much significance. Initial knowledge of the affair reached us at seven o'clock, through the medium of the *News of the World*, which carried two small photographs, one showing the scene of the murder, the other the victim, taken from life. Between the two pictures, in rather well inked print, was a *Wanted*:

Wanted for Murder!

> *A young man of medium height (five feet, seven inches), black hair, dark eyes (supposed brown), full black moustache on upper lip, thin firm lips, long arms; when last seen dressed in grey waterproof and number seven shoes.*

It was superscribed *Police Order*, and signed *Seymour R. Jamison*, the Scotland Yard Inspector in charge of the case, and one of Pons' most critical admirers, who very often brought his problems and difficulties to Pons' attention.

Pons, I remember, made some commonplace remark about the matter, and put the paper aside. Rain fell outside, and the twilight was still with that hush which falls along Praed Street just before darkness, so that the distant rumble of the Underground at Paddington made a muted hum in the room.

It could not have been half an hour later when there came a sudden ring at the bell and, before either of us could move to answer it, there followed a wild clatter on the stairs. Pons, who was standing near the window, pulled aside the curtain and looked out. A cab stood below in the driving rain. A moment later the door flew open, and a wild-eyed young man, with a cap pulled low over his forehead, burst into the room.

"Which of you is Solar Pons?" he demanded, looking anxiously from one to the other of us.

Pons stepped away from the window, manifestly identifying himself.

"I am James T. Rudderford," said our visitor, flowing his words together in an agony of haste and obvious fright.

"Wanted for murder, I observe," said Pons. "Please sit down and compose yourself."

The young man pulled his cap from his head and stood staring at Pons with a mixture of fear and perplexity in his eyes, as if he did not know whether he had better turn in flight now or carry on. He did not move to take the chair Pons indicated.

Pons, however, was reassuringly casual. "But for the moustache that you shaved off somewhat awkwardly not long ago – cutting yourself in three places, incidentally – you might fit Jamison's *Wanted* description as well as any of a thousand or more other young men now in London."

Our visitor collapsed into a chair and covered his face with his hands. "Mr. Pons, I didn't do it."

"I should not have thought you came here to confess," said Pons quietly.

Rudderford raised his head and stared at Pons. "You believe me!" he cried in wide-eyed astonishment. "You don't know then. Every bit of evidence is against me, Mr. Pons – every bit!"

"Suppose you tell us just what happened," suggested Pons.

"Mr. Pons, I am a ruined man. Until yesterday I was moderately wealthy. Today I haven't a halfpenny. I have lost everything through speculation. I do not usually speculate, sir, but I took Deming's word. I had known him for some time, and I had no reason to believe that he was not honest." He shook his head, and his not unhandsome features clouded with sudden anger. "I confess I went up to his office this afternoon to kill him. I'd have done it, too – but someone had got there before me."

"Ah!" exclaimed Pons, his interest manifestly quickening. "Let us start from the beginning, Mr. Rudderford."

"It wasn't until four o'clock that I discovered Claybar Mine had gone under. At first, I couldn't believe it; Deming had assured me that it was a dead certainty to go up. When I saw I was done for, I just simply lost my head. I know I took my revolver, put on my waterproof, and ran out of the house without my hat. I believe I ran all the way to Deming's office. There was no one on the main floor in the halls, and the elevator was not running; so I had to go up the stairs. On the first flight I met an old charwoman descending. There was no one else.

"I got to the fourth story and opened Deming's door slowly, just in case someone were in the outer office. But no one was. I crossed to the inner office, which stood open. I got half way across that room when I moved into line with the desk in the inner office, and the first thing I saw was Deming's head on its side on the desk, mouth and eyes wide open. For a moment I didn't know what to think; I hesitated; then I went boldly on. I was so angry that it didn't seem to matter what he was doing, and I think I had the idea he was having me a little by some kind of act. But at the threshold I saw what I hadn't been able to see before. Deming was dead. He had been stabbed in the back. Well, sir, when I saw that, I saw it was only by a miracle I had been saved from doing that very thing, and I turned and went back the way I had come.

"When I got down to the main floor, there was a newsboy in the hall – took refuge from the rain, I think. He stepped in front of me and flourished a paper. I brushed him aside and ran out into the street. At seven o'clock I saw the *News of the World*, with my description. I saw then what a net I was in, shaved my moustache, and came directly here."

"Obviously the newsboy described you to Jamison – an observant lad. And your footprints were taken on the stairs. Those are the circumstances of the evidence Jamison has to offer. You have a strong motive, you acted on impulse, you had the intention of committing the crime – yes, you have put yourself into a difficult position. But not a hopeless one."

"What shall I do, Mr. Pons?"

"Since you are doubtless being earnestly sought all over London, I suggest you stay here. I think Dr. Parker and I will go over to Deming's office and have a look around."

Pons doffed his smoking-jacket, and put on a light coat and his waterproof. Waiting for me at the door, he turned to our still agitated client and reassured him. "I should not trouble myself too much if I were you, Mr. Rudderford. Let us just see what I can do. Meanwhile, there are books here, if you care to read."

We descended to Praed Street and walked rapidly toward Paddington Station. The rain by this time had deteriorated into a heavy mist, which shrouded everything; wherever one glanced, heavy drops of moisture clung, reflecting light dimly in the murky atmosphere; all sounds were muffled and strange, and there lay in the air from time to time a stray scent of flowers or foliage, as if something of the country air had managed to invade London. We took the Underground at Paddington, rode to Newgate, and walked rapidly over to Paternoster Row.

The building in question was a recently-erected office building, five storeys high. The constable at the door was young Mecker, still comparatively new to his work, but, as Pons had noticed earlier, rather observant for his limited experience.

He greeted us with a polite "Good evening," adding, "I have orders to let no one pass; but I daresay you may go up. Inspector Jamison's there with the police coroner."

Pons paused to shake some of the moisture from his waterproof and light his pipe. "No doubt the murderer has already been apprehended. I could not help seeing Jamison's remarkably clear description of him in the *News*."

"We've already got thirty suspects," answered Mecker morosely.

Pons smiled dryly. "You should have at least two hundred more by midnight."

"Oh, surely not if they measure his shoes, Mr. Pons; sevens aren't that common."

"Not at all; but that won't be done at once in most cases; and the rest of the man is alarmingly prosaic."

We went up the stairs, seeing at different places sections blocked off, clearly indicating that footprints had been taken there.

"Jamison is thorough," said Pons.

Jamison was walking through the outer office as we entered: a bluff, hearty man, with a closely-clipped moustache; the police coroner could be seen in the inner room, though it was obvious that his work had been completed.

"Pons!" exclaimed Jamison. "Whatever brought you down here tonight? I'm afraid this little matter has nothing of interest to offer. Simple vengeance by a swindled investor. We'll have our man in a few hours."

"I wish you luck, Jamison. You don't feel, then, that the description you offer through the papers is – shall we say, a little general?"

"Not at all. Taken over-all, not at all general, no, sir!"

"Ah, well, a difference of opinion adds zest, eh, Jamison?"

"You'll want to see the body, I suppose?" asked Jamison a little stiffly.

"I did have that in mind."

Jamison led the way into the inner office just as the police coroner came out.

The body of the dead man lay in the position Rudderford had described to us. Projecting from his back was the handle of a common carving knife, driven to the hilt into Deming's body. Pons walked around the body and came back to stand looking at it. It was clear that the knife had been driven into the victim with great force, and I thought of Rudderford, who could easily have had strength enough to use the weapon so forcefully.

"It is not clear who discovered the body," said Pons.

"The charwoman."

"At about what time does the coroner place the murder?"

"At or near five o'clock."

"Where was the charwoman at that time?"

Jamison made an impatient movement. "She was upstairs, cleaning the floor above. She had a good alibi, if you are thinking of her in connection with this. Deming's secretary left at half after four, and stood in the hall talking with the char, who had just come in and was going on upstairs; they talked until quarter of five. When she left, the char went upstairs. The char, incidentally, offers a good alibi for the secretary, for she says she saw Deming at work through the half open door. The broker upstairs, a fellow by the name of Welkins, was still in his office and vouches that the char got there at about quarter of five. She cleaned his office and then the hall; Welkins says he saw her cleaning the hall and stairs as late as twenty past five. Then she came down, cleaning as she went. When she came in here, she found Deming like this. That was about half after five. Welkins was still in his office then, working late, and he called us at once when he discovered why the char had screamed."

During this résumé Pons had been looking around without comment. He had examined the body to his satisfaction, and was now scrutinizing the desk, which was occupied by books, papers, a desk-pad, and the various accoutrements to be expected there. However, there remained unaccounted for a rather singular object which lay behind a book at the rear of the desk. Pons leaned over and picked it up; it was a single black narcissus, still rather fresh, for it gave off a faint perfume.

"Where was this when the body was found?"

"Near the head."

"So?" Pons placed the flower parallel to the head and stepped back. Jamison nodded thoughtfully.

"Yes, about like that. A little closer to his head, if anything."

"It was moved then. By whom?"

"The coroner, I think."

"Interesting. What do you make of it?"

Jamison was a little taken aback. "Why, nothing. Nothing at all." He hesitated and gazed at the flower again. "However, if you think it significant, I should be obliged to know why."

"Are you aware that a black narcissus is a rare and costly flower, and somewhat out of place in a situation like this? Surely you are not accustomed to finding black narcissi beside your corpses, Jamison! I should place this at about one pound ten."

Jamison made a sound of disgust. "Oh, rot, Pons! Deming was rich enough to buy a carload of the things. Why shouldn't he bring one of them to his office?"

"Ah, and if so, why shouldn't he put it into water, if not in his lapel? No, I'm afraid that will not wash, Jamison. Observe: it is still quite fresh. As a matter of fact, it was removed from the florist's not later than four o'clock this afternoon and reached this desk at approximately five, leaving, as you might have noticed, spots on the desk blotter – raindrops, I submit."

"What you mean is that the murderer brought it."

"Surely it would seem so? Why not just telephone Deming's secretary and ask her if Deming himself brought it after luncheon? Or if it was here in his office when she left for the day. I'll wager she will admit to knowing nothing whatever of this curious flower."

Jamison looked at Pons in bafflement, his inability to follow the trend of Pons' thought quite discernible on his bluff features. There was, too, a suggestion of aggressive defiance. He turned just as Meeker, having been relieved by another constable below, came into the room, and gave the constable an order to telephone the secretary, who had been asked to remain at her home pending conclusion of the initial phase of the investigation.

Pons now returned to the body and bent to examine the hilt of the knife, looking at it from all sides.

"You noticed this legend burned into the handle, I daresay?" he asked thoughtfully.

"Yes. *From Emily.*"

"Does it not suggest to you that Deming knew someone named Emily?"

"Oh, that is possible, but surely you don't propose that the murderer left a calling card?"

Pons smiled grimly. "I should hardly need to suggest so obvious a fact. I gave that to you."

"Look, Pons – the knife..."

"I am not speaking of the knife," interrupted Pons. "But of the black narcissus."

"Oh, that..." Jamison sighed.

At this moment Meeker appeared on the threshold. "Deming's secretary says that Deming did not like flowers, and there was certainly no flower of any kind in either office when she left late this afternoon."

"I put it to you, Jamison," said Pons, "that the significance of the black narcissus cannot any longer be avoided. I earnestly suggest that you concern yourself with discovering the meaning of the flower. I commend to your attention especially the files of the newspapers, which might possibly reveal a connection between Deming and the flower."

Thereupon Jamison burst into a flood of remonstrances, to the effect that, since the murderer was already being sought by the police, surely there was no need to trouble one's self about the appurtenances which had in any case only a dubious relation to the crime. Pons paid little attention to him; he walked to the outer office, seated himself at the secretary's desk, and took up pencil and paper.

Jamison watched him write, silent now, and biting his heavy lips in vexation.

Pons looked up presently, after having written rapidly for a few moments.

"If you have some knowledge I do not have, I think it only fair that you tell me," said Jamison then.

"Quite right. In the first place, then, the young man for whom you are advertising did not commit the murder."

"I am somewhat familiar with your methods, Pons, but I don't follow you."

"There is for one thing, the matter of footprints," said Pons. "I doubt the possibility of tracing them through to the inner office, however wet the shoes were, but if by chance the prints could be traced, I think you would find that they stopped at the threshold. It may be possible to so trace them, and I suggest you try to find the print of a number seven shoe in the inner office anywhere beyond the threshold. That should settle the matter to your satisfaction since the knife could not have been hurled from the threshold."

"Mecker took the prints on the stairs, after we had the newsboy's story. But how do you suspect that? I confess I see nothing to indicate it."

"Obviously, because the man you want told me so himself." Jamison looked the astonishment he felt.

"And by reason of the fact that he should seek my help, he is innocent; he would never otherwise have done so. From him, too, I learn that at the time he made entry to the building, he encountered a woman he took to be a char coming down – an old woman wearing a shawl over her head."

"We have a record of her."

"Ah, who was she?"

Jamison shrugged. "We don't know."

"Ah, well, I will tell you. It was she who murdered Deming."

"Fantastic!"

"Slowly, slowly, Jamison. You proceed from the theory that the young man committed the crime. I proceed from the premise that he did not. We are thus left with no alternative but the old woman. However implausible or impossible that may sound, I think you will find it to be the ultimately correct explanation. And to facilitate that end, I have here prepared two notices, which ought to appear in all the papers tomorrow. I have taken the liberty of attaching your name to one of them, Parker, and yours to the other, Jamison."

He passed over to Jamison the two notices he had written, and I read them over the Inspector's burly shoulder.

"Found: a large kitchen knife, of the type commonly used for carving fowl, with *From Emily* burned on the handle near the blade. Owner will please apply to Dr. Lyndon Parker, Number Seven, Praed Street, Apartment 2B." The second notice was more concise: "Will the florist who yesterday, between opening hours and five P.M., sold a single black narcissus to an elderly lady wearing a shawl, please communicate at once with Inspector Jamison at New Scotland Yard."

Jamison looked up, perplexed. "Still going on about that narcissus, Pons."

"I believe it holds the key to our puzzle." Pons smiled. "You'll see that these notices reach the papers, I hope. And if you do set Mecker to looking for footprints of a size seven shoe in the inner office, I would appreciate having a report of his findings in the morning. Furthermore, you can oblige me by coming around when your notice is answered."

"Very well. I'll do it."

Pons touched a match to his pipe, which had gone out. "I think we've done all we can. Ready, Parker?"

We found young Rudderford in an agony of apprehension on our return, but Pons had no great difficulty disposing of him, telling him only that he must be prepared to make a truthful deposition about his part in the matter, and delivering himself of a few remarks about the potential murderer and the fear of punishment. Following Rudderford's return to his own home, Pons spent some time going through a bulky compendium of newspaper accounts of his own compilation – a collection of scrapbooks containing many thousands of stray bits of information relative to frauds, murders, larcenies and other offenses against the law. He was still at this long after I went to bed.

In the morning Pons examined the papers for the notices he had written. He found them easily, and observed to Jamison's credit that the evening's *Wanted* had vanished. We prepared ourselves to await an answer to the advertisement for the knife's owner, though Pons was not at all sure that such an answer would be forthcoming, admitting the possibility that the owner of the knife may not have missed it, or may quite probably have been the murderess herself.

At shortly over an hour after noon, Jamison appeared.

"Well, Jamison?" asked Pons, looking at the Inspector through the haze of smoke in the room, though the expression on Jamison's face told its own story.

"You were right, Pons," said Jamison, sitting down. "Mecker did manage to trace footprints to the threshold, but there they stopped. There were nines and tens in the inner office, and that's all we found, though we looked half the night. The weather made it possible even after the prints had dried."

Pons nodded cursorily. "It is the notice in which I am interested. Any answer?"

"A florist on Cheapside telephoned at noon to say he had sold a black narcissus to the woman you described. Cost: one pound. It was sold at around four o'clock yesterday afternoon."

"Capital!" exclaimed Pons.

"I'm not so sure, Pons. Admitting that the young man for whom we advertised did not commit the crime, we are confronted with the fact that an old woman – an old woman, mind you, who yesterday bought a black narcissus, for what reason I have still not been able to ascertain – stabbed Deming with a common carving knife, and with such strength that the knife went into him up to the hilt. Is that tenable?"

"That is the situation as I see it, Jamison. You need only ask yourself what peculiar conditions need to be satisfied to make it possible." He reached down among a stack of papers near his armchair, and, after rummaging among them, he came forth with one and pointed to a photograph. "Could this person, for instance, have done it?"

Jamison favored the photograph with a long, cold stare, and I did likewise. The photograph, in a paper of two days past, was that of an old woman. Beneath it appeared her name: Emily Riswall, and above, in black-letter: *Escaped from Strathbone Asylum for the Insane*.

Whatever Jamison might have said was cut short by a sharp ring at our bell.

A few moments later, Mrs. Johnson ushered in a thin, slatternly woman, who stood hesitantly on the threshold. "Come in, come in, my good woman," said Pons.

Thus invited, she ventured three steps – just far enough to permit the door to close behind her – and stood looking from one to another of us.

"You are looking for Dr. Parker, I presume," continued Pons.

"Yes, sir," she said nodding.

"You've come for your knife," continued Pons, in his role.

She nodded, and Pons went into his laboratory and brought out an exact duplicate of the knife which had been used to kill Deming; he had evidently prepared this after I had gone to bed the previous night. He handed it to her and waited while she looked it over, turned it to where *From Emily* was burned on the handle, and nodded with a satisfied, if somewhat worried, air.

"It's mine, all right."

"May I ask how you came to lose it?"

"It was stolen from me."

"Ah? Only the knife?"

For a moment our visitor hesitated. "Well, sir, I guess the same person what took the knife took the two pound I had hid in the tea-pot."

"Took a knife and two pounds, eh?" Pons looked at her earnestly. "Someone who knew the house, I take it, and knew where you kept your money."

The woman nodded emphatically. "Yes, sir, and so I thought. I kep' an eye on 'Enery – that's my 'usband – because I thought he'd done it, 'specially when he called home that he couldn't get home on account of the rain yesterday. The night of the same day the money was took – that was yesterday, after I come back from a neighbor's house – I found 'alf a pound back in the tea-pot. Then I knew 'twasn't 'Enery, because he'd have used it all." She looked at the knife. "And this knife, now – I wouldn't care much for it, but seeing as it was a present from my dear sister Emily, I took a fancy to it."

"And your name?" asked Pons.

"Clymer. Mrs. 'Enery Clymer."

"Your sister's?"

"Her's was Riswall. She married a good-for-nothing who shot 'imself and she went out of her 'ead, poor thing." She sniffled a little. "She's been in the asylum these ten years."

"I think you've proved your right to the knife, Mrs. Clymer. You may keep it."

"Thank you, sir." She backed toward the door, a little suspiciously. "Good day, sir." And she was gone.

Jamison stared after her in bewilderment. By this time the Inspector was convinced that Pons was correct, but he had not yet discovered the essential explanation of the mystery. However, he was not to be kept long in ignorance.

"A curious affair," mused Pons, sitting down again, with one volume of his encyclopedia of clippings. "I take it you spent very little time on the black narcissus, Jamison."

"Mecker is looking the matter up."

"Well, we have it here." He was leafing through the pages as he spoke, and now stopped. "It would appear – this is from the *News of the World* of about a decade ago – that the Black

Narcissus was the name of a spurious mine, through which Deming, who promoted it, mulcted investors of a good many thousand pounds. Among stockholders suffering the greatest losses when it crashed in 1918 were Sir Evelyn Mansfield, Selwyn Carington, Thomas Gainbridge, and James Riswall. Riswall lost his entire savings and shot himself on the same day. – Observe the similarity of the pattern, for that was your young man's experience; his name, by the way, is James T. Rudderford, and he is prepared to make a deposition as soon as you call on him. – Shortly after this event, mention of the *Black Narcissus* so enraged Riswall's widow that she made a murderous attack on Deming, inflicting some injuries. As a result, she was confined to Strathbone Asylum for the Insane, laboring under an obsession to revenge her husband by killing Deming. You will observe, Jamison, the outcome of the obsession, and the singular significance of the flower left on Deming's desk."

"It's clear now, Mr. Pons – or reasonably clear, at any rate," said Jamison, with some trace of bewilderment still in his eyes. "But we haven't got the murderer, after all."

Pons shrugged. "Technically, there is none. The woman will be found, I think, somewhere about the home of her sister, whose statements you will have to take. You might watch for her there."

IV

THE ADVENTURE OF THE NORCROSS RIDDLE

"The science of deduction rests primarily on the faculty of observation," said Solar Pons, looking thoughtfully at me with his keen dark eyes, the ghost of a smile at his thin, firm lips.

"Perhaps you're right," I answered, "but I find that much of my so-called observation arises out of intuition. What do you make of that?"

Pons chuckled. "I don't deny it. We are all intuitive in varying degrees. But for accuracy in conclusions, observation must stand first." He turned and rummaged through the papers scattered on the table beside his chair; from among them he drew an ordinary calling card, which he tossed over to me. "What does your intuition make of that?"

The card bore an embossed legend: "Mr. Benjamin Harrison Manton," and in one corner, in smaller print, "Norcross Towers." I turned it over. The caller had written on its back, *Will call at three*.

"My observation tells me that the gentleman used a broad-point pen; the character of the writing indicates that he is firm and steady. I see he uses the Roman *e* consistently; my intuition tells me he is an intelligent man."

Pons' smile widened, and he chuckled again.

"What do you make of it?" I asked, somewhat nettled.

"Oh, little more," replied Pons matter-of-factly, "except that the gentleman is an American by birth, but has resided in England for some length of time; he is a man of independent means, and is between thirty-five and thirty-nine years of age. Furthermore, his ancestry is very probably Southern United States, but his parents were undoubtedly members of the American Republican political party."

"You have seen the man!"

"Nonsense!" Pons picked up the card. "Observe: The name *Manton* is more common to the Southern part of the United States than to any other region; undoubtedly it is English in ancestry. In that part of the States, political sentiment is very largely Democratic, but it is not amiss to suggest that Manton's parents were Republican in sentiment, since they named him after a Republican president.

"Well, that is simple," I admitted.

"Precisely, Parker. But there is no intuition about it. It is mere observation. Now test yourself; tell me how I know he is of independent means."

"He calls at three," I ventured. "Certainly if he were not of independent means he could not break into an afternoon like that."

"He might well get away from his work to visit us," objected Pons. "Examine the card more closely."

"Well it is embossed; that is a more expensive process than simple printing."

"Good, Parker. Come, you are getting there!"

"And the card itself is of very fine quality, though not pretentious." I held it up against the window. "Imported paper, I see. Italian."

"Excellent!"

"But how do you know he has lived in England for some time?"

"That is most elementary of all. The gentleman has purchased or rented a country place, possibly an abandoned English home, for 'Norcross Towers' is certainly the name of a country house."

"But his age!" I protested. "How can you know the man's age merely by glancing at his calling card?"

"That is really absurdly simple, Parker. In the States it is considered fashionable even today to name children after the president in office at the time of the child's birth; doubtless the American tendency to hero-worship plays its part in that, too. Harrison was president from 1889 to 1893; hence it follows that our man was born in one of the four years of Harrison's term. The age is more likely to be thirty-nine years, because the tendency to name children in such fashion is strongest during the inaugural period."

I threw up my hands. "The contest is yours!"

Pons smiled. "Well, here it is three o'clock, and I should not be surprised if our client is at the door."

As he spoke, there was a steady ring at the doorbell and, after the usual preliminary of shuffling feet on the stairs, Mrs. Johnson finally ushered into our rooms a youngish, black-haired man, whose smooth-shaven face was partly concealed by large, horn-rimmed glasses with dark panes. He was clothed in the best fashion, and as he stood before us, leaning on his stick, he held in his hand a motoring cap, indicating he had come some distance – possibly from his country place.

Our visitor looked from one to the other of us, but, before Mrs. Johnson had closed the door behind her, he had fixed his gaze on Pons, and it was to him he now addressed himself.

"You are Mr. Solar Pons?" he asked in a low, well-modulated voice.

Pons nodded. "Please be seated, Mr. Manton."

"Thank you." With simple dignity our visitor seated himself and immediately threw a dubious glance in my direction.

"My assistant, Dr. Parker," said Pons. "Anything you say is eminently safe with him."

Manton nodded to me and gave his attention again to Pons. "The matter about which I have come to consult you is one of disturbing mystery. I don't know that anything criminal is at its root, and I cannot afford to have any word of it leak out."

"You have our confidence," Pons assured him.

Manton nodded abstractedly, and for a few moments he was silent, as if trying to decide where to begin. Finally, however, he looked up frankly, and began to speak. "The matter concerns my country estate, Norcross Towers, which fell into my hands a little over six months ago. I might say that it was purchased to please my wife, who had lived there before I married her, and is again mistress of her old home. I have been very fortunate in business, and I am able to keep both town and country houses; but since I am usually kept in the city, I don't often have time to join my wife at Norcross Towers.

"However, a month ago I drove to the Towers for a short vacation. Though the estate had been in my possession for some months, I had not yet had time to go over it thoroughly, and this I now set about to do. One of the first places to attract my attention was the fens, which had claimed the life of my wife's first husband."

Pons, who had been sitting with closed eyes, looked suddenly at our visitor. "Are the fens on your estate called 'Mac's Fens'?"

Manton nodded. "They were named after my wife's first husband – by the natives in that country."

"Then your wife was Lady McFallon."

"I married her six months after her husband's tragic death."

"Scott McFallon was the man who with one servant and his hounds set off across the fens near his home and sank in a bog. His servant, I understand, pointed out the exact spot where he went down."

Manton nodded again. "Yes, that is quite right."

"Go on with your story, Mr. Manton."

"The fens," Manton resumed, "are quite large and, in common with most fens, almost entirely marshland, with a few scattered patches of firm ground. On this considerable tract of land stand the ruins of a very old building at one time used as an abbey. It is of stone, and one wing of the place has a kind of intactness. I had taken it into my head to examine this ruin, and I started out alone for it one afternoon in my car; I had had a road built to wind through the fens to the village of Acton, to reach which previously it had always been necessary to make a wide detour. The new road was open to the public, of course.

"As I drove toward the ruin, it occurred to me that I had forgotten to instruct my secretary about a business matter of some importance; so I decided to drive straight on to Acton and wire him, examining the ruin on my return. But dusk had already fallen when I returned, and I had no intention of prowling about the building with a flashlight. Just as I was approaching my home, a car came speeding past me, going in the direction of Acton. I thought nothing of it then, for it was possible that someone was taking this convenient short cut to the village, though it is not often used."

"You made a note of the car?"

"Not definitely. It was a large touring car – a Daimler, I thought; but I could not be sure. However, I did see three people in the car, for I noticed this especially because one of them seemed to be ill."

"What gave you that impression?"

"He was sitting in the rear seat with a companion, and was almost completely covered with rugs and coats. As I flashed by, it seemed to me that his companion was trying to soothe him."

Pons nodded, and indicated that Manton was to continue.

"I speedily forgot this incident, and went into the house for dinner. Throughout the meal, I observed that my wife ate very little, and I became alarmed at the thought that something troubled her. I had noticed something like this before – a certain uneasiness and nervousness – but had put it down to some passing physical disorder. I could now see, however, that she was deliberately trying to appear normal, and eat dinner as if she were perfectly herself. This is unusual for my wife; she is a remarkably straightforward woman, and illness in the past has always caused her to refrain from taking heavy meals. I asked her whether she felt ill, and whether I could do anything, but she denied that she was ill, and only redoubled her efforts to appear at her ease.

"I tried to forget this incident, and retired to my study, where my wife shortly followed me. Now, Mr. Pons, my study overlooks the moor, and is in a direct line with the ruin. I was sitting directly opposite a low window facing the ruin when I closed my book at about ten o'clock. Judge my surprise, gentlemen, to see in this ruin two lights, one of which was put out even as I looked. Presently the other began to move, going from one room to another, according to its appearance, among those which were left intact in the wing still standing. Then it, too, was put out.

"My wife, meanwhile, had caught my look, and since she sat opposite me and could not see the lights, she asked what I saw. 'There's someone in the ruin,' I said.

"I caught an exclamation from her, and then in some confusion she said, 'Oh, I forgot to tell you, but I rented the ruin for two months.'

"I was astonished, but I recovered quickly enough, and asked to whom she had rented it. There was quite a pause before she replied, with some apprehension, that she had rented it to a professor of psychiatry who had brought a lunatic and his keeper out there for the purpose of isolated observation of his patient. Though I had been somewhat upset at first, I now recalled the car which had passed me on my homeward way that evening, and I assumed at once that the sick man was none other than the psychiatrist's patient. I could not forbear suggesting to my wife that she might first have consulted me, whereupon she seemed hurt and said that we could put them out. Of course, I would not hear of it.

"'I'd like to have a talk with the professor, though,' I said.

"'I wouldn't disturb them, Benjamin,' she answered.

"'Oh, I don't suppose there's any harm in going out there. After all, it's our property and they're our tenants temporarily.'

"'But there's no need to disturb them, Benjamin,' my wife insisted.

"I could not help feeling that for some reason unknown to me my wife did not want me to go to the ruin, but as I said no more, the matter was closed for the time being. Shortly afterward, I went to bed. My wife usually stays up quite late, reading and embroidering, and I thought nothing of her staying up that night.

"Some time during the night, I was awakened by the sound of tapping on glass somewhere about the house. I am a very light sleeper, and I sat up in bed to listen. I heard a window open downstairs. I looked at my watch; it was a quarter of twelve. Then I remembered that in all probability my wife was still in the study. I called down to her from my doorway, and Anna answered at once. Reassured, I returned to bed.

"Next day, my wife asked for a thousand pounds. Though it means little to me as money, this sum rather staggered me, and I was naturally curious to know what Anna wanted with so large a cheque. She evaded all my questions with banter, but I believed I would most likely learn to whom Anna signed over the cheque; so I gave it to her. When the cheque came back a month later, I discovered that Anna had cashed it at my bank, and that in consequence I knew nothing of where the money might have gone.

"Last night another chapter in this curious puzzle took place. As before, I was awakened close to midnight by the sound of tapping on a window, but this time I slipped from the room into the hall just after the window was opened. I went down the stairs as the window was closed again. Below me, I could see my wife's shadow, cast by the lamplight in the room, and distorted by the firelight from the hearth. To me it seemed that she was reading something, but my thoughts were interrupted by a low moan from her. At the same instant I saw her fall to the floor. She fell toward the fireplace, and I ran to her assistance.

"She had fainted. As I bent forward, I caught sight of what she had been reading; it had fallen from her hand into the fire, and was now almost entirely consumed. Nevertheless, I snatched it, put out the fire with my hands, and on the corner of paper as yet untouched by the flames, I read: *five thousand pounds at once... what will happen if...* – disconnected certainly, but enough to assure me that my wife was an unwilling party to some conspiracy. I thought immediately of the thousand pounds of the previous month, and of the ruin on the fens, which I feel instinctively is connected with the mystery in some fashion. The inhabitants of the ruin have never been seen; by day there is no sign of life about the place.

"My wife, meanwhile, was coming around, and as she regained consciousness, she looked toward the fireplace; this made me determine to say nothing about the note, for I felt that if she wanted me to know about it, she would speak. She did not. I could think only that some diabolical circumstances were keeping her from confiding in me. There can be no question of doubtful conduct on her part; I know that as only a husband can know that. I have had countless proofs of her devotion to me, and I hope I have given her all reason to feel that I love her fully as much.

"This morning, Mr. Pons, my wife asked for five thousand pounds. I quibbled a little, but in the end I handed over the money. Then I came directly to the city and poured out my story to Lord Crichton, who advised me to come to you as a man of the utmost discretion. I left my card on my first visit. Now that you have heard my story, perhaps you could come to visit us – say as friends of mine in the trade – and see what you can make of the matter at close range."

Manton leaned back and watched Pons.

"The matter certainly has points of interest," mused Pons. "I see no reason to forego it."

"Can you come with me at once?"

"I believe we can. But first, a few questions."

"Go right ahead, Mr. Pons."

"I am under the impression that before her first marriage, your wife was the young social leader, Anna Renfield. Has it occurred to you that she is being blackmailed for some past error?"

"It has," replied Manton gravely. "But unless I have been grossly deceived, Anna was held up as an example of all that is best in a young lady."

Pons nodded, and appeared to reflect for a moment. "You say you married Lady McFallon six months after the tragic death of her husband. Were you aware of the financial condition of the late Scott McFallon?"

Our visitor nodded. "When I came to England seven years ago, and came to know the lady who is now my wife, I learned that her husband's affairs were in a bad way, and that it had become necessary to sell Norcross Towers."

"You were not then aware that other factors entered into McFallon's weak financial condition at the time of his death?"

"Such as what?" asked Manton bluntly.

"His lack of honesty with friends and patrons to the extent of causing many of them to lose heavily because of certain ill-advised – if not criminal – activities?"

Manton shook his head. "I knew nothing of it."

"Perhaps it has so happened that some group of persons has discovered or manufactured evidence to show complicity between McFallon and his wife, and perhaps this is the nature of the blackmailing attempts."

Manton sprang from his chair in extreme agitation. "I can't consider such a suggestion, Mr. Pons," he said sharply. "I cannot for a moment believe that Anna was in any way a party to any of McFallon's schemes. If you come to Norcross Towers with that idea, Mr. Pons – " He shook his head violently. "No, it's better to drop the matter at once. Anna's past is spotless; if McFallon was guilty of dishonest or criminal acts, then she knew nothing of it, believe me. You cannot think it."

"You forget that I am only suggesting possibilities, and it's entirely possible that forged evidence would cause her to fall a ready victim, fearing that connection with scandal, however ill-founded, might reflect upon your name or your business."

Manton looked down at Pons, a light breaking over his features. "Mr. Pons, I believe you have hit it!" he exclaimed. "That must be the reason she didn't want to tell me – for fear of injuring my position – for she knew nothing could ever come between us."

"I am not at all sure that my supposition is correct," objected Pons. "I merely consider possibilities. There are more to examine."

Pons reached for the telephone and called Scotland Yard. I heard an answering voice which, from my place close to Pons, I recognized as Inspector Jamison's. Pons asked for information concerning Scott McFallon, and we sat in silence while Pons waited until Jamison had given him the data he wanted.

He turned from the instrument smiling cryptically. "Apparently death was an escape for McFallon. The day before the bog claimed him, an order for his arrest was signed. He would be in prison today if he had come alive from the fens."

"Good God, Mr. Pons!" exclaimed Manton. "My wife must never know that – she can't have suspected anything bad of McFallon."

Pons nodded and rose to dress for the long ride before us. Norcross Towers was a large rambling structure, a typical English country house, not far from the highroad, which connected with the road Manton had had constructed across the fens to Acton. The two-storey building was surmounted at the rear by twin turret-like towers, from which the estate no doubt derived its name. The house was of old grey stone, made extremely attractive by great masses of ivy that flung its vines far up along the old walls. As we came up the flagstone walk toward the house, I noticed that all the windows within range were set very low, close to the ground.

Mrs. Manton was the type of woman most often described as ash-blonde. Her features were thin, well formed, and her body was very lithe. She had lost neither the dignity of bearing nor the singular beauty which had helped to make her a social leader before her marriage. We met the lady in Manton's study, where we were introduced under our own names as brokers, for Pons considered it unlikely that Mrs. Manton would recognize either of us.

It was dusk when we arrived at Norcross Towers, and the first duty before us was dinner, over which we spent an hour, chatting about stocks and bonds, a subject about which Pons knew much more than I had given him credit for, and, for the benefit of the lady, the news of the day. However, Pons and I excused ourselves immediately after dinner and retired to our room on the first floor, where Pons had insisted it be, for he planned on some nocturnal reconnoitering, and had no wish to be forced to descend the stairs each time he wanted to prowl about.

In our rooms, Pons gave a sigh of relief. He changed into an old hunting outfit, complete with a rifle, and stepped out of the low window to the adjoining terrace. I watched him make his way over the lawns to the road leading across the fens, and saw him at last trudging away down the road. I settled myself to read and await his return.

But it was after midnight when Pons came back, and I was dozing in my chair, book in my lap, when he slipped into the room. I awoke with a start to see him standing before me, removing his hunting jacket, and regarding me with a tolerant smile.

"You examined the ruin, I suppose?" I guessed.

Pons nodded. "There's certainly some kind of patient there. The fellow is in an improvised bed, and if I'm not mistaken, he won't last long; he is quite wasted by disease. He looks sixty, but cannot be much over forty."

"And his keeper?"

"A burly fellow, but never a country man. I daresay I should not be wrong in asserting that he is not unfamiliar with Limehouse or Wapping. The patient's doctor is there, too – a great hulk of a man, who shows some traces of culture. He is well-dressed, wears pince-nez on a gold chain, and has fascinating – that is to say, hypnotic – eyes. There is nothing definite to be said about him, save that under pressure, he might well become a very ugly customer. I should not like to cultivate his acquaintance.

"All in all, it has the appearance of what it is meant to be: a case of experimentation on the health, mental and/or physical, of the patient, though he seemed to protest his imprisonment. Unfortunately, I could hear nothing of the conversation, for the room was tightly shut – they are occupying but one room, incidentally – and the three spoke in low voices. It's entirely possible that we may be assuming too much in suggesting a connection between the trio and the unknown blackmailers, about them. I have the feeling I have seen the three before, but I'm hanged if I can place them at the moment."

"They must be in it," I put in. "I see no reason for this kind of treatment of a patient, lunatic or not. The man is exposed to consumption in this atmosphere; it is perfectly ridiculous."

"Consumption!" exclaimed Pons. "Yes, the patient out there strikes me as a consumptive; if he is, then his doctor is no more a physician than I am, and the patient's presence there is vitally necessary to the blackmail plot. It may be that the patient is the directing genius, but that is unlikely, for he would not endanger his life by staying out there." He shrugged. "Ah, well, let us just sleep on it."

The next day Pons drew Manton aside. "Do you think it possible for me to have a few words with the servant who accompanied McFallon on the day of his death?"

"Why, the fellow has been dead for years. He had a stroke two days after his master was drawn under by the mire out there," said Manton.

For a moment Pons stood as if petrified, his eyes fixed on our host in open astonishment, his pipe hung loosely from his mouth. Then he clapped his hand to his head and exclaimed, "What a fool I have been!"

Without a further word, he astounded Manton and me by stepping from the study window and vanishing into the mists of early evening in the direction of the ruin on the fens.

"Do you think he has discovered something?" asked Manton guardedly.

"Unless I'm greatly mistaken, he has. Pons displays every sign of being off on a strong and perhaps conclusive trail!"

Pons' face on his return was jubilant. His easy grace had returned, and his attentions were all for Mrs. Manton. He managed to seat himself next to her at the table that night, and he chatted with her amiably throughout the meal. It was as she was rising to retire that Pons bent to assist her, and muttered into her ear five words, which, however lightly they were said, I managed to overhear.

"He died tonight of consumption."

I think Mrs. Manton would have fallen, had not Pons been at her side. Manton, however, noticed nothing; for her recovery was instant, and there now passed between our hostess and Pons a glance of understanding which had our host as its object.

Sometime after Mrs. Manton had left us, Pons turned to Manton and said quietly, "I think your charming wife will no longer be bothered by the rascals out there on the fens."

"You've cleared up the matter, then?" asked Manton eagerly.

"I have."

"In heaven's name, what could they have held over Anna?"

"Forgery, my dear sir. And what an elaborate forgery!"

"Poor Anna!"

"But they will be well on their way to the coast by now," continued Pons.

"What!" cried Manton, springing to his feet. "You didn't let them off?"

"In the circumstances, I thought it best," said Pons calmly. "The rascals would be certain to drag up the scandal of McFallon's questionable activities, with which they are thoroughly familiar."

Manton nodded glumly.

"But sit down, my dear sir, and let me tell you the clever story the fellows had forged to deceive your wife."

Manton sat down expectantly.

"Two blackmailers, familiar with McFallon's history, met a young man whose resemblance to your wife's first husband was very remarkable. These two persuaded this third man to fall in with their plan and impersonate McFallon in order to blackmail the present Mrs. Manton. Their plan was this: they were to go to Mrs. Manton with the clever story that her first husband had not been lost in the bog, but had fled to the Continent to escape the consequences of his stock juggling – 'certain unpleasant circumstances,' they told your wife. Now these fellows were supposed to have encountered McFallon on the Continent, persuaded him to return to England with them some time ago, and forced him to reveal his presence to his wife through his writing, carefully copied from the real McFallon's. Then the blackmailing was to begin, to rise from small sums to larger and ever larger sums, forcing the lady to give and give under fear of the exposure of her first husband's presence here on the fens, and the scandal of a bigamous marriage.

"How long this might have kept up, it is difficult to say; for all went well for them at the beginning over a month ago. Your wife believed their fantastic story, and fell prey to them. Unfortunately for the villains, the fellow they had chosen to play the part of McFallon was a consumptive. The damp air of the fens brought about a quick collapse in his constitution, and only tonight he died and was buried in the bog. The rascals are gone, and my advice to you, Mr. Manton, is to say no word of the affair to your wife. She will soon know that her trouble is over, and she will feel better if you know nothing of it." He sighed. "And now let us get to bed, for I should like to be in London early tomorrow."

"What a curious tale," I said, when we were once more alone in our room, "and yet, in a way, very clever. The idea of having McFallon vanish with the servant as accomplice is perfectly logical in the circumstances of McFallon's imminent arrest; his supposed stay on the Continent and his meeting with those rascals when he could no longer return to England because his wife had remarried after the unexpected death of his accomplice prohibited her from knowing the true state of affairs; those fellows forcing him to aid them, for he was noble enough to keep away all these years and now fell victim to them – why, every step is perfectly logical!" I exclaimed in admiration.

I stopped suddenly and looked at Pons, whose face looked gray and gaunt in the dimmed light of the room. "Why, Pons!" I cried. "It was true!"

"Every word of it!" Pons nodded. "Except that McFallon killed himself rather than be instrumental in his wife's suffering. He rests now in the bog, and no one will ever know he has not been there all these years!"

"Good God! And you let those scoundrels get away?"

Pons turned his inscrutable eyes on me. "I had all I could do to keep my hands from their throats – but there are better ways of handling these matters. I sent a wire to Jamison before lunch; they'll be taken at Dover."

V

THE ADVENTURE OF THE RETIRED NOVELIST

Though Solar Pons does not consider it among his best adventures, the case of the late famed man of letters, Mr. Thomas Wilgreve, has always held for me a fascination of which I cannot rid myself. It was late one night in October, 1926, when Pons and I were returning from Covent Garden that Pons gripped my arm, not far from our lodgings in Praed Street, brought me to a halt, and pointed upward to our windows, bright with light. Silhouetted against one of them was the profile head of a man. Pons studied it for a moment; then he turned to me with raised eyebrows.

"Do you recognize that profile, Parker?"

"Well, it is certainly not John Barrymore's – unless he is in disguise," I answered. I shrugged and admitted that I did not recognize him, despite the feeling that there was something very familiar about the silhouette.

"In his own field he is a distinguished gentleman. That long, singularly lean face, that straight nose, those bushy eyebrows and that affected mane of hair all suggest a picture reproduced in rotogravure by the metropolitan papers at least once a month. What would you say if I were to suggest the author of *Victoria*?"

"Thomas Wilgreve! Of course – I knew I had seen that profile somewhere."

"It does suggest Barrymore," admitted Pons, smiling dryly.

In spite of his leonine and impressive appearance, Thomas Wilgreve was very taciturn and almost humble in bearing, as is the case with so many men of genuine stature who have little inclination to be pompous and self-important, and no stomach at all for arrogance. He apologized for taking the liberty to invade our rooms, singling out Pons by the same means used by Pons to identify him, and explained that it was very seldom that he left his home in St. John's Wood and that, once having left it, he was loath to return without accomplishing what he had set out to do. He waited while Pons and I took off our outer clothing, and then a little diffidently resumed.

"What I came to see you about was to ask whether you can investigate a small matter that seems to concern me in some inexplicable manner."

Pons hesitated, avoiding Wilgreve's inquiring eyes. "I should say it depends upon the nature of the affair."

"I've an idea that this matter will interest you, Mr. Pons," said the retired novelist. "It takes a bit to stir me, for I'm used to the most intricate subtleties and variations of writing and the imagination, and ordinary events appear to me for the most part singularly banal."

The novelist paused and took from his wallet a piece of paper. He put on his pince-nez, and read it over very carefully to himself, as if to make certain beyond question that he had got the right paper. Then he passed the paper on to Pons, who read it and handed it over to me, after which he took it back and studied it, an enigmatic smile playing over his saturnine face. The paper was a short, informal note, an invitation –

"My dear Wilgreve,

I am briefly up from the country, and have but a limited time at my disposal. Yet I do want to see you very much. I find it absolutely impossible to run out to St. John's Wood, but I hope you will not find it too much trouble to join me for dinner and perhaps the evening on Friday, the seventh. I will wait for you at Claridge's, the usual place.

Lakin."

"Lakin is the Essex novelist and poet," said Pons thoughtfully. "I take it you went, he was not there, he had not been there, he was not up from the country."

"Yes, yes, exactly," said Wilgreve, smiling delightedly. "Your talents are amazing, sir – but of course, it is elementary, is it not? It would almost have to be so, would it not? Well, that is the way things turned out; I went, he was not there, he had not been there, no word had been left, I waited a reasonable time, I returned home. I made no attempt to solve the riddle; I was annoyed, I thought someone had taken the opportunity to make a joke at my expense. Yet I had to admit that it was well done; the writing was very much like Lakin's – I had never a doubt of it when I read it. It was, in short, precisely the kind of note Lakin would have written; next day I telephoned him, and discovered, as you guessed, that he had not been in London at all."

He became a little more animated, taking off his pince-nez and leaning forward to tap Pons' knee. "Now then, Mr. Pons – almost two weeks later, that is, last night, – an extraordinary event took place. I had come out to the stoop for a breath of air, when I was a witness to a sudden accident – or rather, to what appeared to be an accident. Before I quite knew what had happened, two gentlemen came running to where I stood and insisted that I accompany them as a material witness, the child's life might be in danger, not a moment was to be lost. I did not hesitate, despite my reluctance; I stepped back into my house, turned out the light, and pausing only to take my hat, I accompanied them. I see now on mature reflection that it was a foolhardy thing to do; but in the excitement of the moment, what more natural! In any case, I was hustled into a waiting car and driven some ten blocks, where I was taken into what appeared to be a small waiting-room, where one of the gentlemen very courteously asked me to stop, an officer would be along to take my statement as soon as possible. Then, in a very agitated manner, he vanished into an inner room. I saw no one for an hour; then I got up and tried the inner door; it was locked; my knocks brought no response. I tried the outer door in some alarm, thinking that I was the victim of some scheme; but it was open, I was free to go. Naturally, I did not know what to do; I confess that I waited a while longer, and then took my departure, utterly mystified.

"When I let myself into my house, Mr. Pons, I took off my hat in the darkness and then went over to turn on the lamp. Now, sir, my reading light is a table-lamp with a green shade; it throws a strong light within the room, but seems to throw only a subdued glow to anyone outside. As I reached down for the switch, I was aware of a warm glow; I touched the bulb – it was warm – as warm as if it had just been put out. Yet I had turned it out approximately two hours before! Hurriedly I checked all the doors and windows, but nothing was amiss; all were locked save the front door through which I had come."

"Ah!" exclaimed Pons, his eyes narrowing, the smile on his lips persisting.

"I thought you would be interested, Mr. Pons. Now, then, after I had made this search, I observed that the door to the attic stood open. I live in a one-storey bungalow with an attic of good size. I do not keep much in the attic – some books, papers, magazines – the natural accumulation of anyone in my profession; and some of the old furniture that was in the house when I bought it. This furniture had been pulled around, despite some manifest effort to conceal the fact."

Pons touched his ear lobe thoughtfully. "When did you buy the house?"

"About ten and a half years ago."

"You bought it furnished, apparently. From whom?"

"From the executors of an estate."

"Whose estate?"

"I believe it was a widow's – a Mrs. Paul Greenbie."

A smile touched Pons' lips, and his interest manifestly grew. "You say you kept 'some' of the old furniture in the attic. What did you do with the rest of it?"

"I sold it to a dealer on Cheapside. As far as I know, he still has it."

"The address of your place, if I recall it correctly, is seven Cavendish Road."

Wilgreve nodded.

"I take it you are aware of no enemies who might choose this way of troubling you?"

Wilgreve shrugged. "None. People who differ from my ideas, of course, and who can be bitter; but no one who could be called an enemy."

Pons produced the letter once more. "Do you have the envelope in which this was mailed?"

Apologetically, Wilgreve surrendered it.

"Now, just let us see what we can make of this," pursued Pons, scrutinizing the paper and envelope carefully. "The writing is effortless; so that it is not too much to suppose the gentleman an accomplished forger. It is certainly no task to find samples of Lakin's writing, but more of one to copy it expertly enough to take in an old friend. We may assume that the writer, aided by a confederate, is anxious to obtain entrance to your house without needlessly setting you on his track. If this were not so, he could very easily have invaded your home, bludgeoned you, and gone about his nefarious business without troubling about the consequences. No, for a very good reason, he did not wish you to know that he had an interest in your premises, and he went to considerable pains to deceive you – witness this forged note, and even more, the obviously staged accident.

"Moreover, he has studied your habits; he will have known you are of a retiring and sedentary nature, and so contrived ingeniously to decoy you away from the house. Whatever it is he wants there remains to be discovered."

"But that is what is puzzling," interrupted Wilgreve. "I own no valuables, I do not keep money in the house, my manuscripts are given to charitable institutions for sale – I have nothing of value."

"Does not then the possibility suggest itself that you may possess something of value without being aware of it?" asked Pons.

"No, sir," answered Wilgreve with alacrity. "I am fairly well-informed in the matter of antiques and the like; I own nothing of value save a few signed first editions – and these, you will admit, have at best a fluctuating value."

Pons nodded, his brow furrowed in deep thought. He held paper and envelope up to the light. "Mailed in St. John's Wood, I see. This would suggest that you or your house at least have been kept under observation. A good grade of paper, too."

"Yes, it is precisely the kind Lakin uses."

"Indeed! What care!" said Pons, shaking his head. "Tell me, Mr. Wilgreve, how many people would you say were involved in the 'accident' you supposedly witnessed?"

"Why, I suppose five or six – "

"The writer, his confederate, and perhaps four cronies – or actors employed for the occasion. Most likely actors. Could you identify any of them?"

"I doubt it," replied Wilgreve. "The two gentlemen who approached me, perhaps, – but no more."

Pons was now silent for so long that Wilgreve was finally moved to inquire whether or not he would undertake to investigate the matter. But clearly Pons had already made his decision; he nodded and asked for the name and address of the dealer to whom Wilgreve had sold the furniture.

"Now, then, Mr. Wilgreve, I shall want to examine your attic."

"I will expect you tomorrow, Mr. Pons."

"The matter may be more urgent than you think. There is no time like the present, Mr. Wilgreve. Come along, Parker."

He came to his feet with animation, brushing aside Wilgreve's doubt, and reached for his Inverness.

The novelist's home was easily identified from his description of it, not so much because his description had been so explicit, but because it was the only house on the street which was obviously of one storey. It was tastefully but simply furnished, but Pons scarcely glanced around him, merely flicking his eyes toward the lamp which Wilgreve said was warm to his touch; he went directly to the attic stairs and vanished into the darkness of that room under the roof, both Wilgreve and myself following to the threshold, from which we observed Pons using his pocket flash to make the most careful examination of the furniture stored there, painstakingly scrutinizing piece after piece, without a word in our direction, until he had finished almost an hour later.

"Have you discovered anything?" asked Wilgreve when he came toward us.

"Yes. Within a few days you may expect an inquiry about that part of the furniture you sold."

"Shall I answer it?"

"By all means," said Pons, smiling cryptically.

Then, pressing the novelist to lose no time in notifying Pons if any further suspicious circumstances designed to take him from his home took place – though clearly he doubted that anything further would happen – he bade him good night, and we left the house.

Upon reaching our lodgings once more, Pons sat for some time in cogent silence. He looked at the letter which he had retained, examined the envelope repeatedly, observing casually that the writer had been in dress clothes, for a smear of ink carried the impression of a weave with which he was familiar, and finally ended his period of thought by telephoning the director of Actors' Services, late as the hour was, and asking that four or five actors who could reenact a street accident – preferably someone who had done similar work before – be sent to Praed Street in the morning. Saying nothing further about Thomas Wilgreve's curious narrative, he then retired.

Promptly at nine o'clock in the following morning, three men and a woman from Actors' Services presented themselves at Number seven. Pons was waiting for them, and lost no time in examining them. Had any one of them done anything of the sort before? Three had not, but one gentleman said that he had been required to take part in the re-enactment of an accident in St. John's Wood only two nights ago. Clearly, this was what Pons had expected; he dismissed the other three with their fees, and bade Mr. Nickerton, the fourth member of the group, to sit down.

"Now, sir, I want to place before you six photographs. I want you to study them. I want you to tell me whether you have ever seen any one of those faces before."

Nickerton's lined face betrayed his perplexity, but he did not demur while Pons went to the cabinet where he kept his files of data on crimes and criminals, a practise fairly common among both professional and amateur sleuths in London, as well as the custom of the police. From his files he took the photographs in question and, without a word, came back to the table and arranged them before Mr. Nickerton.

The actor thereupon studied them in silence for some time; four of them he discarded immediately; of the other two, he was clearly not certain. Pons began to fidget a little, tugging at the lobe of his ear, and finally he could contain himself no longer.

"Well, it is perfectly obvious that you detect some similarity, Mr. Nickerton. Perhaps it would help if you looked at those faces as if they wore moustaches or beards – whatever it is that impedes your identification."

Mr. Nickerton's response was prompt. "If this gentleman wore a moustache, I would say it was he who directed the re-enactment of the accident in which I took part last Wednesday."

"Capital!" exclaimed Pons, obviously pleased.

Forthwith he permitted Mr. Nickerton to take his leave, while he put all but the identified photograph back into his files. I reached over and took up the photograph; it was that of a distinguished-looking man of middle age, wearing a monocle, full-faced and keen of eye.

"And who is this?" I asked.

"You may well inquire," answered Pons, chuckling. "It is none other than the author of Mr. Wilgreve's curious tale – Guy Pilkington, one of the most accomplished forgers in England, if not, indeed, in Europe. He was released from prison only a few months ago. He had forged a cheque on the Bank of England, and would have got away scot free if he had not had the bad fortune to become involved in an accident on the road to Dover."

"What can he want of Wilgreve?"

"I think that is reasonably elementary, Parker," said Pons shortly. "He was a one-time associate of Culross Parey, who died in prison about eight years ago. You will remember Parey as the star performer in many a celebrated and daring theft.

He was imprisoned for the theft of the Peacock's Eye; you will remember he went boldly to the house of its owner, presented a demand in its owner's writing, and made off, in the character of a diamond merchant, with the stone. A child's chance photograph of the house while he stood on the stoop was the one piece of evidence too damning for him to overcome. Parey was a brother of Mrs. Paul Greenbie. But come," he said, suddenly animated, "we have work to do. Let us be off."

We had not far to go, for Pons led the way to the Praed Street station, and there we took the Underground. At Moorgate we came up once more into the morning's now thinning mists, and walked down Princess Street to Cheapside. Pons had no difficulty locating Number 231A, and briskly entered the shop.

A rotund little man wearing a skull-cap and octagonal glasses rose from his place behind a counter, and came around to confront us.

"Mr. T. Woodly, I presume?" inquired Pons.

"Yes, sir. What can I do for you?"

"I am Solar Pons, Mr. Woodly. Some time ago you purchased some furniture from Thomas Wilgreve, the novelist, of St. John's Wood. If you are still in possession of those pieces, I should like to examine them."

"They are very ordinary pieces, Mr. Pons," said Woodly dubiously. "I can show you many better things."

"No doubt. But it is these pieces I wish to see. I take it you still have them?"

"Lot forty-seven, Mr. Pons. You'll find it ticketed if you go down the shop and turn into the room at the right. There are only four pieces – an old arm-chair, a sofa, and two occasional chairs."

"Thank you. I'll just go along and look at them."

Forthwith Pons strode into the darkness of the shop's rear, turned to the right at the end of the little more than passage which made up the width of 231A, and found himself in a sizeable store-room. With the aid of his pocket-flash, he located lot number 47, and thereupon he began to scrutinize the furniture with the same microscopic care with which he had looked at those pieces remaining in Wilgreve's attic. Not a sound escaped him, save only a small cry of interest, followed by the appearance of his head above the back of the armchair, to caution me to watch for Mr. Woodly. I saw him take from his pocket the ponderous pocketknife which was all things to Pons and begin to work at the fastenings of the chair, but what he did there, I could not see; however, in a few moments he left his place and came whispering to me for a scrap of paper, which I tore from my notebook and gave to him. I saw him last writing something on the paper, after which he completed his work on the furniture and joined me.

Mr. Woodly waited for us. "Well, sir, you found it as I told you, eh? Quite ordinary. I have some good Sheraton..."

"Thank you, Mr. Woodly, but I am not interested at this time. However, I daresay you will shortly have a further enquiry about this furniture, and unless I am very badly mistaken you will have a handsome offer for it. By all means get as much as you can for it; the purchaser will be very anxious to possess the lot."

With this cryptic statement, Pons left the shop and strode out into the occasional sunlight now breaking through the light fog of the October morning. He walked with a gleam of good humor in his eyes, so that I knew his examination had not been fruitless. Yet he said nothing, and I would not ask until we had reached our rooms and discovered that Mrs. Johnson had left a note to say that Thomas Wilgreve had telephoned; he had received an inquiry about the furniture, and had answered it, in accordance with Pons' instructions.

"You might just telephone Wilgreve, Parker, and ask him to step around here at two o'clock this afternoon if he cares for an explanation of his mystery," said Pons.

"You've solved it then?"

"Oh, yes – disappointingly elementary, and yet not without aspects of interest." He shrugged. "And by the way, I wish you would telephone Lord Venler and tell him that I would be obliged to him if he would call at our lodgings this afternoon at the same hour."

"But what is it all about?"

Pons chuckled. "Well Parker, you have all the facts. It should be obvious to you as it was to me from the moment Wilgreve concluded his curious narrative."

"I can make nothing of it, save that apparently something of value is connected with the furniture."

"Come, come – you are warm, but how carefully you tread!" Laughing, he retreated to his crime file, and left me to the telephone.

The novelist, curious and still perplexed, arrived but a few moments before Lord Venler; he had hardly seated himself when Mrs. Johnson announced Lord Venler, a tall, grim-faced man in his sixties, wearing impeccable afternoon dress. He fixed his keen grey eyes on my companion and bowed.

"You wanted to see me, Mr. Pons?"

"Yes. I believe I have something that belongs to your lordship."

So saying, Pons reached casually into the pocket of his jacket and took from it a rough stone, which he put on the table before Lord Venler. His lordship's expression was almost ludicrous in its amazement. His eyes widened, his lips parted, he took a step forward; then he snatched the stone from the table and held it up before his eyes. Only after he had thoroughly examined it did he turn to Pons.

"It is the Peacock's Eye! Where did you find it?"

"Just where Parey put it – into the padding on the back of an old armchair in his sister's house in St. John's Wood. You will remember that Scotland Yard was able to account for every moment of Parey's time except for a half hour which he claimed to have spent on the Underground; he spent it in his sister's house, quite possibly unknown to her, and hid the stone in the armchair there."

"But he died without revealing anything!"

"Quite so. But one of his associates was in prison with him – the man who wrote the actual note, Guy Pilkington. There was always a reasonable doubt that Parey committed that forgery; it was too skillful; your writing was perfectly reproduced, and so, too, your signature. Pilkington was released from prison but a short time ago, and began his search for the stone as soon as he could do so. That brought him to Mr. Wilgreve, the novelist, and Mr. Wilgreve sought the aid of my modest powers."

After Lord Venler had gone, Pons gave his attention to the novelist. "Do you understand the matter now, Mr. Wilgreve?"

"Yes – except for knowing why Pilkington was so cautious."

"Why, to avoid the very contingency he precipitated by his caution – sending you to any authority who might be able to rationalize the problem and so reach the Peacock's Eye before he did. Hence his extreme care about Lakin's signature and his carefully staged accident, which, if you had not gone from that office to which they had taken you, would doubtless have been very reasonably explained to you. You left the waiting-room before Pilkington and his confederate could complete the mumbo-jumbo of taking your deposition; doubtless Pilkington's companion was at fault, for Pilkington himself would never have been guilty of permitting you to go before he could allay any suspicions you might have. Pilkington might have obtained a key to your house from Parey; he might have managed an impression unknown to Parey or even to yourself; that he had one is apparent. We may logically assume that though Pilkington learned that Parey had hidden the stone in a piece of furniture, he knew, no more than I, *which* piece."

Mr. Wilgreve stood, preparing to take his leave. "Then it was he who wrote to inquire what I had done with the rest of the furniture?"

"Precisely."

"And he will go to Woodly and buy the furniture, I suppose. I should like to see his face when he opens up the armchair."

Reaching for his pipe, Pons smiled. "He should have no cause for complaint," he said dryly. "In place of the stone I left him a receipt, over my signature."

VI

THE ADVENTURE OF THE THREE RED DWARFS

The affair of the Three Red Dwarfs, as it is chronicled in my notebooks, stands among those cases most typical of Solar Pons' method, and ranks, in the brevity of its problem and the almost pedestrian acuteness of Pons' observation with the adventure of the Black Narcissus, which it followed. It was one of those cases marked by unusual features which Inspector Jamison of Scotland Yard habitually brought to the attention of "the Sherlock Holmes of Praed Street," as the papers were even then beginning to call Pons.

Jamison came to our lodgings at 7 Praed Street one afternoon in early May, following a period of enforced idleness which had irked Pons, coming into the room puffing heavily, his chubby face red with the exertion of climbing the stairs.

"Ah," murmured Pons, eyeing him with delight, "there's been a murder."

Jamison followed Pons' gaze to the small spot of blood on his trousers at the knee.

"The body was on the floor, I see," Pons continued, "and since it bled profusely, I should not be surprised to learn that the victim was stabbed to death."

Jamison looked at Pons in admiration and amazement.

"Was it a man or a woman?" asked Pons.

"A man," replied Jamison hurriedly. "But how you heard, I don't know."

An expression of annoyance crossed Pons' face. "You have only to use your eyes, Jamison," he retorted. "Those stains on your trousers are obviously bllod-stains. The condition of your knees shows you to have been creeping about on the floor. The fact that you were creeping about on a floor where you stained your trousers with blood suggest that there has been a murder rather than a suicide, for in the latter case you would not have come to me. If there was so much blood on the floor that you could not avoid it in your examination of the body, I infer that the victim bled profusely, and that in turn leads me to suspect that a knife was used and drawn from the wound."

Jamison nodded glumly.

"Suppose you tell us about it," suggested Pons.

"The matter is right in your line," began Jamison.

"And have you given up, then?"

"Certainly not. I have my own theory of the crime."

"So? Let us have the details." Pons lit his pipe and sat back in his chair, contemplating Jamison in silence.

"Well, it's like this, Pons," began Jamison. "You know those two authors – the collaborators – up in St. John's Wood? The same two the papers had so much about a few days past?"

"Brighton and Lane, eh? Writers of realistic fiction, and quite prolific, I believe. I am under the impression that Lane is also an artist and has had several exhibitions. They recently published a monograph on chess which struck me as rather well done. Which was murdered?"

"Lane, the younger of the two. Stabbed twice. The first wound was not fatal, but the second must have killed him almost at once, for it penetrated the heart. In the second wound we found the weapon – an Italian stiletto, his own property. Besides the wounds we found some suspicious bruises on his head and on his left wrist. There was nothing about that could have made the marks nor was there anything he could have hit while falling, for he lay well away from the wall, toward the middle of the room, and there was no furniture near him."

"Any sign of a struggle?" interrupted Pons.

"None. The room is as spick and span as if nothing had ever happened there – not a mark. Just between us, it's my idea that Lane killed himself."

Pons looked at Jamison incredulously. "Don't you think that it would be more reasonable to believe that Lane would have made sure the first time, had he wished to kill himself?"

"I don't know. The circumstances are peculiar. Brighton called us. He was quite incoherent, and said that something had happened to Lane, and that we'd better come at once. When we got there, we found him nervous as a cat. He was pacing the floor holding a paint brush in one hand and a pot of paint in the other."

"Most singular," murmured Pons. "You asked him about it, I hope?"

"Oh, yes. He explained that he'd been painting, and indeed, we could see his work in the kitchenette."

"Hm!" said Pons. He pondered a moment in silence. Then he asked, "What was the coroner's decision?"

"He tends toward murder – as I said, I don't agree. Lane had been dead an hour when we arrived."

"An hour!" exclaimed Pons. "And where was Brighton all this time?"

"Oh, everything's satisfactory. Brighton was puttering around in the garden all the time, and only discovered his colleague when he entered the house. The body was on the floor of a typical lounging room looking out on St. John's Wood terrace. He called us directly after finding Lane."

"Of course, you asked him whether he had heard a disturbance in the house?"

"Yes, certainly. He had heard nothing. As a matter of fact, he did not even know that Lane was in the house, for he had gone out early in the morning, and Brighton had not heard him come in."

Pons considered this. "The body, you say," he went on presently, "bears bruises, which look as if they might have been inflicted in a struggle. Yet there are neither signs of a struggle in the room, nor is there any evidence of noise suggesting that there was a struggle. Decidedly perplexing. Have you examined into the motive of the murder?"

Jamison nodded. "Yes, we've unearthed a motive, Pons. It was Brighton who set us on that. It seems that over a month ago Lane wrote an article on a fellow journalist, dished him up pretty well done, I'm afraid. Of course, no names were mentioned, but for those in the know, the journalist is pretty obvious – so I am given to understand. At any rate, two weeks ago Lane got a short note from this fellow, telling him that scores would soon be even."

"You have the note?" Pons cut in.

"No. Brighton says that Lane destroyed it; Lane looked on the matter as a joke."

"Of course, you have the man's name?"

"We're not sure of that. Brighton says the fellow Lane had done up was a journalist on the *Mirror* staff – name of John Estenham. But Brighton says he did not see the note, and therefore he doesn't know whether the signature was that of Estenham."

"Estenham?" repeated Pons musingly. "The name is familiar. Did Brighton say – does the man chronicle the races?"

"Why, yes," said Jamison, "it seems to me that Brighton said something about it. Yes, I believe he did."

"Then you may dismiss Estenham from your list of suspects; he was killed three days ago in a motor crash at the Sussex Chase. Have you no other suspects?"

Jamison shook his head. "None. But we haven't gone far with the enquiry. Brighton says he cannot think of anyone who'd want to harm Lane, and he can't believe that Estenham had a hand in this business."

"We can rule Estenham out," said Pons shortly. "Of course, you formed some opinion of how the crime was committed?"

"From the look of things it's pretty obvious," said Jamison. "Lane entered the house, removed his outer clothing and made himself comfortable in the lounging room. Shortly after, someone entered from the street – there might have been an argument, a struggle, and Lane was killed. It is either that, or Lane killed himself. If the unknown had seen Lane enter the house, and knew also that Brighton was working in the garden, it would have been a comparatively easy matter to follow and kill Lane."

Pons closed his eyes for a moment in reflection. Abruptly he rose and went over to a wastebasket, in which he began to rummage, and from which he at last extracted a thick book catalogue, which had come in yesterday's post. With this he returned to his chair. He began to page through the catalogue.

"Ah," he murmured at last, "here we have it. 'Chess... *Chess and the Human Mind – A Monograph*, by H. C. Brighton, with a commentary by Gerald Lane.'" Pons read for a moment in silence; then he looked up and said, "I think we'll run up to the scene for a bit, eh? What do you say, Parker?"

I nodded. It was a foregone conclusion that the possibility of an adventure with Pons took precedence over anything else I might have in mind.

Our taxicab drew up before a modern, one-storey house of white stucco, set modestly away from the street. There was a roofed-over terrace at one side of the building, and beyond this, the latticed-in garden could be seen. It was on the terrace that Brighton met us. He made a curious figure as he came rushing from the house clad in a flowing lounging robe of black silk and scarlet crepe. He was handsome, but his features were somewhat disfigured by the large horn-rimmed glasses he wore.

"Mr. Solar Pons at last," he said in a hurried voice as he came on. "Perhaps now we'll have some light on this horrible affair." He glanced significantly at Jamison.

"Mr. Brighton, I take it?" said Pons dryly.

"Yes, yes, certainly," replied Brighton in a nervous, jerky voice. "I suppose you would like to see the body at once." Then, without giving Pons time to answer, he turned and led the way quickly into the house through the French doors which were thrown open on the terrace.

Jamison had given us an idea of the position of the body. We saw it now, with a sheet covering it, and beside it stood a constable on guard. Pons nodded silently to the constable, and bent to pull the sheet from Lane's body. The young, fair-haired man lay as Jamison had described him, partly on his side, partly on his back, his right arm flung out, his left turned in toward the body, indicating in its direction the stiletto in the body. Pons looked searchingly at the corpse, throwing an occasional glance at the French doors, through which the murderer might have entered. Then he bent to scrutinize the two bruises of which Jamison had spoken, one on the head, the other on the left wrist. He pondered a moment over the bruise on the wrist, but at last he rose from his crouching position and re-covered the body. He stepped carefully away from the blood-stained floor and turned upon the bespectacled author, whose sharp eyes had followed Pons' every move.

"Was Mr. Lane left-handed?" Pons asked abruptly.

"Yes – yes, anyone can tell you," replied Brighton in a breathless voice.

Pons nodded abstractedly and continued, “I understand that you were in the garden prior to your discovery of the body. You were not aware that Mr. Lane was in the house?”

Brighton shook his head. “I had no idea Gerald had returned.”

“You heard and saw nothing, then?”

“No. If you care to verify, you’ll see that the greater part of the garden extends to the rear of the house, out of sight of the terrace. I was at the extreme end of the garden and neither saw nor heard anything unusual.”

“Nothing unusual,” repeated Pons. “Did you hear anything usual? Some familiar sound or sounds that struck you, but which you were able to accept unconsciously?”

Brighton appeared to think. “Why, yes, now that you put it that way. There was a peculiar sloshy sound – as if someone were washing something with a soggy rag, slapping the rag against some surface. Sort of a dull sound, accompanied occasionally by the sound of running water. This lasted for some length of time, and ceased only when I entered the house.”

“What did you think it was?”

“I assumed that one of the neighbors was washing something – their houses are not so very far away – or that Gerald had returned. It did not strike me that the sound was continual for over an hour, but it must have been, for I remember hearing it but at the same time not noticing it during my work. I heard it, too, when I entered the house.”

“Quite so. And what time was it when you entered the house?”

“I think it was just about noon. I couldn’t say exactly, but it was between a quarter of twelve and noon.”

“Now tell us just what you did when you discovered the body,” suggested Pons.

Brighton stuck his hands deep into his pockets. “Of course,” he began, “I was deeply shocked, more than I can say. Gerald and I have been living together for six months, and we had become quite attached to each other."

"You found the body at noon," Pons cut in. "Exactly what did you do?"

"I called Scotland Yard at once," replied Brighton in an injured voice which Pons affected not to notice.

"Very good," interrupted Pons again. "You called the Yard, and Jamison responded. I daresay it took the Yard some time to get Jamison out here – what did you do in the meantime?"

Brighton hesitated; his face began to color slightly. "Well, Mr. Pons, it was a funny thing. The sight of Gerald dead there on the floor simply bowled me over. I was so nervous – I am very nervous, you will have noticed – and I was very much upset. After I had called the Yard, I tried to collect my thoughts, and out of everything, one thought stood out."

"And that?"

"Two days ago Gerald had expressed a wish that three dwarf figures which he had procured in Germany should be colored for him – he wanted them a cardinal red; now, this thought came to me again and again, and what I ended up in doing was to paint those figures. They're out in the kitchen now. I painted them – I was just finishing when Mr. Jamison came, as he can tell you."

"And these figures," said Pons, "where were they standing?"

Brighton indicated a mantel above a fireplace across from the open French doors. "They were on that mantel."

Pons nodded. "I understand that apart from his work as an author, Mr. Lane was accomplished also as an artist of no small repute. Might I ask why he did not himself paint the figures?"

Brighton contemplated the covered body on the floor. "Gerald was a very busy man, Mr. Pons. Nor was such work quite within his scope. Landscapes, seascapes – yes, those Gerald could do, but to coat these figures and still retain the original delicacy of their construction and execution, this

Gerald knew himself incapable of doing. But I've done such things before; you'll see them in all the rooms."

"Indeed," murmured Pons.

Brighton fixed his large eyes on Solar Pons and regarded him unblinkingly. Pons stepped to one side and walked a short distance to a door leading into an inner room; through this he peered momentarily. From the door he turned and said, "I understand that you've been occupying this house for six months – you furnished it, I take it?"

"Yes," answered the author. "I furnished my room and the dining-room; Gerald furnished his room and the lounging room; we went together on the kitchen and the smaller room."

"Ah, so?" murmured Pons, obviously interested. "I should like to see Mr. Lane's room."

"Very well," assented Brighton. "Please follow me." He turned, passing Pons, and entered the inner rooms through the door at which Pons was standing.

Pons followed.

Alone, Inspector Jamison and I turned at once to each other. "It doesn't seem we're getting very much ahead," said Jamison.

"Lane's left-handedness ought to mean something since Pons mentioned it," I suggested.

"It indicates for one thing that there was certainly a struggle," said Jamison, and would perhaps have said more, had not Pons popped into the room at that moment.

"Have you looked into the adjoining dining-room, Jamison?" asked Pons.

"Haven't moved," said Jamison.

"So? Well, take a look at it."

Pons stepped aside and Jamison moved briskly forward. Brighton appeared in the doorway and watched the proceedings with a puzzled face. In a moment Jamison was back.

"Well, Jamison?" asked Pons.

"Funny room, Mr. Pons. Highly decorative, I'd say."

"Quite so," said Pons. His eyes were eager, and he now moved forward again and took his stand at the French doors, looking out across the terrace to a yard adjoining the garden, separated only by a hedge, where a child was playing at building a sand or mud castle.

"Is there anything you could suggest?" asked Jamison in a troubled voice.

Pons turned slightly. "I would call your attention to the peculiarity of this room."

Jamison looked bewildered; he cast a rapid glance around him. "But there's nothing peculiar about this room," he protested.

"That is the peculiarity!" returned Pons.

At the same moment Pons stepped from the room and ran lightly across the terrace. He vaulted the hedge and entered the adjoining yard, where he squatted beside the child and his mud-castle.

"Dear me," murmured Brighton. "What a strange temperament Mr. Pons has. Rather... rather..." He broke off and looked helplessly at Jamison, who was standing and staring at Pons in sheer amazement. "Do you think he's quite – quite right?" suggested Brighton hesitatingly, blinkly owlishly through his glasses. "His actions, now..."

Indeed, Brighton was in a measure justified, for Pons was obviously assisting the child to build his mud-castle. I stepped closer to the French doors, the better to observe the two. Pons was evidently absorbed, but I could see that he was talking to the child at the same time. The child, however, appeared older than I had guessed at first sight – a boy, about four years of age.

For fully ten minutes Pons stayed with the child. When he came back, it was only when he stepped into the room that the tension broke.

"Well, Mr. Pons, whatever this rooms lacks in peculiarity you – you certainly make up for," said Brighton uneasily.

"Indeed, Mr. Brighton," said Pons, smiling. "My peculiarity, however, has just enabled me to discover the source of the curious sloshing sound you heard this morning."

"You don't mean the child?" put in Jamison.

"Precisely. The sloshing sound rose from the child's patting the sand onto the castle, which you will see is already quite far advanced, showing that it has been in the process of erection for some hours. The sound of running water came from a hose, which he can turn on or off at the nozzle whenever he wishes. It follows, then, that the child was building his castle at the time of Mr. Lane's death."

Jamison and Brighton turned quickly to Pons.

"You questioned the child?" asked Jamison.

Pons nodded. "He heard the struggle of which we already have evidence; hence it follows that the struggle was muffled, since the child, directly across from the open French doors heard it, and Mr. Brighton, in the rear, did not."

Pons turned to Brighton. "There has been some mention of a note – a threatening note received by Mr. Lane shortly before his death."

Brighton nodded. "Yes, but it has been destroyed. It was directed to Gerald by some journalist. Mr. John Estenham, I think, for Gerald had lately written a sharp burlesque of Estenham."

"Mr, Estenham was killed three days ago at the Sussex races," said Pons. "Were you aware of this?"

Brighton nodded easily. "Yes, I knew that."

Jamison bristled. "Why didn't you tell us that this noon? When we questioned you?"

Brighton looked surprised. "Why, I thought you knew, of course. If you read the papers – of course, everyone reads the papers."

Jamison subsided. Pons repressed a smile.

"Had Mr. Lane no other enemies?" asked Pons.

"I wouldn't say Estenham was an enemy, Mr. Pons. It's a case of journalism. If he did send that threat, I don't think he sent it seriously. No, I don't think Gerald had any enemies."

"Very good. I should like to have a look at the burlesque that Mr. Lane wrote; I daresay there's a copy of it about."

"Yes, there's a copy in my room," said Brighton. "I'll get it for you."

Hardly had the author disappeared into the dining-room before Pons was up and out through the terrace like a shot. He vanished around a corner before either Jamison or I could move.

A few minutes elapsed.

Brighton returned and looked absently around the room. "Where is Mr. Pons?" he asked.

Even as he spoke Pons stepped into the room from the terrace. He was wiping his hands on a large handkerchief, which he proceeded to stuff into his top-coat pocket. I saw that both his pockets were heavily weighted down; from one a corner of newspaper projected.

"Ah, Mr. Brighton," he said, "you have the burlesque."

Brighton extended the folded clipping to Pons without a word. He fixed his large, unblinking eyes on Pons, and continued to regard him as he read here and there from the article.

"'The great Mr. Pain,'" began Pons, "'has again caused somewhat of a furore by a report on the races, with which he is entirely too familiar. We are told that Mr. Pain has profited by the races; indeed, Mr. Pain is now engaged in financing a new theatrical project, in which he will take the leading role, while directing the show and incidentally also financing it... Mr. Pain is a great asset to certain of us; no doubt of it.'

Hm! Hm!" muttered Pons, and read the remainder of the article in silence. Looking up at last, he said, "I notice that this article isn't signed."

"That's quite usual, Mr. Pons. Very often we do not sign our articles. Often, too, its position in the paper will determine the writer. I think that is how Estenham recognized the author of this satire."

"Indeed," murmured Pons. "I understand that Mr. Lane himself had quite an interest in the theatre?"

Brighton nodded. "Gerald had been an actor since he could walk. His mother was the actress, Jenny Lane. You remember her."

"Quite so. And did Mr. Lane also report races occasionally? This article shows quite a knowledge of racing."

"Gerald used to report races in his earlier days. I think that he still followed them quite eagerly, and often placed money there."

"Thank you, Mr. Brighton. One more thing. I understand that the stiletto which killed your colleague was his own property. Exactly where was this weapon before it was taken up today?"

"Just over on that small stand there," said Brighton, indicating the stand in question. It stood just at one side of the entrance to the room from the hall."

Pons moved rapidly to the stand and examined it. Jamison followed him with his eyes.

"The murderer picked it up as he came in and came directly at Lane," suggested Jamison.

Pons nodded abstractedly, but made no reply. I could see from the puzzled expression on his face that he was in deep thought. Finally he left off his examination and looked over at Brighton.

"I think that will be all. We can do no more here," he said, turning to Jamison. "You might call at our lodgings in about an hour, Jamison. I may have something for you. In the meantime, you may have the body moved."

In our rooms once more, Pons proceeded to empty his topcoat pockets of the heavy objects wrapped in newspaper. I stared at Pons in curiosity, but I forbore to question him, preferring to wait until he himself spoke of his find. But I was to be disappointed, for, after slipping into his dressing-gown, Pons gathered up his burden and disappeared into his laboratory, where I soon heard the sound of running water, punctuated at intervals by muttered ejaculations from Pons.

It was three-quarters of an hour before he finally emerged, and by that time my curiosity knew no bounds.

"Well," I asked "what have you been doing?"

"Putting our little problem together in its proper order, Parker."

I saw now that he held in his hand a curiously carved manikin, a troll figure, Austrian in origin.

"The other two are in the laboratory," said Pons. "This is the only one we're concerned with."

"Lane's three dwarfs, are they?"

He nodded silently. He placed the dwarf upon the table and regarded it fondly.

"I thought they were red," I put in.

"So they were," said Pons. "I have just now removed the paint."

"Why?"

"To ascertain which of the three made the bruises on Lane's body, and to prove to myself that the figures were painted not because Lane wished it so, but because one of them was stained with blood."

"Good heavens!" I exclaimed.

"This wood, as you see," Pons went on imperturbably, "takes stain very easily. Even now I have not been able to get all the paint off; yet, it's easy to see under scrutiny where the original blood-stain was. I have no doubt that Brighton carefully washed off what blood he could, but he could not wholly remove the stain. Therefore, rather than destroy these attractive figures, he thought to cover them with paint so as to hide the blood-stain."

"Then Brighton is the murderer!"

Pons chuckled. "Brighton hasn't the courage to kill anything – yet he has the cleverness to try to foil the police investigation by cloaking what little evidence there is."

"He knows who killed Lane, then?"

"He knows all about the matter, Parker," replied Pons. "Let me assure you that it's not as mysterious as you have perhaps imagined."

At this moment there was a ring at the doorbell, and shortly after, Jamison strode into the room, excitement showing in his face.

"There's been a new development, Pons," he said eagerly.

"Indeed?"

"You remember those red dwarfs Brighton mentioned?" Pons nodded.

"Well, they're gone. Someone's made off with them. Brighton is quite upset about the affair."

"I'm sorry to hear that," replied Pons. "Because I took them myself."

"You!" exclaimed Jamison.

"Yes. Here's one of them," continued Pons, handing to Jamison the dwarf he had been discussing.

"But this isn't red," protested Jamison.

"No, certainly not. I cleaned them in order to get to the bottom of this matter."

"You have the murderer!" exclaimed Jamison.

"There is no murderer," said Pons.

"Ah, it was suicide after all! I was right at first, then?"

"It was not suicide," continued Pons with maddening imperturbability.

"Well," said Jamison in justifiable exasperation, "I'm certain he didn't die of heart failure."

"But almost the same, Jamison," chuckled Pons. "The entire matter was somewhat of an accident." Pons reached down into his wastebasket and drew forth a newspaper, through which he searched diligently before finding what he sought. At last, however, he folded the paper and extended it to Jamison, indicating a paragraph to him. "Read it aloud," Pons suggested. "I'm afraid I had a slight lead on you at the outset."

"'The artist and author, Mr. Gerald Lane, was today fined twenty guineas for assault and battery committed on the person of Mr. Eldridge Morton, the art critic, whose comments on his work aroused the temper of Mr. Lane. Mr. Lane, it will be remembered, was recently severely reprimanded in this court for a like offense; he is well known in artistic circles for his furious outbursts of temper.'"

"You see it now, I hope," said Pons.

Jamison shook his head. "It doesn't help me in the least," he said. "But surely this fact alone did not lead you to the solution of the case?"

"No, certainly not," said Pons. "But reflect, I called your attention to my other point, in noting the peculiarity of the room in which we found the body. If you care now to re-examine the house in St. John's Wood, you'll see that every room furnished by Brighton is marked by a radical clash of colors – no true artist can tolerate such gaudy, showy decorative effects as those colored figures in the other rooms. Lane's rooms are in splendid harmony. Yet we were told that he had wished to have his German troll figures painted a cardinal red – a color altogether out of harmony with his room. That, Jamison, was one of my chief points. There was nothing peculiar about the room, but, after you look into the dining room, that very fact becomes a peculiarity."

"Then Brighton deliberately blocked our investigation," put in Jamison.

"I fear he did," agreed Pons. "But his work was clumsily done; any amateur could see through it."

"Yet I did not."

"Well, it's really quite elementary," said Pons. "At the outset, it should be perfectly obvious that the author of that article in the paper was not Lane at all, but Brighton, and that the subject had nothing at all to do with the man Estenham, but concerned Lane. Note the curious point of the name of the subject, Pain – what more similar in mockery to Lane? Then too, throughout the entire article the parallelism of character between Pain and Lane is too obvious. There was no note from Estenham, of course, but Brighton rather cleverly invented this point to befog the police."

Jamison looked uncomfortable.

"Couple this fact with what we knew at the outset. It was certainly inconceivable that Lane should want to break the harmony of his room by introducing the red figures; this struck me at once. Then I thought of the reputed violence of Lane's temper, and when I read the article itself, my suspicions were definitely formulated and I lacked only the proof, which I already had in my pocket. Now that I've cleaned the figures, I have ascertained that on one of them there is still evidence of a blood-stain."

"Then it was this that made the bruises on Lane's body," Jamison cut in.

Pons nodded.

"But if the entire matter was an accident, why should Brighton strike him like that – assuming it was Brighton who inflicted thc bruises?"

"It was," Pons assented. "That, however, is equally elementary. You have only to recall Lane's violent temper and imagine what a rage he flew into when he discovered that the author of the satiric article was Brighton. He found this out and rushed home immediately to take issue with Brighton. He was in a violent temper, naturally. Brighton was probably not in the garden at all, but was somewhere in the house. By the time that Lane had his outer clothing off, Brighton had heard him, and he came into the room where we found the body, wondering what had brought Lane home. Thus it was that the child next door heard the struggle that followed and Brighton did not, because Brighton was there, in the room.

"At the moment that Brighton entered the room, Lane undoubtedly caught up the first weapon that came to hand – his stiletto. Brighton instinctively moved to protect himself, and took up the only weapon within his reach, one of the little manikins on the mantel behind him. He had no wish to injure Lane, knowing that the violence of his temper passed quickly, but he did not want to be slashed if he could help it. Therefore, he struck at Lane's left hand – Lane was left-handed – hoping to disarm him. When this was not effective, most probably Brighton seized hold of Lane's left hand, dropping the manikin, and struggled with him – the result was the first wound inflicted on Lane.

"Undoubtedly, in the course of the struggle, Lane pressed Brighton pretty hard, and Brighton clung all the while to Lane's left hand, so that in the end, when Brighton was forced to the wall, it was pure accident that the stiletto impaled Lane. You probably noticed in your examination of the body that the left arm was twisted toward the stiletto; I daresay that's as good a point as any – it strikes me as more or less throwing the weight of evidence on the fact that Lane's hand was clasped about the weapon when it entered his heart. And then it is needless for me to say, I suppose, Lane must have fallen near the dwarf that Brighton had dropped, so that it became blood-stained.

"Of course, it's clear that, after his first fright, Brighton became calculatingly cool; the man who wrote the monograph on chess emerged then, and laid elaborate plans to foil an investigation. And in this he might well have succeeded, had his artistic leanings not bidden him keep the figures, the one of which was so blood-stained that he could not wash it all away, by painting them.

"His motivation in hiding the facts was, naturally enough, the fear that the facts might be misconstrued."

Pons paused and lit his pipe.

"You might take the manikins back to him, Jamison," he added. "And pray don't think of prosecuting Brighton, for a capable barrister will efficiently clear Brighton of all blame in the matter, especially since there is Lane's previous record to bring forward."

VII

THE ADVENTURE OF THE SOTHEBY SALESMAN

It was on a warm summer night in mid-August that the curious matter of the Sotheby salesman came to the notice of my friend, Solar Pons. Fortunately, Pons had no problem in hand; he and I had spent the greater part of the day in Soho, moving idly from one place to another. Shortly after eleven o'clock that night we returned to our lodgings in Praed Street and found the telegram which was to introduce us to the mystery at Sotheby.

> CAN YOU COME DOWN TO SOTHEBY AT ONCE EXTRAORDINARY AFFAIR HAS TAKEN PLACE HERE SOMETHING QUITE IN YOUR LINE
>
> Jeremy Hudson

"Sotheby," I said. "Where is it?"

"Just south of Aldershot," answered Pons. "It's only a village, if I'm not mistaken. Can't have more than a thousand inhabitants."

"I don't remember having any acquaintance with Hudson."

"I daresay you haven't. He's an interesting chap; police inspector at Aldershot. His mind has on more than one occasion struck me as promisingly acute. I'm certain that if he must resort to me, the problem is more than ordinarily interesting." Pons looked at his watch. "We've just time to make the twelve-ten at Victoria."

Within a half hour we were well on our way to Sotheby. Pons was in good spirits, anticipating an interesting puzzle, and he had put me in much the same frame of mind. At Woking Pons was fortunate enough to procure a copy of *The Aldershot Chronicle* from a local lad, and there we found reported what was undoubtedly the matter which had incited Hudson's wire.

CURIOUS AFFAIR AT SOTHEBY
Salesman Slain in Empty House

> The body of Mr. Peter Woodall was found late this afternoon in an empty house on Pearsall Street, the property of Mr. William Hendricks, who lives next door. The dead man was identified as a salesman by several merchants of Sotheby who came to view the body. It was later ascertained that the late Mr. Woodall was native to Aldershot, and Police Inspector Hudson was summoned to take charge of the investigation.
>
> An early examination shows that Mr. Woodall was killed by a rifle shot, and that he had already been dead some time, between eighteen and twenty-two hours, when found. The *Chronicle* was sent to examine into the matter.

"Hm!" muttered Pons. "This is the seven o'clock edition of the paper, and the man had been dead between eighteen and twenty-two hours when found late this afternoon. That would put the murder at somewhere around nine o'clock last night."

"It sounds perplexing enough."

"The matter certainly presents interesting angles," agreed Pons. "The first question which naturally arises concerns the reason for the salesman's presence in an empty house obviously not his own property."

"And who would be sufficiently acquainted with his movements to be on hand to shoot him when he arrived?"

"Well, I daresay speculation is idle. Let us wait until we reach the scene before we search for conclusions."

At the small station of Sotheby we were met by Inspector Hudson in person. He was a tall, heavily-built man near middle age, with plain, unattractive features. He wore a slight black moustache on his upper lip. He was obviously glad to see us, for he ran toward Pons with outstretched hand as we stepped from the train.

We were soon comfortably seated in Hudson's car, rattling away toward the scene of the murder, which was, it developed, on the farther side of the village.

"We've seen the first reports of the matter," said Pons, tapping the paper he still carried, "but, of course, we can learn little from them. Has the coroner determined when the man was killed?"

"Yes. It was between nine and ten last night – probably closer to ten."

"Indeed. The paper says he was killed with a rifle. Has the calibre been ascertained?"

"Not definitely, Mr. Pons. The size of the hole in Woodall's head indicates either a .22 or a .25."

"The bullet is lodged in the head, then?"

"Yes."

"Well, then, perhaps the man was not shot in the house," ventured Pons.

"Some of us have thought he was shot elsewhere and dragged into the building. But I am not inclined to agree with that theory, for I've examined the grounds minutely, and it is definitely certain that Woodall came alone to the house, walked along the side wall and entered through the back door."

"I take it you went over the footprints?"

"Certainly, Mr. Pons. Besides, there had been rain two nights ago, and the ground under the eaves at the side of the house where Woodall walked was somewhat muddy. Some of this mud can be found adhering to Woodall's boots."

"Excellent, Hudson!" exclaimed Pons, his keen, dark eyes twinkling.

"Yet," continued Hudson, "if the man had not been shot elsewhere – and presumably he had not – I find it difficult to determine why the rifle bullet did not go through his head. – But here we are," he added, as the car drew up before a small estate fenced off from the street by a row of white staves.

A constable at the gate saluted us as we passed. We walked up a poorly marked path and entered the house through the front door, Hudson pointing out from the windows as we went from one room to another the path taken by the victim in going around to the back door.

As we entered the kitchen, two constables who were standing beside the body directed the light of their flashes upon the recumbent form on the floor. The body was that of a middle-aged man, small of build, dressed in shabby clothes. It was difficult to imagine this unprepossessing man – for such he must have been in life – a solicitor of trade. His features were colorless, and must have been even in life. His hair was thin and sandy, and he had an incipient moustache of the same tinge. He lay almost in the center of the room, crumpled on his side, his legs twisted beneath him, his arms flung grotesquely outward.

At Inspector Hudson's order a lamp was now lit, for there was no electricity, and the room immediately came to life. It could now be seen that the back door opened directly on the kitchen, for it was standing ajar, and the light from the lamp threw a feeble glow outward and revealed a path of cobblestones leading away from the door. The utterly bare walls of the room were broken only by the door leading into the inner rooms, and a window looking out on the side of the house. The window, set low in the wall, had been lowered from the top as far as it could go.

The lamp was placed on the floor beside the body, and Pons sank to his knees the better to examine the dead man. He peered intently at the black wound in the dead man's left temple, from which little blood had flowed. Then he examined the dead man's clothes, rummaging through the pockets, but he found nothing save a small penny box of matches which was two-thirds empty. Having completed this scrutiny, he took up the lamp and, holding it aloft in one hand, crept around and around the body in ever-widening circles. At intervals he placed the lamp on the floor, in order to scrutinize anything that might catch his eye. It was an hour before this process was completed, but at last Pons rose and gave the lamp to one of the constables.

Then he took from his pocket his own flash and vanished into the interior of the house, where we could hear him tramping from room to room. At length he went outside, for we heard the front door open and shut, and presently the light of his flash appeared at the window, where we could see him examining the tracks made by the late Mr. Woodall in approaching the kitchen. At last he himself pushed wider the kitchen door and stepped into the room.

For some moments Pons stood gazing with rapt interest at the lowered window, his eyes slightly narrow now, his lips pushing out and in his customary fashion when deep in thought. Then he turned abruptly to Hudson and inquired, "Who lives next door on this side?"

"The owner – a Mr. William Hendricks."

"And on the other side?"

"Mr. Jonathan Green, one of the merchants who was able to identify the body."

Pons turned this information over in his mind for a moment without comment. Then he continued, "I understand Hendricks discovered the body late yesterday afternoon. How was it that he came to the house?"

"The same question occurred to me," answered Hudson. "He told us he came to shut the window, which he first then saw to be open."

"Ah, so!" exclaimed Pons. "It was not, of course, usual for this window to be open?"

"No."

"So I thought. I noticed that all the other windows on the ground floor were securely latched, and it struck me as strange that this one should be open. What do you make of this window's being open, Hudson?"

"Why," said Hudson in some surprise, "I assume Woodall opened it."

"Quite so, Hudson," said Pons. "But surely it is obvious that Woodall was shot immediately upon entering the house? For undoubtedly you have seen that the salesman, upon coming into the kitchen, struck a match and that, by the light of this match, the murderer shot him down?"

Hudson sprang forward with an exclamation. Pons extended a match, burned a good two-thirds of the way from the head, which he had evidently found on the floor during his previous examination.

"You intimate that someone waited for Woodall?" asked Hudson in some trepidation.

"Precisely. The fact is self-evident. Someone came to this house and opened the window; this was certainly not Woodall, for he was unfamiliar with the house. Therefore, whoever opened that window knew that Woodall was to come here tonight..."

Pons stopped suddenly, still looking intently at the open window, then clapped one hand to his head, and ran swiftly out of the open back door, to the amazement of Inspector Hudson and the constables. In a few moments it was possible to determine Pons' whereabouts, for there came through the window a flash of light behind a hedge some distance from the house. This vanished after five minutes, and there now occurred an interval of fully a quarter of an hour, at the expiration of which Pons suddenly appeared in the open doorway.

"Singular!" he muttered, coming into the room. "Most singular." He flashed a glance at Hudson. "I understand that Woodall was an inhabitant of Aldershot. Do I understand that he made his home there?"

"He didn't have a home of his own, Mr. Pons. But he certainly spent his free time there, staying at a second-rate hotel, *The Antler Inn*."

"You are aware of no enemies he might have had?"

"Entirely unaware of any. Woodall was a meek, timid man, not likely to arouse enmity. It is always the strong man who has enemies, seldom the weak."

"True," assented Pons. "But surely this must have blocked your search for a motive?"

"The murder seems marked by an entire absence of motive," admitted Hudson. "But if you've discovered anything," he continued, looking sharply at Pons, "I should be glad if you could suggest it to me."

"I think it quite possible to say that the murderer was concealed behind a hedge dividing this property from that of its owner, Mr. Hendricks. It is obvious that he waited there for some time – over an hour, I should say. The distance from here to the hiding place is roughly about fifty yards; I think you'll find upon investigation that a bullet from a .25 calibre rifle will not go through a man's head at fifty yards. While he waited, the murderer dropped a fragment of a note."

Pons took from his pocket a small, triangular scrap of paper, which he spread on his palm for Hudson to see.

"You will observe," Pons went on, "that the piece is so torn as to give us three words – the first word, *he*, on the topmost line of this scrap, and two words on a following line, *nine* and *ten*, from which the connective has been torn, but I daresay we would be quite safe in assuming the missing word to be *and*. Then, below, we have the first letter of a signature, the letter *J*. I give you that for what it is worth to you, Hudson; for the present I should like to retain the scrap. Also, I would commend to your attention the clothes of the late Mr. Woodall, and the articles found in them."

"But there were no articles found – only a box of matches."

"That is what I would draw to your notice." Pons turned and looked from the window, where in the grey of the sky white rifts were coming. "Dawn is breaking, Hudson, and I would like to have a few words with Mr. Jonathan Green. I daresay it can be arranged."

"Certainly, Mr. Pons." Hudson turned to one of the constables and instructed him to go to Green's house and rouse him.

It was becoming rapidly lighter as we left the empty house and walked slowly down the path. In the street Pons spoke again.

"You will note that these three houses – Hendricks' two, and Green's – are fenced in as one estate, though hedges divide them."

"Yes," replied Hudson, "I understand that Green bought his house from Hendricks, who built all three. They are similar in structure, too."

We entered Green's property. Just beyond the gate Pons stopped and indicated a short triangular series of footprints leading from the gate and back to it again.

"Let me call to your notice that Woodall first entered here and ventured some distance before discovering his error and retracing his steps."

"The man made a mistake anyone might have made."

"Quite so. But recall the note. One does not appoint a rendezvous at a place with which one of the parties is not familiar. Especially is this true when the rendezvous has been made for night."

"You think there was a rendezvous, then?"

"Surely it is not a coincidence that the fragment of note should mention the hours of nine and ten, between which the coroner has given his verdict that Woodall was killed?"

"But who would write to Woodall?" asked Hudson in perplexity. "Since you put it that way, you certainly bring forward a new aspect. Unless I've been greatly deceived by Woodall's appearance, I find it difficult to concede that anyone might write him to appoint a rendezvous, obviously meant to be secret."

"A good, pertinent question, Hudson. Who would write Woodall?" He paused and looked intently at Hudson with a twinkle in his eye. "Who would write to a common salesman, and sit patiently waiting to dispose of him – a man who had not an enemy in the world?"

"The problem grows more and more puzzling."

"Indeed, Hudson. Where are your wits?" exclaimed Pons in mild irritation. "After all, the note was not found on Woodall's body."

"Someone might have taken it."

Pons shook his head impatiently. "The soft ground shows you that no one approached the deserted house until Hendricks came to examine into the matter of the open window. Besides, the note had been near the hedge since the night of the murder. Now, Hudson, I leave you to ponder over these things; here we are at the home of Mr. Green and, if I am not in error, there is our man in that small room just ahead."

Jonathan Green was a rather handsome man about forty years of age. Slightly built, clothed in a dark blue dressing-gown, he presented a good appearance as he stood waiting for us in his small library.

"We're sorry to knock you up so early, Mr. Green," said Hudson, "but Mr. Pons here, who is looking into the matter next door, wished to have a few words with you."

"Quite all right," said Green in a mild, pleasant tone of voice. "I'm ready to answer any question you may care to ask."

Pons thanked him with a nod. "Forgive me if I come directly to the matter in hand. In regard to the occurrence next door, it rather surprised me that no one had made mention of hearing the shot that killed the poor fellow. Did you, by any chance, hear a shot between nine and ten o'clock on the night of the crime?"

"Yes, I did."

"Did you get up to look about?"

"No."

"Are shots then so common in this part of the country?"

"In a way, yes," replied Green, smiling at Pons' surprise. "You understand, Mr. Pons, we are at one end of the village out here, and it's not unusual for rabbits from the neighboring fens to come prowling about our small gardens at night. Mr. Hendricks has been especially bothered with the pests – they have been eating his vegetables – and he has got into the habit of rising at night to shoot them. I myself occasionally take a shot at them. The neighborhood would not be startled by a shot or two before midnight."

"How long has this been going on?"

"Oh, ever since last spring."

"I think we may take it for granted that whoever shot Woodall knew of that," I put in.

Pons assented shortly and turned again to Green. "Might I ask you what you were doing on the night of the murder, Mr. Green?"

"Certainly," answered Green readily. "I was preparing to go out, but I changed my mind and remained at home."

"Was that after the shot?" put in Hudson eagerly.

Green regarded Hudson inscrutably for a moment before he replied, "Yes, after the shot."

"May I ask where you had intended going?" inquired Pons.

"I'd rather not say," returned Green, coloring a little. "Of course if you must know..."

Pons waved the question good-naturedly aside. "You're not a married man, I see," he said, chuckling.

"No, I'm not," Green admitted. "But it's not my fault."

There was general laughter, only Pons retaining his composure. Pons now produced a pen and paper and extended them to Green.

"Just as a matter of course," he explained, "will you write down and sign a statement that you heard a shot between nine and ten on the night of the crime?"

"Certainly," said Green. He took the paper and pen, and retired to a small desk nearby, where he sat and wrote out the desired statement. He turned and read what he had written: "I hereby depose that I heard a shot between nine and ten o'clock on the night of 17 August." He looked up. "Is that satisfactory?"

"Quite," said Pons, and gravely took the extended paper, folded it, and slipped it into his pocket. "I think that will be all, Mr. Green. Thank you for bearing with us."

On the street once more, Pons turned to Hudson. "Now I should like to ask a few questions of Mr. Hendricks."

Hudson nodded. "He must be up by this time. If not, we'll have no difficulty in routing him."

Pons nodded absently.

"By the way, Mr. Pons," Hudson broke in, "if I might ask, why did you want Green to write out a statement?"

"I thought that quite obvious, Hudson," replied Pons. "You'll note that the statement contains both the words *nine* and *ten*. A brief glance at the fragment of note found behind the hedge has already assured me that its writer and Mr. Jonathan Green are one and the same. The writing is marked by the Roman *e*; the *J* of the signature is precisely the same; there is the identical pronounced upward slant – all in all, there is only a very slight difference between the two writings."

Hudson pondered this briefly before he protested, "But if Green wrote that note, he can't be our man, for the note could not have been written to himself."

"Certainly not. But you forget that, as you yourself proposed, the murderer might have recovered the note in some fashion. Also, you might have noticed on the wall of Green's library just such a weapon as killed Woodall – a .25 calibre rifle."

Hudson gave vent to an exclamation, and slowed his pace perceptibly.

"And to top that, my dear Hudson, it is quite possible that some painful business details between the late Woodall and Mr. Green supplied the motive for this apparently so perplexing puzzle. It would be interesting to build up a hypothetical case along those lines."

"Striking!" murmured Hudson. "I never considered that angle."

"Obviously," said Pons dryly. "Nor would I suggest that you give much thought to it now."

Inspector Hudson turned a chagrined face to me.

"However," continued Pons imperturbably, "if you're determined to get ahead with your investigation, I would advise that you return to Mr. Green and discover just where he was going the night of the murder."

"You think that important?"

"Extremely so. Indeed, perhaps it is most important. Has it not occurred to you that Green might have been on his way to visit the person to whom he had addressed his note?" Pons waved Hudson away. "Don't think of us, Hudson. We'll find Hendricks easily enough. Do go ahead and do as you please – question Green; find out where he was going. Don't be too harsh with him."

"You think it will be necessary to be harsh with him?" asked Hudson dubiously.

"Perhaps. In any case, I venture to predict that Mr. Green will prove remarkably reticent about where he had intended going between the hours of nine and ten on the night of the murder – despite his show of good-natured willingness to tell us a few minutes ago."

"I'll go back," said Hudson with determination.

"Follow us to Hendricks' as soon as you can."

Hudson turned and walked rapidly back along the street, while Pons and I turned in at the third of the houses that were so alike. Our coming had not been unobserved, for no sooner had we closed the gate behind us than a tall, striking figure, dressed in hunting clothes, came striding around a corner of the house and bore rapidly down on us. As he came on, I observed that his face was marked by small sharp eyes beneath bristling brows, a full sensuous mouth, and a dark, heavy moustache. He came to a halt ten feet away and glowered at us suspiciously.

"Mr. Hendricks, I presume," ventured Pons.

The fellow nodded.

"I'm looking into the matter next door and there are a few questions I would like to ask you. I am Solar Pons, and this gentleman is my assistant, Dr. Parker."

"Why, certainly," responded Hendricks, softening at once. "Will you come into the house?"

Without waiting for an answer, he turned on his heel and strode rapidly toward the house, Pons and I trailing him. In a few moments we were comfortably seated in Hendricks' den, a replica of Green's library, differing in that where Green displayed books, Hendricks had filled the room with trophies of the hunt.

"Now, Mr. Pons, I'll answer anything you ask if it bears on this matter," said Hendricks.

"I want to know first whether you heard the shot that killed Woodall?"

"I can't say for certain, of course," answered Hendricks slowly, "but I think I did. At least, I heard a shot between nine and ten o'clock on the night the fellow was killed."

"You didn't investigate?"

"It's common for some of us to rise at night and shoot rabbits grubbing in our gardens. I have the habit; so has my neighbor, Green. I thought Green was protecting his garden when I heard the shot."

Pons reflected for a moment, Hendricks watching him closely. "I should like to know your reaction on discovering Woodall's body."

"Naturally, I was very much surprised," replied Hendricks without a trace of emotion. "I knew Woodall slightly, of course, but not enough to speak to. I notified the police at once."

"What did you think when you saw the body?"

"Well, I didn't think it was a case of murder; I thought the poor fellow had made away with himself – I understand he'd not been in sound condition financially – but the absence of the weapon left no alternative but that murder had been done."

"Precisely," agreed Pons. He allowed his gaze to linger on Hendricks' new hunting boots. "One more thing – I am told you went over to the house to close the kitchen window; you did not close it. Why?"

Hendricks shrugged his shoulders. "Purely an oversight, I suppose. In the excitement of the discovery, I naturally overlooked it; later on, I realized that it was the best thing I could have done, for it left the scene just as I found it."

"The windows were always kept locked, then. Were the doors also kept locked?"

Hendricks leaned eagerly forward. "There you have it, Mr. Pons. Those doors were always locked. Yet, Woodall didn't break in the back door – so it must have been open when he got there. Question is, who opened it?"

"Who has the key?"

"It's kept in a drawer in my room."

"The drawer is kept locked?"

"No."

"So that anyone in the house had access to it?"

"Yes, but there are only three of us. My wife, my man, and myself."

"Very good, Mr. Hendricks. I should like to speak to your wife."

"Very well," answered Hendricks and left the room to get her.

Mrs. Hendricks was a slight woman, somewhat younger than her husband, and singularly attractive. My first impression, which I felt Pons shared, was that Mrs. Hendricks had been weeping; for this seemed evident, despite the patent efforts she had made to disguise the fact. She greeted us in a light voice, which impressed me favorably.

Before Pons could begin to question her, there was a sharp rapping at the front door, and Hendricks departed to answer it. As he left the room, I noticed that his wife followed him with her eyes – and I was struck with her gaze, for it was venomous with hatred.

"Mrs. Hendricks," Pons spoke quickly, "do you realize that you have unintentionally caused the death of a man?"

"What do you mean?" she asked breathlessly, her face paling so that the artificial color flamed on her cheeks.

"You unlocked the back door of the empty house so that someone could keep an appointment with you," began Pons, only to be interrupted by the woman.

She sprang up in uncontrollable agitation and came over to Pons. She put her hand on his arm, and looked at him, wide-eyed. "How much do you know?" she demanded.

"Everything," answered Pons, looking sternly at her.

For a moment there was silence. She swayed a little, and I thought briefly that she might faint, but she did not. "My God!" she breathed. "Surely you can't blame me?" She stepped back. Then, with an abrupt gesture, she allowed her kimono to slip down over her shoulder, exposing her skin, upon which were ugly, dark welts.

There was an exclamation from Pons. I felt a sudden wave of pity for Mrs. Hendricks.

"I have to live with him," she said passionately. "I hate him – he beats me." She stopped and looked at Pons steadily for a moment, struggling to regain her composure. "You know all – about the note?"

"Yes," said Pons in a low voice, for we could hear the footsteps of Hendricks and Hudson approaching along the passage.

"I lost it," she went on hurriedly. "I know *he* found it. And his temper – I knew that might happen. But I called Jon in time!" She stopped and hastily rearranged her kimono.

"I think that will be all," said Pons kindly, as the two men entered the room. "Please return to your room, Mrs. Hendricks."

The woman got up obediently and, without a glance at her husband, who had shot a quick, suspicious look at her, left the room. Pons turned to Inspector Hudson.

"Well?" he asked, "Did Green tell you?" Hudson shook his head glumly. "Not a word. And got quite angry, too."

Pons smiled. "But I shall have something of interest for you soon, Hudson. Will you be so good as to call two of your constables?"

"Certainly, Mr. Pons." He was as surprised as I at Pons' request, and he could not help betraying his perplexity as he left the room to call the constables from the empty house next door.

"I hope you're getting on, Mr. Pons," said Hendricks. "This business is awkward for me."

"I shall have the matter cleared up before long," answered Pons.

At this moment Hudson and his two men entered.

"Ah, Hudson," murmured Pons. "Please step forward. You may arrest Mr. Hendricks and charge him with the wilful murder of Mr. Woodall night before last."

There was a hoarse bellow of rage from Hendricks, but the constables were upon him before he could reach Pons, and in a few moments he was securely manacled between them.

"It would be well if we removed from Mr. Hendricks that part of the evidence he has not destroyed," continued Pons, as if nothing had taken place. "Some inconvenience will no doubt be caused, but in the circumstances it would be better to remove the prisoner's right boot, on the sole of which you will find a fragment of flint pressed into the hard leather; comparison with the print beside the hedge will prove that it was made with this boot."

Only after Hendricks was taken away did Pons consent to expound the case to Hudson, who came bristling with questions to take us back to the station.

"Let us start at the beginning," began Pons. "You will remember, I called your attention to the articles found in the dead man's pockets, and to his clothes?"

Hudson nodded.

"Very good. I did so because it was perfectly obvious that his entire lack of the smallest necessities, his threadbare clothing, supplied the answer to the primary question of why Woodall was in the empty house. He was there for shelter; having no means and a little pride, perhaps lacking friends and, knowing this for an empty house, he planned to spend the night here. He entered as we know by way of the back door. In the kitchen he struck a match to look around him and was shot down by a good marksman at fifty yards – from the hedge next his home.

"Since the purpose of the salesman in coming to the house must certainly have been kept secret, it follows then that the note written by Mr. Green, a fragment of which we found near the hedge, where Hendricks carelessly dropped it, could not possibly have been addressed to Woodall. After our conversation with Green, I was satisfied that he had not written a note to lure someone to the house to be killed, as at first it appeared. Instead, a new element entered into the matter. I had now to determine who opened the back door and the kitchen window. The key to the door was kept in Hendricks' drawer, where he, his wife, or his man had access to it.

"Thus, by simple elimination, it became evident that Mrs. Hendricks had opened the door; therefore, it followed that Green's note had been addressed to her, for surely Green was not arranging a tryst with Hendricks or his man. In turn, it follows that there was something between Mrs. Hendricks and Mr. Green. However, if Mrs. Hendricks had, on receiving Green's note appointing the empty house as a safe place to meet – I daresay they had met there before – gone over and unlocked the back door, so that Green could enter and wait for her, surely she did not open the kitchen window, for this would have attracted her husband's attention.

"It was evident that, owing to the habits of Mr. Hendricks – you remember the *he* of the note, a pronoun I take to refer to Hendricks – no definite hour of meeting could be appointed; hence the rendezvous was made for some time between nine and ten o'clock that night. Now, if neither Mrs. Hendricks nor Woodall opened that window, who did? Could it be anyone but the man who intended to take his chance shooting through it without breaking the pane? Hardly, I daresay. This man was Hendricks, for he had found the note Mrs. Hendricks lost, and in his jealous fury, he determined to put Green definitely out of the way.

"But he failed to reckon on his wife who, when she missed the note, called Green to warn him away. Hendricks, knowing nothing of this, concealed himself behind his hedge, and, when he saw a figure enter the grounds and pass into the house, he prepared to shoot. And at the moment when Woodall struck a match to look about him at the place he had chosen to spend the night in, Hendricks fired and killed him. That is all there is to the matter."

Pons paused briefly before he added, "By the way, Hudson, if you want to do me a favor, let me suggest that you keep the relations of Mrs. Hendricks and Green as much out of the picture as possible."

To this Hudson unhesitatingly agreed.

There was an epilogue to this curious affair. Hudson was as good as his word, for there was no mention of Mrs. Hendricks and Green in the prosecution, and much trouble was saved by Hendricks' confession, for he made no mention of his motive in killing the salesman.

A year after the death of Hendricks, Pons received in the mail a clipping telling briefly of the wedding of Mr. Jonathan Green and the widow of the late Mr. William Hendricks. There was no signature, nor any indication of who might have sent it, but Pons never had a doubt of the sender. Nor had I.

VIII

THE ADVENTURE OF THE PURLOINED PERIAPT

We had been talking about the science of deduction that noon hour, when we turned into Praed Street not far from our lodgings, and Pons touched my arm with a gesture designed to direct my attention to a young man walking not far ahead of us.

"Now then, Parker, let us see what you make of that fellow going there. You know my methods; apply them."

"He seems a perfectly ordinary young fellow," I answered at once. "Like thousands of others."

"Yes, indeed. But do not speak so hastily. Look again."

I saw that the object of our scrutiny walked along with occasional glances at the numbers, and said that manifestly he was looking up an address.

"Elementary. Anything more?"

"He seems to be of modest means; he is not yet thirty years of age; he is obviously English."

"You see nothing further?"

"Nothing but the obvious details relative to the color and make of his clothes." I glanced at him. "I suppose you are about to tell me a host of incredible conclusions to which you have come in these few steps."

"No, no, you over-rate my poor powers, Parker. I was about to add only that he is unmarried; he lives in the suburbs of London; he cycles to work; he is very probably a book-keeper; and he is employed in our immediate vicinity. Moreover, he is not imaginative, but rather prosaic; he is precise and methodical, but sparing at the expense of neatness, and he is at the moment doing without his luncheon in an effort to accomplish something which has nothing to do with his work, for he is too conscientious to take time away from his work to pursue an inquiry into what is a purely personal matter."

For a moment I was too astonished to reply. Then I protested. "Oh, come, Pons – I have every respect for your use of the science of deduction, but I cannot follow you in all that."

"I assure you it is all extremely simple, my dear fellow. Surely no wife would permit her husband to go to work in such unpressed clothes, any more than she would allow him to wear a shirt which carries on the cuff the kind of inkmarks commonly found on the cuffs of those engaged in book-keeping? By the same token, the fellow is sparing at the expense of neatness, for he has not had his suit pressed, nor his shirt washed; yet he dresses rather well, if in singular dreariness of color, betraying a lack of imagination."

"He cycles, you said."

"Surely that mark on his trousers' leg is nothing other than the mark of one of those clips designed to keep the trousers free of the wheel."

"I missed that. But how, then, do you know he lives in the suburbs?"

"Because a cycle is the readiest way to work from the suburbs, if one is employed in the heart of the city and is at the same time of such modest means that a certain care in spending money is advisable."

"Very well, granting that – I fail utterly to understand how you can say with such positive assurance that he is employed in our vicinity."

"Ah, but surely that follows inevitably. If he cycles to work, obviously he has his cycle at hand. Since he does not use it to look up an address which I fancy will turn out to be our own, certainly it is not too much to deduce that his place of employment is so close to the address he seeks that it would be superfluous to use his cycle!"

I shook my head. "I am afraid I am destined always to fall short of your kind of observation, Pons."

"But you have your diagnoses to uphold, Parker, and they should be your primary concern." He smiled. "Ah, see; it is as I thought. He has reached number seven; he pauses; he is going in. Now we shall soon learn what it is that troubles him to the extent that he is willing to depart from what is doubtless a long-established routine in order to bring the problem to us.

As we entered the outer door to our lodgings, we were seen by Mrs. Johnson, who had answered the bell.

"You're in luck, Mr. Harris. Here they are now." She smiled in our direction and raised her voice a little to say, "Here's a gentleman to see Mr. Pons!" and then vanished discreetly into her own quarters.

"Come along, Mr. Harris," invited Pons, as we ascended the stairs to our own lodgings on the second floor.

"Thank you," replied Mr. Harris soberly, and set out after us with an expression of intense gravity on his serious young features.

In this prosaic fashion began one of Solar Pons' favorite adventures, for Mr. Sidney Harris had come to consult Pons about the loss of a jeweled amulet, to which he referred constantly as "my uncle's periapt." He was a young man whose demeanor gave evidence of every deduction Pons had made of him; he readily admitted that he was employed as a book-keeper for the firm of Chasins and Abramson only three streets away from our lodgings, and he told his story with simple precision.

"I live with my sister, who keeps house for me, and there are living with me my father, who is in ill health, my brother, who is occasionally employed as a clerk in a tobacconist's shop, and my cousin, Richard Murchison. We live in South Norwood, and I cycle to work every day, since my salary does not permit of unnecessary expense in traveling to and from the place of my employment. About three months ago my uncle died; he was Teale Murchison."

"Ah, the publisher of religious books."

"Yes, Mr. Pons. The firm still carries his name, though he was no longer actively associated with it at the time of his death. He was my mother's only brother, and he lived in the country south of London."

"A wealthy, charitable old man," observed Pons. "How does it come that his son lives with you?"

"He has a small annuity, and contributes modestly to the household expenses. We do not own the house; I take it by the month. The fact is, Mr. Pons, Mr. Murchison thought his son a wild boy because he had an unfortunate affair with a young lady, and he cut him off with but a modest allowance."

Pons' interest kindled. "To whom, then, did Mr. Murchison leave his wealth?"

"To charity, Mr. Pons."

"His house?"

"I am his heir, in accordance with the terms of his will. Unfortunately, the house has been put up for sale; it is a large, rambling structure, and there is simply not enough left from my uncle's estate to enable me to keep the house up. We had no knowledge of my uncle's doings. Mr. Murchison was a very religious man, but he was also a very crochety one, with a ready temper and a sharp tongue, which he regretted many times thereafter. I felt very badly about his action in regard to his son, for Richard is not wild in the sense his father had it, and he did not deserve the treatment he received. Mr. Murchison had always had a fondness for me; he believed that I was a 'steady' young man." He said this with an apologetic grimace, which made him instantly more likable.

"I had hoped to be married on some part of my uncle's wealth, but now I shall have to put that off until after the house is sold, for, of course, I intend that my cousin Richard shall share whatever can be realized on the sale of the house. I had intended, as soon as I learned of the terms of the will, that Richard should share with me. However, when we went to my uncle's bank after the will was read, we discovered that he had only two months previous to his death converted all his cash reserve, all his stocks and bonds, into gold pieces, and had then gone about London bestowing his wealth upon various charities. We traced some of it, but naturally made no attempt to trace it all, since my uncle had constantly spoken of giving everything he owned to charity, and it was, finally, no surprise to learn that he had done so. However, he thought very well of me, as his only sister's first child, and he left his house and furnishings to me. Among the possessions he bestowed upon me was a valuable little periapt of beaten gold, set with four emeralds and a single ruby. I have no idea as to its worth, but it was set apart in the will as mine, with my uncle's instructions that I follow his precept and carry it more or less as he did, in the nature of a good-luck piece. I accepted my uncle's periapt, and have carried it ever since."

"How large was this amulet?"

"About two inches in diameter. I believe it was hand-made, except for the settings."

"A plain gold piece set with jewels?"

"Not quite, Mr. Pons. My uncle had had some religious verses inscribed into the back of it."

"Let us come now to the incident of its loss."

"That took place this morning. I did not have to reach my desk this morning until eleven o'clock, since I had worked over-time last night. As a result, I departed from my usual custom of taking a steam-bath near my place of work, and took a bath at home. As far as I know, I was alone in the house, except for my sister, who rapped on the bathroom door while I was in the tub, to say that she was going marketing. Since I meant to change clothes, I had emptied the pockets of my suit, and had ranged their contents on my bureau. Among them was my uncle's periapt. About ten minutes after my sister had gone out, I came out of the bathroom and went into my own room. Almost instantly I discovered that my uncle's periapt was missing. I thought I had mislaid it, or that it had fallen from the bureau; but it did not reappear. In my agitation, I forgot to put on the fresh clothes I had laid out, and came away again in my old suit, as you see me. I thought the matter over in the hour before my luncheon, and determined to put the problem before you."

"The door was not locked?"

"Neither back nor front door, Mr. Pons. My sister had not gone far away; I was in the house; I suppose she did not consider it necessary to lock the doors."

"So that anyone could have walked into the house and taken the periapt?"

"I am afraid so."

"Did very many people know of your having this trinket apart from the members of your household?"

"Not more than half a dozen or so in the neighborhood, and perhaps one or two people in the office."

"Yet a child, who had no previous knowledge of it, could have walked into your room and made off with it."

"I am afraid that is the case, Mr. Pons. Perhaps the problem affords nothing in the way of evidence, but I hesitated to go to the police and have the pawn-shops watched, because I do not really know that my uncle's periapt has as much actual value as it has intrinsic value to me. It is rather a matter of sentiment than of actual monetary worth. I would like to have it recovered, and, while I cannot afford much additional expense, I am sure we could come to some agreement about your fee."

Manifestly Pons had made up his mind to find the purloined periapt, for he smiled and suggested, "Perhaps we ought just to run out to your home and look around a little in the hope of discovering the lost amulet."

Harris looked gravely at his watch and shook his head. "I am sorry, but I cannot come along. I would be late to my work if I did so. However, I will send a message to my sister to expect you. I am sure I wish you luck, Mr. Pons, for your luck is mine. But I know my uncle's periapt was on my bureau when I went into the bathroom, and it was not there when I came out. That is the long and short of it."

Immediately after luncheon Solar Pons and I set out for South Norwood.

Mr. Harris's house appeared to be one of a great number built in the same plan, in a somewhat undesirable neighborhood, for living space was obviously crowded, and the street outside the house was occupied by a great many urchins of both sexes. We were admitted to the house by a tired and harassed-looking woman whose features plainly and unmistakably identified her as our client's sister. Tired as she was, however, she was in good voice.

"You're the gentlemen Siddie telephoned about. 'Agatha, I'm sending two gentlemen out to look around a bit,' he says to me. 'Whatever for?' I asked him, but he did not answer."

Nor did Pons volunteer any information, though she paused pointedly.

"He said I was to show you right to his room, Gentlemen, and here it is, just as he left it. I ain't had time to put his clothes away, that he was to wear and forgot. Seems to me Siddie gets more forgetful every day."

I confess that at this point, with the vision of our client as a forgetful young fellow, I began to feel that the adventure of his uncle's stolen amulet was certain to turn out to be one of the most trivial of all those exploits upon which I had had the good fortune to accompany my friend, Solar Pons. And our almost instant discovery on entering Harris's chamber came as confirmation of this conviction, for there, in plain sight on Harris's bureau, lay the object of our search!

Pons closed the door behind him, shutting out our client's curious sister, and went directly over to the periapt.

"Ah, I fancy this is what we want."

"And more of a wild goose chase I have never seen," I said in disgust. "That fellow simply mislaid it, and his sister found it and put it back."

"Slowly, slowly, Parker! How delightful and how empty life would be if all things were so simple! But I fear it is not so. You will reflect that his sister has only just now told us she had no time to put Harris's clothes away; it is not too much presumption to believe that she had no time to clean this room, either; there is no evidence of it. Furthermore, the actual reappearance of this periapt is not adequate grounds for adducing that our client did not know what he was talking about. No, you may depend upon it, Parker, our client meant and believed and knew just what he said; as he put it, the long and the short of it is that the periapt was on the bureau when he went to take his bath, and it was not there when he came back; now it is some three hours, almost four, since that time, and here it is back on the bureau once more. Yet it was gone, it had been taken. But manifestly it had not been stolen because of its monetary value."

"Unless no pawn-broker would accept it," I protested.

"In less than four hours, the thief had poor faith indeed if he gave up trying to dispose of it so quickly." He picked it up. "Besides, it has a good value. The jewels are real enough, and if I am any judge, the piece is solid gold. I fancy any pawnbroker would be happy to lend a modestly substantial sum on this piece. Let us just examine it."

He bent over, turned it about, smiled with a most quizzical expression in his eyes, and handed it to me. "What do you make of it, Parker?"

I took it and scrutinized it closely, aware that something about it had caught Pons' interest and imagination. The face of the amulet was not particularly attractive; indeed, I should have said it was singularly unattractive; its ruby was set squarely in the center, and four little emeralds framed it in the shape of a cross. The entire face had a rough appearance, as if it had been pounded and worked by hand, and it badly needed burnishing. I turned it over and discovered that the back of the piece was burnished and carried the religious "verses" of which Harris had spoken. *Ask, and it shall be given you: seek, and you shall find: knock, and it shall be opened to you. Numbers: 8, 2.*

"It appears to be quite valuable," I said, handing it back.

"Nothing more?"

I smiled. "If there is anything more to be learned from that piece, I should be delighted to be instructed."

"Ah, forgive me, Parker; I am your humble servant. I should say only that it is possible to draw a conclusion or two from it. The late Murchison was a wise old bird, who, though he fancied his nephew, did feel that he lacked imagination and was altogether a little obtuse in matters pertaining to his own best interests. Plainly, too, he was a man who believed that one ought to merit his just deserts."

"My dear Pons! You are having me."

"Not at all. It is all written here as plainly as this quotation from the Bible."

"I fail to see it."

"Look again."

He returned the periapt to my hand, and I examined it once more. I could not ascertain what it was that gave Pons any reason to make the deductions he had just made. I said so, with some heat.

"Ah, well, ponder it. Perhaps it will come to you."

I shrugged, a little nettled. "Well, this must certainly go down as our most unimportant and most quickly solved puzzle."

"On the contrary, it has only begun. I daresay we shall have a little excursion before we are done. Come, we are finished here. Let us just go back into the city and surrender the periapt to Mr. Harris."

So saying, he opened the door of the chamber and stepped out just as our client's sister made a show of being busy not far away. It was clear that she had been listening at the threshold. We bade her good-afternoon and set out for Chasins and Abramson's, to deliver his amulet to Mr. Sidney Harris.

Our client was soberly pleased at Pons' discovery, though a little nervous at having been summoned from his work to take time for Pons' questions. He strove to settle upon a fee, but Pons would not ask one.

"By no means, Mr. Harris. I found your little puzzle instructive, and our discovery of the periapt was due to no acumen of mine."

"I cannot understand it," said Mr. Harris for the third time. "I know it was not there, it was not in the room – I searched for it carefully."

"Ah, it is strange how objects can elude one. Tell me, Mr. Harris, do you have the key to your late uncle's house?"

"Yes, Mr. Pons. Would you like to look at it?"

"I have for some time been entertaining the thought of buying or renting a house in the country. It may be that your uncle's home is in the nature of what I had in mind. Do you think we might go down to look it over?"

"When I can get away."

"Ah, but I would rather not lose time. I should prefer to go down within a short time. If you will but lend me the key."

"I think that will be all right, Mr. Pons. You can bring the key back to me here tomorrow."

He detached the key from a ring in his pocket, and gave it to Pons.

"By the way, your late uncle was a Roman Catholic, was he not?"

"Yes, sir. Our family belongs to that faith."

"You mentioned your family this noon. Would it be too much to ask you to describe them to me? Your sister, of course, we have seen."

Harris looked apprehensively toward the clock on the wall of the receiving room, but nevertheless set forth upon the details Pons had asked of him, with such precision that in a remarkably short time he had brought his father, his brother, and his cousin to vivid life, so that it seemed to me I should be able to identify any one of them at sight.

"Ah, that is splendid, Mr. Harris. Is it my impression that your uncle carried this periapt as a kind of good luck charm?"

"So he said."

"Of some years' standing?"

"That was our belief."

"Well, thank you, Mr. Harris. Good-day."

As we were walking leisurely back toward our lodgings, Pons beckoned one of the street gamins to us; I recognized him for the son of a locksmith who had his little shop in the vicinity. The boy came running up, a bright-eyed lad of ten or thereabouts, touched his cap, and stood with his arms akimbo before Pons.

"Alfred, my lad – do you think you might find three other boys and come 'round to 7B posthaste?"

"I think so, Mr. Pons."

"Capital! I have a little mystery to solve. Be off with you now."

The boy cut away and vanished into an alley-way; in a moment his voice sounded at a distance, raising a hue and cry for a companion. Pons looked after him with a whimsical smile.

"Are you taking to the children to assist you now, Pons?" I asked.

"I have used these lads before your time, Parker. And no doubt I shall use them after. They are remarkably alert. I call them my Praed Street Irregulars." He glanced at me quizzically. "Did not something in Mr. Harris's conversation give you pause, Parker?"

"Oh, nothing but his fidgeting. Why, the man carried on as if he feared he would be summarily dismissed if he took time to answer your questions."

"Yes, yes – but it was not that I had in mind. Did it not seem to you a little strange that a man like Teale Murchison should carry a good-luck piece?"

"Many people do."

"True. But surely it is inconsistent with the tenets of the Roman Catholic faith to put any trust in such charms and amulets as this?"

"I believe it is."

"And since we know that the late Murchison was a religious man, a manufacturer of Bibles, no less, this tale of his good-luck charm does not ring quite true."

"What are you getting at?"

"I submit that Mr. Harris's periapt was not designed as a good-luck charm at all."

Somewhat impatiently, I retorted that very clearly it was meant to be coin of the realm.

"Strange you should say so, Parker. Now, I had the distinct impression that the amulet was made up of two gold pieces, melted down – somewhat crudely, to be sure. Moreover, I submit that the amulet is not more than four months old at the most, and that it was made out of two of those gold pieces the late Murchison removed from his bank."

"How can you possibly make that assertion?"

"Ah, it is a simple matter of deduction, Parker."

"Well, it is quite beyond me."

"Indeed, it is so elementary I hesitate to mention it."

But he offered no explanation, and I did not ask one, for it was manifest that he believed anyone alert and observant should have recognized his premises. So it was in silence that we mounted the steps of number seven and went up to our rooms.

We had hardly removed our light coats before there was a rush and a clatter on the stairs, coupled with Mrs. Johnson's indignantly raised voice; the door was thrown open without ceremony, and young Alfred burst into the room, followed pell-mell by a trio of grinning urchins.

"Here we are, Mr. Pons," cried Alfred, closing the door and marching up to the table, followed by his companions, who ranged themselves in a row beside him.

"So I see," replied Pons. "It is a mystery to me how you can manage to act so quickly, Alfred – even to the extent of having a little bread with jelly before you came. Yes, there at the corner of your mouth, my boy."

While he spoke, Pons went about gravely taking from his pocket four guineas, which he placed in a neat row at the edge of the table. Four pairs of bright, eager eyes watched him with keen interest.

"Now, then," continued Pons, standing before them. "How many of you have cycles?"

Two hands went up. "Good. Two will carry the four of you. I have a little errand I want you to do. For the next three hours I want you to watch a house in South Norwood. There are four people of interest to me. The fifth I know. I want you to watch everything these people do, put down where they go, and come back here by six o'clock. Then these guineas will belong to you. Listen to me carefully."

Thereupon he repeated almost word for word the excellent description of his relatives given us by Mr. Sidney Harris, our recent client; and, so armed, the boys descended the stairs with the same clatter and banging which had accompanied their arrival. Pons, appearing well pleased with himself, rubbed his hands in satisfaction and gazed over at me with a twinkle in his eyes.

"The lads are far less likely to excite suspicion than you or I might be. And these are onerous details."

"It would seem to me that Harris might have told you what you wanted to know."

"Not he. No, no, Parker, he is too trusting. He sees no evil; hears none, and plainly believes little. We must have some unbiased comment on these people, and I am sure we shall get it from the 'Irregulars.'"

Promptly on the hour set, the boys returned.

As their acknowledged leader, Alfred instructed them, one after the other, to make their reports. The smallest lad, a red-haired boy called "Pinky," had been detailed to observe Harris's sister, who had emerged once in late afternoon to go to market. Pinky did not have a high opinion of the lady, for he observed that she quarreled with the green-grocer about the price of vegetables. She was also seen to manifest her insatiable curiosity by peering into windows of the neighboring houses. She gabbled for a long time with another woman out marketing, and the boy had crept close enough to overhear the two ladies energetically gossiping about a third. The second lad kept his eye out for the old man, Harris's father; he had come home from the house of a friend, and was clearly enough an ailing man. A husky lad had pushed him home in a wheel chair, and the old man had given him a coin of some kind; he had seemed very friendly and bore very well the immediate scolding set up by his daughter.

The third lad had watched for Richard Murchison, who had arrived home from his work shortly after four o'clock. He was a boyish young fellow, and shortly after he had gone into the house, he came back out once more carrying a letter, which he read. "It was a love letter," said the lad scornfully.

"Ah, indeed! How could you tell, Peter?"

"E 'ad such a silly grin, 'e did, all the time 'e was a-readin' it. Then 'e picked a flower and 'eld it under 'is nose, 'e set down on the kerb and read the letter twice over."

"Ah, observant lad! Poor Richard is a second time bitten in the same place."

Clearly the lad had no good opinion of Richard for his being in love.

Alfred, however, had the longest tale to tell. He had watched Harris's brother, whose name, he had discovered, was Charles. Charles had been at home when the boys arrived, but he did not stay there long. He went down the street some distance to a pub; there he sat for some time scribbling on the back of an envelope. Then he went to a library in the neighborhood and came out whistling. He went back to the pub and set them up for the three or four men in the place at that time. He did a little more figuring and writing on the edge of a newspaper. He crumpled up one of the papers on which he had been writing and threw it away as he came out of the pub; Alfred had rescued it, and now handed it to Pons, who took it eagerly and unfolded it.

"Ah, Mr. Charles's new suit is ready, his tailor writes, 'but please, sir, to come with the money to pay for it in advance.'" He looked up. "Evidently Charles is living on his future."

"That's all, Mr. Pons," said Alfred.

"Well done, boys! And there are your guineas. Now be off with you."

There was a chorus of "Thank you, sir!" and once again that mad clatter on the stairs, followed by Mrs. Johnson's portentous sighs, made pointedly loud from below, so that Pons and I would be sure to hear.

"Mrs. Johnson bears her cross well," observed Pons. "Well, Parker, what do you make of it?"

"Frankly, nothing."

"Oh, it is not as bad as that. I fancy Charles is the man we want. I have no doubt he overheard his brother say he meant to have a bath, and slipped back into the house to take the periapt while Sidney was in his bath. He had begun to wonder about the periapt. That he did not get it back before Sidney came out again was very likely a miscalculation on his part."

"Oh, come, Pons! How is it possible from these lads' tales to deduce that?"

"Why, it is a process of simple elimination. Harris's father and sister are clearly out of it; his cousin is in love, and between his work and his romance – his addiction to romance, you will remember, was responsible for the rift between his father and himself – he has little time for such calculations which plainly occupy the mind of Mr. Charles Harris."

"What are those figures on the envelope?"

"They are calculations concerning the probable state of Mr. Charles Harris's finances, if he can riddle himself into riches. He does not seem to be a poor man, for all that there is no evidence of his having saved money." He threw the letter carelessly to the table and got up. "But come, Parker, we have but an hour or two until darkness to get on with it."

Mystified, I got into my topcoat, and set out with Pons for the street below, where we walked for a short distance before Pons managed to hail a cab. We got in, and Pons gave the driver the address of our destination. It was not South Norwood. It was beyond London, past the outlying districts of the city.

"I thought it was Charles we were after," I said pointedly.

"Dear me, no. Charles is the man who purloined the periapt. We are done with him unless he has more wit than I credit him with. As to that, we shall see in good time. We are off to look over Mr. Teale Murchison's country house."

"Yes, that is a matter I meant to ask about. What the devil did you mean by telling such a fabrication to Harris?"

"Ah, you know my methods, Parker. Ponder them."

Pons sat back and relaxed, his eyes half-closed. Swallowing my chagrin, I did likewise.

In a little over an hour, we were delivered at a fine old country estate, clearly at one time the property of a wealthy man. Pons instructed the driver to wait, and we walked up a flag-stone path under a gracious avenue of trees to the front door, a heavy, panelled piece with bronze finishings. Pons fished from his pocket the key Harris had given him, inserted it into the lock, and opened the door.

"I take it you are looking for something specific," I said as we entered the house.

"Capital! Parker. Indeed I am. I am looking for a seven-branched candelabrum. Or perhaps seven lamps. But I rather fancy it will be a seven-branched candelabrum, after all."

My astonishment did not permit me to reply.

"Let me see – where are we most likely to find such an ornament? The study, perhaps, or the library. Let us just look around."

We went down the hall, peering into one room after another, Pons somewhat in the lead.

"Hm! Surely this looks like it, does it not, Parker?"

We entered a small library, packed with books on all walls save the wall to our left as we entered; that wall opened on to a fireplace, and, above the mantelpiece, one on each side, were affixed two seven-branched candelabra, wired for electricity. I gazed in amazement, for I knew that Pons had never before entered this house, nor had Harris in any way described it except in the most general terms.

"I fancy this is the room we want," said Pons tranquilly.

"How in the devil did you know these candelabra were here?"

"Oh, I did not know they were in this room, Parker. You credit me with too much knowledge. But it was almost inevitable they were somewhere on this estate; surely that was manifest from the beginning!" He turned to look at the candelabra. "I daresay that switch over there controls the lights. Try it, Parker."

I did so, and the candelabra glowed with a soft, yellow light.

"Excellent!" murmured Pons, turning on his heels, his back to the candelabra. "And here on this wall, I fancy, we will find what we are looking for. Let us just examine these books a bit. The light falls here, well above the floor."

He stood back from the shelves and looked the books over without touching them. The contents of the shelves before us were what one might expect of a manufacturer of Bibles; they were ancient, worn tomes of considerable size, and certainly of great weight, apparently of no especial value save as curios, for they were, on closer examination of their scarcely legible titles, old variations of, and commentaries on the Scriptures. Without further study, Pons moved forward, opened the case, and began to turn over the books, taking them from the shelves until he came to a set of four of the largest books which were especially encased and were among those quaint old books which bore locks.

"Ha!" he cried. "I fancy we shall want these, Parker. If you will take two of them, I will take the other two."

I picked them up, and found them as weighty as I had expected. "I am by no means anti-religious, but these Scriptures are as heavy as lead."

"Spoken like a true sinner, Parker."

I laughed and carried on.

Pons carefully locked the door. We got into the cab, and rode back to London, reaching our lodgings before ten o'clock. Pons lost no time in going at once to the telephone and asking our recent client, Sidney Harris, to step around. Then he went calmly to the wireless and turned on the news, to which he listened with unbroken attention for the next half hour, thus effectively keeping me from asking the questions that welled up inside me with insistent urgence.

In less than an hour, Mr. Sidney Harris arrived. He had cycled over, and he rang our door bell with an uncertainty that reflected his feelings. Pons stepped to the door, opened it, and called down to invite Harris up. He entered the room with perplexity plainly evident on his features; he was completely at a loss to know why my friend, Solar Pons, had sent for him, and there was manifest also some apprehension, very possibly because he feared Pons had decided after all to ask a fee for his services.

"Come in, come in, my dear Mr. Harris! I have a little matter that requires your attention. First of all, the key to your late uncle's house. I believe the house would be far more suitable for occupation by your bride and yourself."

Harris goggled at Pons as he took the key and mechanically attached it once more to his key-ring. "I'm sorry," he managed to say. "We are hoping to sell it."

"I fancy that will not be necessary." Pons walked with a cat-like agility around the table, took up one of the ponderous tomes he had brought from the Murchison house, slipped it from its case, and pried open the lock. "Pray overlook the liberties I am taking with your property, Mr. Harris, but I believe your uncle intended you to follow this course."

As he spoke, the book fell open with a dull sound, and there lay revealed not an orthodox book at all, but a cleverly made dummy, into the pages of which had been laid row on row of gold pieces!

"My Lord in Heaven!" exclaimed Harris, staring openmouthed.

"Ah yes, these gold pieces are quite real, believe me, my dear fellow! There are four volumes of them. I discovered them precisely where your late uncle said they would be."

Harris, who had taken a tentative step or two forward, hesitated once more and stared at Pons with that strange mixture of uncertainty and respect which my friend never failed to command by these casual announcements of his remarkable deductions.

"My uncle?" he said, passing his tongue over his dry lips.

"Indeed, yes. He left the word for you as plainly as he could in his determination to tax your ingenuity. I fear he had no very great respect either for your knowledge of Scripture or your imagination. I fancy, too, he had a good time exercising his own ingenuity and wit by setting out to distribute his wealth and ending up by concealing the bulk of it for you to find. Your inheritance was precisely where the late Mr. Murchison wrote that it would be – opposite the seven-branched candelabrum, where the light fell on the north wall of his library."

Harris sat down nervously. "I am afraid this is quite beyond me, Mr. Pons. I am all a-tremble."

"Dear me! Pray pull yourself together. You are wealthy, Mr. Harris. No more will you need to cycle to work daily, and no longer will you need to put off your wedding. But, come, let me explain the puzzle to you. Have you your uncle's periapt?"

Wordlessly, Harris produced the curious object.

"Herein lies the solution of the matter," continued Pons. "I apprehend neither you nor my estimable companion knows his Scripture well. Attend me: *Ask, and it shall be given you: seek, and you shall find: knock, and it shall be opened to you.*

Numbers: 8, 2." He looked up, his keen eyes narrowed. "Now, then, think: what is the source of that quotation?"

Harris swallowed and answered uncertainly. "Is it not from the Sermon on the Mount?"

"Capital! Capital! Of course it is, Mr. Harris. But what then, is it doing in Numbers, which is in the Old Testament?" Harris began to look a little foolish, and I have no doubt I too looked as foolish as I felt.

"There you have it. The quotation is from Matthew: 7.7., the Douay version, which is the version of Scriptures preferred by members of the Roman Catholic faith. Clearly, then, Mr. Murchison meant you to seek and find, and he told you at least initially where to look. Let us turn to Numbers: 8.2."

As he spoke, he lifted from his shelves the Bible in question, turned over a little more than a hundred pages, and read aloud:

"*Speak to Aaron, and thou shalt say to him: When thou shalt place the seven lamps, let the candlestick be set up on the south side. Give orders therefore that the lamps look over against the north, towards the table of the loaves of proposition, over against that part shall they give light, towards which the candlestick looketh.* – Surely that is plain enough!"

At that, Mr. Sidney Harris found his voice. He came to his feet, seized Pons' hand, and began to shake it in the sudden expression of his joy. "Mr. Pons, I owe you more than I can pay you. You have given me a new life, indeed, you have!"

"On the contrary, my dear fellow – it is I who owe you a debt of gratitude for bringing to my attention one of the most intriguing problems in many months. – And, by the way, if I were you I should not permit natural generosity to make it unnecessary for brother Charles to get himself a suitable position and learn to work."

IX

THE ADVENTURE OF THE LIMPING MAN

The ceaseless activity in which Solar Pons was engaged during the summer and early autumn of the year 1923 brought him at last to a stage where he was forced to choose either absolute rest or a nervous breakdown. Knowing how much Pons loathed the thought of inactivity, I put off broaching the subject of a holiday for as long as possible, but at last, early in October of that year, I suggested that both of us run up to the country estate of a good friend, Sir John Mollines, for a brief stay, which I secretly planned to lengthen as much as I could. Sir John's estate lay in Northumberland, near the Scottish border, in the midst of a well-populated district, though surrounding estates were quite extensive and the houses therefore rather widely separated.

Pons opposed the suggestion from the start, but sheer persistence on my part, coupled with his knowledge of his own condition, and my assurance that the nearby village of Durward was in easy communication with London, finally overcame his opposition, and he gave in after a week of dubiety and protest.

By the fifteenth of that month we were comfortably established in Sir John's country house, which was far more than merely a house, what with its library and its stores. At my suggestion, Sir John had given the servants a fortnight's leave, excepting only the caretaker, who remained in his lodge at the gate. We had the house to ourselves, therefore, and it devolved upon me to do the work of cook and housekeeper, not in any sense exactly a new experience for me.

But alas! for plans of mice and men! Pons spent all the first day resting, while I lost myself in a monograph concerning the mental aberrations of men and women of genius; beyond that first day, rest, as I understood it, was not part of Pons' routine. Nothing could keep Pons in the house on the second day. Indeed, he was already gone when I awoke that morning, and he did not turn up until some little time after lunch, and then only ran in with a briefly ironic, "I see you're up!" and left again before I had time even to protest.

It was not until after dark when he came in to stay. He was begrimed and dusty, as if he had walked a long way. He said not a word as he entered, but walked with singular directness over to a sheaf of his papers, and a volume of his file of clippings which he had insisted on bringing along from our lodgings in Praed Street. Armed with these, he came to the table and seated himself opposite me, looking at the dinner waiting for him with remarkable disinterest.

"We have most interesting neighbors to the north, Parker," he said musingly, a thoughtful glint in his eyes.

"Indeed! Were you resting there?" I asked, eyeing his clothes in studied disapproval.

He ignored my thrust. "I fancy you've heard of the Melham family?"

"I must admit I am not a walking directory."

"Come, Parker," he challenged impatiently. "Surely you can't have forgotten the strange disappearance of old Sir Peter Melham! Let me see – " he paused and frowned briefly, as if he had any necessity to recall facts which were doubtless at his fingertips – "that was three years ago, I believe."

I sighed and settled back, shaking my head in disapproval which did not stem his enthusiasm.

"He vanished some time in October, if I recall rightly," he went on blithely. "I brought my notes on the matter down with me, since I rather hoped that Sir John's lodge was near the Melham estate."

"Certainly you aren't planning to reopen that old matter?"

"Not unless I am asked to do so."

"Well, there is little danger of that. The case is pretty well closed."

"Say, rather, it has rested. It is as far from being closed as it ever was. No case is definitely closed until it is solved."

During this brief exchange, he had been going through his papers, and he had now come to his notes relating to the disappearance of Sir Peter Melham. I felt all my hope for his holiday fading, for I saw in his keen eyes once again all the excitement of the chase. As if he had read my thoughts, he looked up and fixed me with a sharp glance.

"Perhaps you would rather hear nothing more of the matter, eh?"

He had me; he knew he had. "I would rather you had forgotten all about it – but now that you've interested yourself, go on."

"Very well, then. I have a good summary of the case here. Sir Peter took possession of Melham Old Place, as it is called, in late May, 1920, after selling his London house; he came with his daughter Maureen, his wife having died many years earlier. Melham Old Place has always been the family seat, and it was at that time occupied by Peter's brother Andrew, a paralytic confined to his bed. Sir Peter was engaged in business on the Continent, and Maureen was to remain with her uncle during his absence. His ultimate destination on the Continent was Prague, though the nature of his business was never revealed. He set out on the night of October seventh, 1920, leaving Melham Old Place with two bags and a portfolio. He was known to have purchased a ticket for Dover at the Durward station, and he was seen to enter the midnight express from Edinburgh shortly after ten o'clock. That was the last seen of him. His punched ticket, with his bags and portfolio – all were found in a first-class carriage compartment in Victoria Station, London, just after the boat train for Dover had taken its departure.

"In his deposition, a guard stated he had punched Sir Peter's ticket somewhere out of Reveling, which is well away from Durward. Sir Peter had not been in evidence; he had assumed that Sir Peter was either in another compartment or in the lavatory at the other end of the carriage. The ticket lay on the seat; he had punched it and replaced it; in Victoria Station he had found the ticket just where he had put it after punching it. The indication, therefore, was that Sir Peter vanished in the vicinity of Reveling."

"Yes, I remember it now," I said. "Quite extraordinary."

"Sensational," corrected Pons. "I have some memory of the investigation pursued by Scotland Yard, whose men were sent as far afield as Prague, to discover if possible what was known of Sir Peter there. But nothing was – beyond his two monographs; so that his destination was never revealed, since it was apparently as much of a mystery to his brother and his daughter, as to Scotland Yard. Of course, the usual rumors began to circulate immediately, and ranged all the way from suspicion of murder – for what motive no one ever tried to account – to wilful disappearance."

"Had Sir Peter anything to gain by vanishing?"

"Nothing, apparently, and all to lose. Of course, old family history is always a source of great interest to rumormongers and those who have little to do with their time. But the history of the Melham family offers comparatively little of major interest. The family first came into prominence through the knighting of Sir Mark Melham – born in 1832 – in 1867. The sons, Andrew and Peter, were born in that year, and Lady Melham died shortly thereafter. Not long after, Sir Mark removed to London, and there he stayed until he died in 1911.

"Young Peter briefly troubled the family in 1887, when, after an affair with a Miss Rose Hadley, he eloped with her. The young lady was the daughter of a woman who had been recommended to Sir Mark as a housekeeper for Melham Old Place. When Peter was next heard from, he turned up with his small daughter, Maureen, saying he had married Rose Hadley, but that she had died shortly after giving birth to the little girl. Sir Mark refused to recognize either his son or his grandchild; he executed a new will in favor of Andrew, cutting Peter off. This was in 1899; Maureen was then three years of age. After this cold reception, Peter entrusted his daughter to her relatives on her mother's side, and returned to London, where he came to some prominence in 1902 by distinguishing himself in the scientific field with two monographs and a minor invention. He supported his daughter and assured her education.

"Sir Mark died in 1911; Sir Andrew inherited the estate, and Sir Peter, now knighted for scientific service to the Crown, returned to Northumberland to suggest a partition of the estate, to which Sir Andrew did not agree. This time Sir Peter took his daughter back to London with him. There was a period of coolness between the brothers for some years, but early in 1919, after Sir Andrew sustained his paralytic stroke, their coolness was forgotten, and they kept up a warm correspondence up to the time of Sir Peter's final leaving of London."

Pons looked up from the papers. "Now does that not present a prosaic background for that inexplicable disappearance?"

"Ah, you consider it inexplicable, then?"

"No, no, nothing of the sort. You misinterpret me. It has been inexplicable up to this time; beyond that I will not go. You know my methods; you know my confidence; you ought not to tempt me in this fashion, Parker. It is quite possible that I may be drawn into this matter – even against my will."

"Against your will, indeed!"

"I fear you are becoming too dogmatic, Parker, especially in regard to your diagnoses. Recreation and rest do not necessarily imply mental and physical stagnation."

"There is no good in your stirring up this old mystery, and surely no one will invite your services at this late date."

"You forget there is Miss Maureen Melham, who must certainly be interested in the fate of her father. She is now twenty-seven, and decidedly attractive, I should say, judging by the glimpse of her I got through my glasses this afternoon." He smiled ruminatively. "I daresay it is no surprise to you that it has come to her ears that I am in the neighborhood."

"Impossible!" I cried. "I have maintained the strictest secrecy!"

"Dear me! How reprehensible of you! Now I, on the contrary, immediately noised my coming about. Our lodge-keeper carried the information over to Melham Old Place with commendable dispatch."

"I think it most unwise..."

"I may as well tell you, Parker, I expect Miss Maureen Melham to call on me not later than eight o'clock tonight. And now, I think we had better do justice to the meal you have had waiting here all this while."

There was nothing more for me to say.

It was almost eight o'clock, and only a few moments after Pons came in that evening, when a faint rap sounded on the heavy oaken panels of the outer door. I rose at once and admitted a young woman whose attractiveness had not been done justice by Pons' comment at dinner. She wore no hat, and her hair was slightly but agreeably disarranged, as if the wind had blown into it and not fully escaped; it was dark, ashen hair, complementing the grey of her eyes. She was dressed in a neat tweed walking suit, the jacket of which was unbuttoned, since the night was warm. In her right hand she carried a stick, which she tapped almost with impatience against her walking shoes as she stood looking from one to the other of us. Her eyes, however, with true woman's instinct, fixed on Pons even before he spoke.

"Miss Maureen Melham, I take it," said Pons, placing a chair for her and courteously inviting her to be seated, so that her face was illuminated by the lamp on the table, and so betrayed a distinct uneasiness. Her lips parted twice, but no words came. She flashed a glance at me, looked to the windows, looked back at Pons.

"Pray be at ease, Miss Melham," said Pons. "I observe you are carrying a heavy stick, obviously for protection; you may safely discard it here. Manifestly, you consider the stick necessary. Why?"

"In the light of past happenings, Mr. Pons, I cannot help but feel that I am in physical danger."

"Yes, I observed you were followed here tonight."

She started. "How could you know that?"

"Ah, I was behind you all the way from Melham Old Place. Apart from myself, whom I modestly assume to have been invisible, there were two people interested in your actions. I understood that your young man was the one, and had no difficulty concluding that he is not in favor at your home, for he met you some distance from it. But the other follower – I found him quite interesting."

"There was another? Besides yourself?" She was plainly frightened.

"Oh, yes. A short man, quite old, I should say; he walks with a slight limp."

Miss Melham's expression was briefly of fear before she controlled herself; nevertheless, she half-rose from her chair, and her hand clenched around the heavy stick. "It is he!" she cried. "The limping man. The man I came to see you about tonight."

"No, Miss Melham, forgive me," replied Pons calmly. "The man who followed you tonight carried no cane; I understand the apparition you have seen of recent weeks is in the habit of carrying one."

The girl nodded and looked at Pons in some perplexity.

It was as apparent to her as it now was to me that Pons had withheld something from me at dinner, that he knew something more of the immediate background for Miss Melham's visit than he had cared to tell me.

"The man who followed you tonight bears a close resemblance to the man I saw about the premises of Melham Old Place once or twice this afternoon. Indeed, I should say the two men are one and the same. His left hand, I could not help seeing, is or seems crippled. Who is he?"

"He is Jasper Bayne, my uncle's valet and secretary."

"And presumably he has a reason for following you?"

"Yes. My uncle, Sir Andrew, is opposed to Hugh – my 'young man,' as you call him, whom I hope to make my fiancé – and it is very likely that he sent Jasper to follow me and find out whether I met Hugh."

"Surely your uncle can have no valid opposition to a family as good as the Bettertons?"

"But he does. I have always been given to understand that Hugh's family is among the best in Northumberland, and therefore my uncle's opposition to him is most astonishing; he offers me no reason for his stand."

Pons' interest quickened. He leaned forward. "Ah, perhaps your uncle offers a substitute?"

"Yes, and that is the most puzzling feature of the matter, Mr. Pons. He does offer a substitute."

"Do not keep us in suspense, Miss Melham."

"It is Robert Bayne – Jasper Bayne's son."

"Capital! Capital!" exclaimed Pons, smiling. "And young Bayne? What does he say of the matter?"

Miss Melham was briefly taken aback, not understanding that Pons' enthusiasm was prompted by his delight at this perplexing ramification. "As for Robert – he is a very sensible and well-educated young man. He does not relish the idea any more than I do, and he cannot understand why my uncle, who, though always fond of Robert, has never before given any indication that he would like him as a member of the family, should suddenly come out with such an idea. We have always been friendly, but there has never been any thought of marriage between us. Finally, though neither his father nor my uncle knows it, Robert is already secretly married."

"It would appear then very much like an understanding between your uncle and Jasper Bayne."

"Very much so, Mr. Pons. And that is all the more reason why I cannot understand it. Why Mr. Bayne should presume to think I would marry his son, and why my uncle does nothing to prevent Bayne from such presumption, actually going so far as to oppose my engagement to Hugh, are questions I cannot answer."

Pons smiled. "Ah, well, perhaps my poor talents may discover the answer for you."

"I would appreciate it very much if you could, Mr. Pons."

"But at the moment I am far more interested in the apparition of the limping man of whom you spoke."

"Yes, it was really about him that I came to see you. You have heard the legends, I suppose?"

Pons nodded. "It would be well, however, to review the entire matter. Let us begin with the first occurrence you can remember."

"That was last August. I woke up one night and I heard a faint tapping, as if someone were walking about with a cane.

I listened. It seemed to come from the long hall on the ground floor."

"You investigated?"

"Not then. The noise did not disturb me at first. I wondered who could be about so late – it was after one in the morning. Two nights later, I heard the same sound at about the same time. That time I got up and went into the hall on the second floor, where I sleep. But as soon as I opened my door, all sound ceased. On the following night, I heard similar sounds again, and after that, heard them regularly.

"I could not help beginning to analyze the sounds. It seemed clear that whoever it was walked with a stick. The more accustomed to it I became, the more I began to notice that the faint footfalls accompanying the taps of the cane were characterized by the peculiar irregularity of a man with one game leg." Our visitor's voice sank lower, and she leaned forward a little. "It was then, Mr. Pons, that I first thought of my father – since then, I cannot think of anything else!"

"Indeed! I was not aware that your father was in any way crippled."

"Oh, but he was, Mr. Pons. A month before we left London he fell and severely hurt his leg; since that time and up to the time of his disappearance, he habitually used a stick. The limping sound I heard during the night was one peculiar to him." She hesitated.

"Pray continue."

"I was afraid, Mr. Pons. I don't know why, but you are aware, of course, that I know nothing of what happened to my father, and for a while I thought that he was coming back – back from – the other side. I have always believed him dead."

"And you thought his restless spirit walked?"

"I did, Mr. Pons. It was foolish, I suppose; but I could not help it. I saw nothing all that time, I just heard those dreadfully suggestive sounds; what was there left for me to think? For, each time I mentioned it, no one else had heard it, and I was looked at askance, as if I had taken leave of my senses."

"And then?"

"Then, Mr. Pons, on the night of September seventeenth, I woke up and heard the sounds approaching, as always, along the second storey hall. The tapping of the cane and the dragging footsteps paused outside my door, and it seemed to me that someone fumbled at the knob; then the sounds passed on. I got up cautiously and opened the door. There was no one – nothing in the hall.

"I was naturally much disturbed, and next morning I spoke to my uncle. He was also troubled, and immediately recalled the old family superstition – that whenever bad fortune comes upon our house, the spectre of the last member of the family to die appears to give warning by his presence."

Something in her manner bespoke her spirit. "You were not convinced, Miss Melham?"

"Certainly not. On the contrary," answered the young lady with considerable heat, "I began to think someone had got into the house with the deliberate intention of planning mischief."

"Is that not a curious change in your point-of-view?"

"Not as curious as it might seem," she answered readily. "My uncle's heart is not strong; it has never been strong since his initial attack. Any untoward event might bring on a fatal seizure."

"But surely you would benefit?"

"Not solely. There are several large bequests – to Bayne, to the widow of an old friend and neighbor, and so on."

"Go on, Miss Melham."

"Then for a time nothing happened. In the interval – on the twentieth, to be exact – I proposed that Hugh call on Uncle Andrew to suggest our engagement. Up to this time, you see, I had no suspicion that Uncle would oppose Hugh. But the suggestion that I made threw Uncle Andrew into a frightening fury; I could not understand it, and believed at first that he thought me guilty of a secret affair with Hugh. Naturally, this hurt me very much."

"That is most interesting," commented Pons. "Up to that time you had no reason to complain of your uncle's treatment?"

"None."

"You found him trying honestly to take your father's place?"

"Mr. Pons, almost from the day of my father's disappearance, Uncle Andrew has done everything in his power to keep me happy and satisfied here."

"Ah, and before then?"

"Well, before then, I think there was something of that old coldness about my mother that influenced him; he was kind, but reserved, somewhat aloof. As soon, however, as the full responsibility for me fell to him, Uncle Andrew thawed out and became very considerate and kind. That was all the more reason why I could not understand his abrupt rage."

"And what did you do?"

"At first I refused to consider what he had to say, but when I saw that he was genuinely upset and distressed, I promised to think the matter over if he would give me a month. He made some small objection, but finally consented. His attitude made me feel very awkward and strange; it seemed so different from his previous treatment of me."

"Yes, I daresay it did. And about the limping man?"

"I heard him again on the night of the twenty-first, on the second floor. And that night, when I threw open my door, I saw him, too. He stood at one end of the hall, and as I looked at him, he seemed to disappear. I don't know what happened; it was just as if he disintegrated, Mr. Pons. But above everything else, I noticed one horrible, frightening thing. Though I had only a momentary glimpse of him, dressed in a long white gown of some kind, with a darker gown over that, and carrying a heavy cane – Mr. Pons, I could have taken oath that he was the image of my father!"

"You were fully awake?"

"Fully. I made no mistake. Even the posture was familiar."

"You have considered the possibility of hallucination?" persisted Pons. "And the known fact that very often in such cases one sees what one expects to see rather than what is actually there to be seen?"

"I thought of all that, Mr. Pons."

"You made no attempt to ascertain how the figure you saw vanished?"

"None. I cried out, and directly thereafter, my uncle called to me from his room. I ran there, which was only a few doors away from my own, and told him what I had just seen."

"Ah, and he?"

"He was not surprised. He seemed, in fact, to be expecting it. He fell back upon that old superstition and intimated that his own death was presaged in this apparition."

"He did not doubt that it was a spectre?"

"Not for a moment. He was insistent. He admitted, too, that he had not been feeling well, but he would not hear of getting the doctor when I suggested it, as I did, of course, immediately. After all, whatever differences there are between us, Uncle Andrew is all I have left."

"Did it occur to you to ascertain whether Jasper Bayne had seen the ghost?"

"It did. Mr. Pons, he not only had seen the ghost, but ventured to go so far as to tell me I was the cause of its appearance!"

"Ah, Mr. Bayne is exercising the fancied prerogatives of all servants who have become part of the household. What had your uncle to say of this?"

"He reprimanded Bayne, of course."

"And no doubt he was thereafter twice as uncivil to you?"

"Yes."

"And the apparition?"

"Continued to appear, though at longer intervals."

"Thus far you have not given any explanation of your impression that you are in physical danger, Miss Melham."

"Our lodgekeeper warned me one day that Jasper Bayne meant mischief, and since then I have continually carried this heavy stick."

"Has Bayne given you cause to believe the lodgekeeper's warning?"

"Not apart from his hostility. He does not seem to like me. But then – I have been aware of being watched from time to time; I have never seen anyone, but I know someone watches me."

"Inside or outside?"

"Both, Mr. Pons."

"Ah. And what is it you expect of me, Miss Melham?"

"I would like you to discover who it is walking about at night – phantom or man – and why."

Pons looked at her with a certain commiseration. "Does it not seem to you that there may be unpleasant aspects beneath the surface in this matter, Miss Melham? It is altogether probable that I may unearth facts which, to put it bluntly, may be most objectionable."

"That makes no difference in my attitude, Mr. Pons. Will you or will you not help me?"

"I will."

"Very good. Thank you. Then I must warn you against Uncle Andrew. I know he would be furious if he discovered I had enlisted any outside aid in laying our ghost. If you visit Melham Old Place, as you undoubtedly must, please come in secret, and preferably by night; Uncle Andrew is suspicious of strangers, and he has always been highly sensitive about his partial paralysis."

"I understand."

"If possible, I would like you to come to the house tomorrow night – at or near ten o'clock. If you will go to the south wall, you will find the French windows left partly open. I will be waiting for you in that room."

She rose to go, and I got up to show her out.

"You may expect me, Miss Melham," said Pons, as our attractive visitor moved toward the door in my wake.

"I rely on you. Good night, Mr. Pons."

I came back into the study and found Pons bent over his notes.

"Does it not seem to you that the night-jars have become suddenly active?" he asked, a smile at his thin lips.

From outside came the weird call of a night-jar, and immediately after, another and yet another; then came three short harsh calls. "The region is infested with the birds," I said.

"Ah, but such regularity! I fancy the cries are a signal for lovers' meetings. Now, then, come here, attend me, Parker." He thrust a paper toward me, and then, as I bent toward it to see that the paper he tendered me bore no writing whatever, he spoke again in a scarcely audible voice. "Raise your eyes very slowly. There is a man looking in through the window opposite."

Though I started slightly, I did as he suggested and saw, framed in the darkness of the window, faintly glowing from the light within the room, the pale white of a man's face. It vanished even as I looked, but not before I had seen two high black lines of Mephistophelian eyebrows and eyes regarding us with burning hatred!

Instantly Pons was up and out of the house, leaving me in some agitation and concern lest he had entered into danger, and unable to forget that malefic face at the window. When Pons at last returned, my relief knew no bounds.

"Thank heaven, you are safe!" I said. "Who was he?"

"Jasper Bayne. He followed Miss Melham here, and followed her back. I followed him. I cannot believe he means her harm, for his actions were rather protective than otherwise. She met young Betterton, but Bayne did not interfere, only keeping well out of sight. He watched her into the house, and it was not until her window showed a light that Bayne himself went into the house. I continued to stand watch, and observed shortly after Bayne's entrance a dimmed light make its appearance on the second floor, perhaps three windows – and three rooms – removed from Miss Melham's."

"But surely Bayne does not sleep on the second floor?" I cried, somewhat surprised that a gentleman who had given so much evidence of being class-conscious as Sir Andrew, should tolerate a servant's sleeping on the same floor as the members of his own family."

"Dear me, no! Certainly not. I submit he went up to report what he had seen of Miss Melham to Sir Andrew."

"The two have an agreement, then?"

"Of some kind, undoubtedly, I fancy. But what do you make of the affair, Parker?"

I had been giving the matter considerable thought. "It seems very simple at the outset, but you have so often warned me about coming to hurried conclusions that I hardly know whether I should say what I think or not."

Pons laughed. "If you have so little confidence in it, it must assuredly be a faulty theory."

"Well, it strikes me that Bayne has a hold of some sort on Sir Andrew Melham, and that, as a price for his secrecy, he demands that Sir Andrew's niece marry his son Robert, which would give the estate to his own line, since Miss Maureen is the only heir."

"And the spectre with the limp?"

"Surely it is Bayne in disguise?" I ventured. "For that might frighten Miss Melham into submission to the plan."

"Ingenious, Parker, if a little obvious. I congratulate you. But you seem to have forgotten that the central mystery is not that of the arrangement between Bayne and Sir Andrew; we must assume that such an arrangement exists, for whatever reasons. But there remains the fact that the limping man made his appearance *before* there was any suspicion that there was an understanding between Miss Melham and Hugh Betterton. It is always possible that Bayne may be the apparition, but in view of this circumstance, his motive must be questioned."

"What do you make of it, Pons?"

"I fancy it is a little early to formulate an opinion." He shook his head. "But I much fear that the matter is far from as simple as it seems to be. Miss Melham is stirring far more deeply than she dreams."

"You have a theory, then?"

"Yes. It should be obvious, Parker. You have all the facts; you know my methods. Apply them."

With that I had to be content.

It was almost two o'clock in the next night when Pons appeared, following his rendezvous with Miss Melham. The expression of annoyance on his face apprised me that his expedition to Melham Old Place had produced anything but satisfactory results.

"A most disappointing affair," he said bitterly, moving his notes to one side. He struck a match and held it to his pipe; then he leaned back and regarded me for a moment in thoughtful silence.

"The spectre did not appear then?"

"On the contrary, he came on schedule. But my own plans were subject to events over which I had no control. Miss Melham did me the unexpected honor of having her young man present – for help, if necessary, as she explained. Despite several pointed hints from me, he stayed. Since no amount of suggestion on my part was likely to send him away, I resigned myself, with results which were well-nigh disastrous.

"The room in which I met Miss Melham and Mr. Betterton is a kind of study, opening off the drawing room, and looking out upon one end of the great hall on the lower floor of Melham Old Place. At the other end of the hall, a double stair leads up to the second storey, or rather, to a landing half way up, and from there on it becomes a single stairway. Next the foot of this stair, on the far side of the house, are the servants' quarters and, adjoining them, precisely opposite the drawing-room, are Jasper Bayne's rooms. All the other rooms on the ground floor are unoccupied. We stationed ourselves in the drawing-room, prepared to watch the hall for the appearance of Miss Melham's spectral man, and there we sat quietly until midnight.

"At that hour, matters quickly came to a head. The spectre duly appeared – but on the far side of the double stair. He was descending slowly, moving along the wall toward us, and came steadily down into the hall itself. I need hardly say there was no suggestion of the supernatural about him, save that his face was not very visible, because it was sunk into the folds of a dressing-gown about his neck. He came on, limping and tapping his cane much as Miss Melham had described him. He came, in fact, almost opposite us, when the futility of my plans became evident.

"Young Betterton, doubtless carried away by the sight of what Miss Melham had so often talked about, darted past me with a cry and lunged for the limping man. The spectre raised his cane and swung at him with telling effect. Betterton fell, but before I could dash to his aid, Miss Melham was inconsiderate enough to faint in my arms. As a result, the spectre vanished in the melee, and on top of this ridiculous spectacle, the door of Jasper Bayne's room opened and he himself strode out into the hall, holding a lamp high in one hand, and fiercely grasping a stick in the other. He took in the tableau at a glance.

"'Mr. Solar Pons, I believe,' he said coldly.

"I nodded to him, and began to retreat to the drawing-room with Miss Melham, when she came to and struggled upright.

"'I do not think you are welcome here, Mr. Solar Pons,' said Bayne with ill-concealed anger. 'Nor is he,' he added, pointing to Betterton.

"Miss Melham dismissed Bayne rather sharply, and we turned our attention to Betterton, who, for his pains, had received an unpleasant clout on the head, which, I'll wager, he will not soon forget, and which, with any luck, will incline him less to impulsive action. As far as the identity of the spectre is concerned, the entire evening was wasted. Besides accomplishing nothing, the household is now on guard, and we can expect nothing of any moment for some time to come."

"You did not see what happened to the spectre?"

"Ah, yes, I managed that. There are several points of interest to be noted. For instance, the cane which struck young Betterton is at least a very material object. I have no doubt we may assume that the spectre who wielded it is fully as material. He appeared, as I said, midway up the far side of the double stairs. Obviously then, he could not have walked the length of the great hall, gone upstairs, and been half-way down before being noticed, since we were watching for him. I fancy, therefore, he must have come not from the lower floor, but from the second storey. And as to his disappearance – this took place just across the hall from where we were hiding in the drawing-room; in fact, it was almost precisely before Jasper Bayne's door."

"Surely that is conclusive!" I cried. "He simply got rid of his dressing-gown and came back out."

"Slowly, slowly, Parker. Not at all. He wore a dressing-gown and pyjamas. He was therefore abed, or at least he was in his room. If it must be admitted that the spectre came from the second storey, it could not have been Bayne, for we had his quarters under eye throughout the preceding two hours. No, I think we cannot suspect Bayne of playing ghost. His lamp was certainly not alight before the spectre appeared, for we would have noticed its glow beneath the door. And if Bayne did play the ghost, he certainly made an uncommonly swift job of getting rid of his paraphernalia and lighting his lamp. Yet, it is equally certain that the spectre disappeared into his room."

"I hold to Bayne, Pons."

"If so, what motive did he have to carry on his deception over a month before Miss Melham made known her attachment for Hugh Betterton?"

"As to that, I can't say. What of Sir Andrew?"

"Ah, you have reached that point, eh? I took occasion yesterday afternoon to consult the physician who attended Sir Andrew during his paralytic stroke, and I have his absolute and unconditional assurance that Sir Andrew could never possibly walk again. I fear Sir Andrew is out of the question."

"Then we have a third party to consider."

"Obviously. And his identity ought to be clear enough. I am, however, not quite certain of the motive behind this complex and dark business, and I fear the matter must just rest until tonight's excitement at Melham Old Place is forgotten. If only Miss Melham had left matters entirely in my hands! As it is, I should not be surprised if events have been precipitated and we shall shortly hear from Miss Melham."

Pons spent the next two days making inquiries in Durham and about the countryside. He learned that Jasper Bayne was the son of the late Sir Mark Melham's secretary, and that he had grown up with the Melham boys, and had been as disturbed and grieved by Sir Peter's unsolved disappearance as Sir Andrew had been. Pons was able to make several routine examinations of Melham Old Place by means of his binoculars, but could detect no signs of unusual activity.

However, matters were soon to be brought to a head.

On the night destined to resolve the mystery, a violent storm broke out. The day had been sullen and close; Pons had seen the storm approaching early in the evening and was in the house when it burst. We sat for some time listening to the furious driving of the rain against the windows, beating upon the glass and the shutters before a wind almost of gale proportions. I saw that Pons was listening intently, and indeed the wind was distinctly foreign to us, unused as we were to such blasts in London. I could not read, and Pons appeared to be ill at ease.

"I should not be surprised if something happens over there tonight, Parker," he said at last, turning to me.

"Why tonight?" I asked, smiling. "Because of the storm?"

"Dear me, no. But Miss Melham's month is up today. She may well be asked for her decision in regard to young Betterton. Since we know she has no intention of giving him up, and that young Bayne has no intention of marrying her, since he could not even if he wanted to, her decision will break the tension and will doubtless effect a rift between Bayne and Sir Andrew. What may come of that should be of considerable interest."

Pons looked up at the clock, while I turned his words over in my mind. It was ten minutes of midnight. "Well, it is almost twelve; if he still walks, the limping man will soon be on his rounds."

At this moment there came a furious pounding at the door. Pons was up on the instant, and I followed him into the hall. As he swung the door open, the limp figure of Miss Maureen Melham fell forward into the room. Pons caught her and supported her, heedless of the rain driving in through the open door. She was dripping wet, and breathing rapidly, obviously having run through wind and rain to the house. I closed the door and turned to find her clutching the lapels of Pons' dressing-gown.

"Mr. Pons! Something terrible has happened. Don't lose a moment! Jasper Bayne has been murdered, and my Uncle Andrew is dying – shot, too!"

She brushed her hair from her eyes and stood away from him, for he took time only to seize his waterproof before he left the house. Miss Melham would have taken after him, tired and wet as she was, but yielded to my insistence that she wear my own waterproof; then the two of us ran blindly through the rain and wind, over open fields softened by the rain, through underbrush of the scattered copses on the way to Melham Old Place.

We were drenched to the skin when we got to the house. But Pons' wild run had got him there in ample time before us to have the situation already well in hand. A man had been dispatched to the headquarters of the county constabulary; another had been sent for young Betterton, since Pons had assumed that Miss Melham would want him to take over when Pons had finished. We had entered by the French windows and had come out into the lower hall where a huddled group of servants stood at a distance from the body of Jasper Bayne, which lay at the foot of the stairs, clothed only in night-gown and dressing-robe. Bayne lay on his back, his arms flung wide; his face was no longer malevolent, being now white and pale, and his cold, sightless eyes were devoid of the hatred I had first seen in them. Even the black Mephistophelian brows were no longer terrifying. An irregular red stain on his breast told where he had been shot.

Pons was bustling about in a perfect storm of action – running in and out of Jasper Bayne's room, and up and down the stairs. "Yes, yes," he said excitedly, as we came up to him, "he was shot on the landing, and rolled down."

"But by whom?" I demanded.

"By whom but the limping man? The whole, ridiculous jigsaw is clear as day, Parker; I have been only a little short of being obtuse. Now, then – we can do nothing for Bayne. Let us attend to Sir Andrew."

So saying, he hastened up the stairs, whither Miss Melham had already gone, and followed her into Sir Andrew's room, the door to which stood open.

Sir Andrew Melham lay in his low bed, breathing painfully. Miss Maureen knelt beside him.

"Your field, Parker," said Pons.

I bent above Sir Andrew, trying not to disturb too much Miss Melham's attention to him, for there was evident between them now a strong attachment, she held one of her uncle's thin hands in hers, and was trying hard to keep back her tears. The old man's thin outlines were plainly visible through the few coverings, which I turned back to attend to his wound. But it was manifest at a glance that he was dying. I staunched the flow of blood from his wound, and stood back.

Despite the look of age upon him, Sir Andrew's eyes were sharp and piercing. He looked past me to Pons, who had seen the weapon on the floor, identified Pons, and spoke to his niece.

"You had better go, Maureen. I wish to speak to these gentlemen, alone."

Miss Melham bowed her head and relinquished her hold on her uncle's hand. Sir Andrew's eyes followed her to the door; only when it closed behind her did he turn to Pons once more.

"Mr. Pons – you know?" he asked, watching him with his sharp eyes, which looked so vital and alive in his wrinkled features.

"Yes, Sir Peter!"

The dying man nodded. "I am Sir Peter Melham, yes. You can guess what we did, Bayne and I. We were mad, Mr. Pons – mad! It was the estate, of course. My brother swore that my daughter would not inherit at his death. I can't know

now whether he meant it; but I thought he did, then, and it maddened me." He put one hand weakly over his eyes.

Pons said nothing.

"It is said the devil protects his own – and he put one in this house to protect me. But I killed him tonight, you see, and now myself, to keep everything from coming out." He challenged Pons. "For the love of God, sir, will you keep it from her?" He made a feeble gesture in the direction of the door through which his daughter had passed.

"I think it can be done, Sir Peter."

The dying man made an attempt to rise on his elbows, but it was too much for him; before Pons and I could reach him, the wound began to gush blood anew, and he fell back, coughing and collapsing into his bed. Sir Peter Melham was dead.

When we came from the room, we found the police and Hugh Betterton in charge. Pons went directly to Miss Maureen Melham, doubtless to tell her Sir Peter was dead. Then he stepped over to the county police and the coroner, and drew them aside; they went together up to Sir Peter's room, and it was some time before they came down to where I waited.

An hour later, we were on our way back to Sir John Mollines' country house. The storm had passed now, and the moon shone from the western heavens, casting a dim, eerie light on the landscape, which was still so wet that our progress was slow. We walked for some distance before I spoke at length to say that the solution of the puzzle left me with little to conjecture, though I must admit I was not entirely clear as to what had taken place.

"Ah, it was simple enough," said Pons. "Suppose you go back three years to that October night when Sir Peter left Melham Old Place on the way to Prague. It should be relatively easy, in the light of tonight's events, to follow him. At Durward he purchased his ticket for Dover; he stepped into the train from Edinburgh, and that was the last seen of him. Sir Peter got into the train, and as soon as it began to move – perhaps even before – he got out again."

"But surely he would have been seen!" I cried.

"The hour was late. He may have waited until the train had pulled out of Durward and got back through the countryside. His motive for making away with his brother was obvious; he himself told us of it before he died. He had Bayne's aid, and Sir Andrew undoubtedly lies buried in some remote spot on the estate. The boldest stroke of the whole wretched business followed, when Sir Peter took his dead brother's place. As you were told, they were twins; their resemblance was marked; moreover, Sir Peter had watched his brother long enough to have memorized his actions, and he knew that since Sir Andrew no longer had regular medical attention, he was safe. His greatest difficulty lay in deceiving his daughter, but he succeeded. Next to that, his inability to enjoy relaxation imposed such a strain on him that he had to resort to walking about by night.

"So the stage was set for Jasper Bayne's betrayal. You can well conceive what Sir Peter's feeling must have been when he discovered that Bayne had promised himself that Maureen Melham must marry his son, Robert. From that time on the breach between the murderers widened, and doubtless then, too, Sir Peter's nocturnal ramblings were made with less care and more agitation, as he passed to and from Bayne's room and his own, and so he was mistaken for his own spectre by his daughter. On the night we almost had him, he was doubtless on his way to Bayne's room, and remained hidden there until the household was once again quiet.

"What happened tonight must be clear. Miss Melham gave her supposed 'uncle' her decision; he in turn informed Bayne when Bayne came to his room; Bayne delivered his ultimatum, which was the threat of revelation – very probably not to the police, since that would involve him, too – but to Miss Melham, in the knowledge that she, to conceal her father's crime, would acquiesce to Bayne's plan, for Bayne never did know of his son's marriage; and Sir Peter gave Bayne his answer – which was to pursue him from the room and shoot him as he was descending the stairs, after which, as we have seen, he shot himself."

"Amazing!"

"A remarkable but annoying affair in which I failed to distinguish myself, because I disregarded one of my own primary concepts – that what is most baffling on the face of matters is often most simple in essence."

X

THE ADVENTURE OF THE SEVEN PASSENGERS

There is a certain name which, when mentioned in his presence, invariably causes my friend Solar Pons to look up with a challenging glint in his eyes but a certain grim tightness of his lips, starting in his mind a reminiscence which embraces some of the most interesting cases of his entire career as an investigator of those curious manifestations of criminal activity which reveal the workings of the human mind. Pons had several encounters with the work of the Baron Ennesfred Kroll, who first came to Pons' attention in a social capacity, for Pons had met him at a ball given at the German Embassy late in 1929, where Kroll, who was a social lion, was a compelling figure, despite his stooped shoulders and his sinister appearance, moving among the throngs at the Embassy ball with a singular ability to attract people to him. Pons regarded Baron Ennesfred Kroll as the prototype of the arch-criminal, and found himself ultimately involved in several adventures in which he recognized the hand of the baron, before he was enabled to trap him. Of these, perhaps two – those chronicled in my notes under the headings of "The Adventure of the Seven Passengers," and "The Adventure of the Lost Holiday," – are most fascinating.

The curious affair of the seven passengers was brought to Pons' attention early one morning in January, 1930. Pons had preceded me to the breakfast table that morning, and was engaged in reading the reports in the *Times* relating to the Naval Limitations Conference then in progress in London.

"Anything new?" I asked, as I sat down opposite him.

Pons shrugged. "Not in the city. An interesting murder in Kent, a robbery of some ingenuity in a small village south of London; beyond those, nothing. But here," he continued, tapping the paper at his elbow, "is an admirable opening for something of major interest."

"What is that?"

"The Naval Conference. I fancy an astute spy could cause a considerable disturbance among the envoys of the nations represented here, if he were to announce the plans of the Conference before the proper time."

Pons had just tasted his egg, murmured the customary compliment for Mrs. Johnson, our estimable and long-suffering landlady, and was about to go on with his breakfast, when there came a sudden ring at the doorbell.

"Ah!" exclaimed Pons, his face brightening. He pushed his chair slightly away from the table, and sat listening with a smile of anticipation to the deliberate footsteps of Mrs. Johnson on the stairs.

Her rap was followed by the appearance of her head with its wisps of hair escaping from her heavy coils. "A gentleman to see you, Mr. Pons," she said, and thrust in our direction a card, which I took and handed to Pons.

Pons' eyebrows raised a little in surprise, and a little gleam of satisfaction appeared briefly in his eyes. "Show him up, by all means, Mrs. Johnson."

"I see you are pleasurably surprised," I observed.

"Elementary, my dear fellow – but still, a deduction. We are about to have a visitor from Downing Street." He dropped the card on the table. "I should not be at all surprised if the Naval Conference has encountered some difficulties."

I took up the card. "Mr. Evan Holdridge St. John," I read. "That is both an imposing and attractive name."

"Withal somewhat affected, one might add. Do not be disconcerted to find him something of an elegant."

At this moment there was a light, discreet tap on the door. Pons called out; the door opened, and a young man not quite six feet in height, a dark blonde, and by no means unhandsome, walked into the room. He was faultlessly dressed in morning clothes, and carried a stick and gloves. Certainly the word "elegant," which Pons had just used, was not in error in describing him.

"Pray sit down, Mr. St. John," invited Pons. "Dr. Parker and I are still at breakfast, but I could not very well disregard a call from Downing Street, no matter at what hour."

Our visitor, who had seated himself at Pons' invitation, leaned forward, supporting himself on his ebony stick, and glanced cursorily in my direction, biting his lips somewhat uncertainly.

"I assure you Dr. Parker is the soul of discretion. Perhaps I am not amiss in supposing that you are working with the Naval Conference, and that something has gone wrong?"

St. John sighed, covered his eyes with one hand, and shook his head. "The bottom has fallen out of it. Everything has gone wrong," he said in a voice that trembled with conviction.

"Dear me!" exclaimed Pons, leaning back and folding his hands. "What precisely?"

"Important papers – I may say, the most important papers of the Conference so far – have unaccountably disappeared. Perhaps it is not too much to say that the entire future of the Conference rests upon these papers."

"Not mislaid, of course?"

Our visitor tapped his shoe impatiently with his stick. "Certainly not, Mr. Pons. The papers were stolen!"

"Ah, that is more like it," said Pons. "Perhaps you would like to tell us exactly what occurred."

St. John nodded and began at once. "We were on the train this morning, coming from..."

Pons interrupted him with a grimace of exasperation. "Pray be so good as to start from the beginning, Mr. St. John. You say 'We' – who, besides yourself? You were on a train – it follows that you spent the night out of the city; yet you are presumably in close attendance upon the Naval Conference."

Our visitor flushed, and his hand closed more tightly upon his stick, a gesture of which Pons took no notice. "I take it you are aware, Mr. Pons, that his lordship, the Minister of War, is convalescing at his country home near Windsor?"

Pons nodded.

"His lordship stipulated that he be fully acquainted with the happenings at the Conference; he desired complete, detailed reports in writing. Since it is largely upon Lord Stapleton that the ultimate results of this Conference rest, his lordship had no difficulty in obtaining his request. In consequence, it devolved upon seven carefully selected men to carry this report to him. Every evening, following the Conference, these seven men, of whom I was one, took a carriage at Paddington. Each man carried in a wallet, kept in his inner coat pocket, a portion of the detailed report in code. I myself carried the most important of the papers; the remaining six men carried the rest. I occupied a compartment alone; my companions divided two compartments between them. In this fashion we arrived at Windsor and reported to his lordship. We were required to spend the night there, and took an early morning train back to the city.

"For the last six days, I was not alone in my compartment. An elderly gentleman, apparently a tradesman of some kind, occupied my compartment with me. This man did not attract my attention until I began to find that no matter how irregular our hours were at night, he managed somehow to take the same train we did, and showed up promptly at my compartment, for the occupation of which he had most courteously requested and continued to request. I had never in any way associated any suspicion with him, for he seemed a rather harmless and decrepit old person, but I admit to a certain vague uneasiness during the past week.

"Yesterday, as the papers have been hinting all week, marked the crisis of the Conference, and as a consequence we carried in addition to yesterday's reports a fully detailed report of the entire work of the Conference to date. Thus far, the work of this Conference has been most rigidly excluded from the press, and it was considered best for this policy to continue for at least the period of a year. In the meanwhile, carefully censored reports were to be supplied the press. Should the press at this moment get hold of these genuine reports which were stolen from us this morning as we rode to the city, the entire work of the Conference would collapse."

"It is difficult to conceive in what manner such a collection of papers could possibly be stolen from seven agents," said Pons with keen interest.

St. John gestured with his hands. "They were stolen, Mr. Pons. I can tell you how they were stolen from me, but as for my companions – I do not know." He shrugged his shoulders.

"And how were they stolen from you?"

"Unfortunately," said our visitor in some embarrassment, "I believe I fell asleep. At least, I can remember drawing out of Windsor, and after that no more, until I came to my senses in the midst of the roar of Paddington Station."

"You have no conscious knowledge of falling asleep?"

"None!" exclaimed our visitor, shaking his head. "Absolutely none. I could not even swear that I had slept, but it must have been so. The compartment was very close, for the air was chill outside, and there was nothing open."

Pons began to chuckle. "I fancy you have fallen victim to a very clever little plot. Unfortunately, it is rather old, though to all appearances still very workable."

"Indeed," said St. John, "what is it, then?"

"You were drugged, and I daresay your companions were similarly treated, but they, unlike you, are unwilling to admit that they fell asleep at the post."

"On the contrary, I ate and drank nothing which might have had such an effect on me," protested Mr. St. John.

"Certainly not," agreed Pons. "You very probably inhaled it. Was the old gentleman in your compartment again this morning? Ah, I see in your eyes that he was. And he was nowhere in evidence when you came to your senses at Paddington."

"You are quite right, Mr. Pons. My companion had vanished," answered our visitor, looking ruefully at Pons.

Pons nodded abstractedly. "If I were to ask you to describe your traveling companion I should in all probability learn that his features were very indistinct; he probably wore dark glasses, perhaps also a beard, a heavy coat – an ulster, most likely – and no doubt also a scarf wound tightly about his neck and chin."

St. John colored; he opened his mouth once or twice as if to speak, but no words came.

"Am I right, Mr. St. John?"

Our visitor nodded curtly. "You might have seen the man, Mr. Pons. He wore an ulster, yes. He also wore a scarf and dark glasses. He had a moustache, but no beard. Yes," he continued bitterly, "I have been taken in very thoroughly."

"Well, you noticed his height, I am sure," said Pons, in a kinder tone. "That he could not easily hide from you."

"He stood a good six feet, Mr. Pons."

"Very good. That is one point gained. Now, his voice – was it that of an old man?"

"It certainly seemed so, though I now have no doubt it was disguised."

Pons nodded thoughtfully. "By the way," he said suddenly, "you have not been long in government service?"

"No, Mr. Pons, I have not."

Pons appeared to meditate for some moments in silence. "You are thoroughly familiar with the effect the early publication of these reports might have?" he asked presently.

"Quite, Mr. Pons. The publication of these reports at this time, aside from breaking up the Conference, would no doubt severely strain our relations with certain powers. There is no question of anything more serious, certainly, but this alone, after such long labor, is not easy to contemplate."

"Which countries might pay a good price to obtain secret knowledge of these reports?"

"Germany would pay perhaps the best price," returned Mr. St. John after a momentary hesitation. "Spain, Turkey, and Austria would be interested."

"Very good. Then I think it reasonably sound to assume that the reports were taken not for the press, but for the purpose of selling them to another country."

"Exactly," agreed our visitor.

"Has it not struck you as somewhat disturbing that your strange traveling companion stole the papers of the very day that marked the crisis of the Conference?"

"I confess it has, Mr. Pons."

"Yes, it is certainly more than a coincidence."

Mr. St. John leaned forward suddenly. "What do you mean, Mr. Pons?" he asked in some agitation.

"Surely it must be obvious that, regrettable as it may seem, there has been a leak somewhere?"

Our visitor came to his feet and began to pace the floor nervously. "But surely you don't suspect one of us?"

"Until the papers are actually found, I must continue to suspect everyone who had knowledge of these reports to Lord Stapleton. Who, besides the seven of you, knew of this arrangement?"

"Only Lord Stapleton and the Prime Minister," answered Mr. St. John, his face clouding.

"And the other six men with you – their names, please."

"Mr. Harold Edson, Mr. James Greer, and Mr. Ewart Stephens occupied the compartment behind my own; behind them were Mr. Algernon Chambers, Mr. Michael Caermon, and Mr. Emmett McDonough. All these men have been in the government service for at least four years."

Pons made a careful note of the names upon a pad at his elbow, and then for a few moments remained in pensive silence. At last he turned again to St. John.

"You say you seemed to fall asleep just out of Windsor – or better, you remember drawing out of Windsor. Now, Mr. St. John, do you remember whether your strange traveling companion left the compartment shortly out of Windsor?" Our visitor nodded emphatically. "He did. Yes, I remember that, because he had never left the compartment at any time before. He left just as we were leaving Windsor behind."

"And did you hear anything that resembled a popping sound – let us say, similar to the pop of a champagne bottle being opened?"

For some moments St. John sat in silence. Then he said thoughtfully, "Yes, Mr. Pons, I believe I did. I heard such a sound just as my companion opened the door of my compartment to step into the aisle."

"Ha!" exclaimed Pons in an undertone. "It was glass, then." He looked up at our visitor. "Has the carriage you used been sent out again?"

"No. I anticipated you might wish to examine it, and had it ordered put on a siding. If you care to step out and walk this short distance, you may see the car at Paddington."

"Later," said Pons. "For the present, you may as well return to the Conference. I will do my best, and if all goes well, I may be able to produce results within twenty-four hours."

"I had hardly dared to hope for that, Mr. Pons."

"If I need you again, I daresay I can reach you through Downing Street."

St. John bowed and left the room. Pons strode rapidly to a window overlooking Praed Street and watched the young man walk to his car. He turned presently and said, "We have just time enough to get over to Paddington before lunch," looking at his watch. "You're coming, I hope."

"Of course," I replied. "But you haven't finished your breakfast, after all."

"I've no time now, Parker" said Pons, and rang for Mrs. Johnson to take the breakfast things away.

At Paddington Station, Pons immediately found the official in charge, and we were quickly taken to the carriage, which had been put on a siding below street level. The carriage was, of course, no different from other first-class carriages of the Great Western Railway. After pointing out to us the compartment occupied by the government men, the official took his leave, and Pons immediately set about examining each compartment in turn.

We entered the first compartment and Pons stood for a moment looking about him. Then abruptly he dropped to his knees and began a minute examination of the floor. I watched him crawl about in some amusement.

"Ah, here it is!" he exclaimed at last. "What do you make of it, Parker?"

I followed the direction of his gaze and noticed near the door the tiny fragments of crushed glass. "Glass," I said dropping to my knees at his side. "You were looking for it, then?"

"Surely it was obvious that the seven passengers of these compartments were rather cunningly gassed. Mr. St. John heard a pop – that suggests gas in glass containers – cylinders, I see," he continued, bending forward and picking up a fragment of glass for closer scrutiny. "Note the thickness of the glass – I daresay a condensed gas was used, for this glass suggests pressure. I have no doubt we shall find the remains of one of these cylinders in each of the three compartments occupied."

Pons passed the fragment of glass to me and I examined it cursorily. "What do you think it might have been? St. John seemed entirely unaffected by the gas nor did he mention having smelled it."

"Odorless, obviously odorless. I thought of carbon monoxide, but if I am not mistaken, the use of that gas would result in nausea and subsequent weakness for the victim."

"Certainly, if enough were administered to produce unconsciousness, it would – there are exceptions, of course."

"Our most likely guess is, I daresay, ethylene. It is odorless and colorless, and its effect is similar to that experienced by St. John. It is extremely volatile. I have no doubt that a small cylinder of compressed ethylene would produce exactly the effect desired by St. John's strange traveling companion. Everything was closed, you remember. St. John's companion would only have to crush the cylinder as he left the compartment; in a short enough time, St. John would be sound asleep."

"But the other compartments?"

"That's a matter of conjecture, until we have seen the other six passengers. I daresay our man, having shown himself already so clever, could insinuate a cylinder in the other two compartments with comparative ease. He had only to blunder into them, excuse himself courteously, and crush a cylinder under foot as he withdrew."

"Yes, it is certainly plausible."

Pons rose to his feet. "It is, however, rather curious that none of the gentlemen was smoking. I should say that Mr. St. John's companion took a long chance."

"But how can you tell?" I asked in astonishment. "Why, you have not even been in the other compartments!"

"Ethylene gas is made up of carbon and hydrogen, a combination always inflammable, and in its compressed form, explosive; had one of the seven government men been smoking when St. John's companion insinuated his cylinder of ethylene, I fancy there would have been a pretty disturbance."

Pons now made his way to the adjoining compartment. I followed at his heels. An examination of this and the remaining compartment disclosed the remains of two more cylinders – in each case, just slightly beyond the door; a fact which gave further weight to Pons' deduction. However, nothing further was found, and Pons gave up the examination at last, taking with him only a few fragments of the thick cylinder glass found in the compartments. We left the carriage, and, after notifying the officials that the carriage could once more be put into service, proceeded to our rooms.

Once there, Pons began to telephone the other six government men who had accompanied Mr. St. John on his journey that morning. In each case Pons found that sleep had overtaken the man, for, under Pons' questions, this admission came quickly. Pons also verified his supposition regarding the insinuation of the glass cylinders into the compartments: St. John's singular companion had blundered into both the other compartments, apparently by mistake, had excused himself and gone out. Had the gentlemen heard a popping noise? Yes, it seemed they had. They smelled nothing, no. And everything was closed. Nor had they been smoking.

Pons turned from the telephone after a considerable time and sat for some moments in deep thought. He rose at last and looked over at the clock on the mantel.

"Time for lunch," I said.

He shook his head. "Not for me. I can dispense with it."

"But you've had hardly any breakfast," I protested.

"No matter," replied Pons. "I find it's imperative I see an acquaintance out Hyde Park way at once. Take your lunch, Parker. Pray do not wait for me. It's possible that I shall find a few moments to drop into a restaurant somewhere."

"Well, I hope so. I don't like to see you going off so without your meals."

"Not a good policy, I agree. But am just beginning to suspect that this matter is not quite as simple as it at first appeared." Pons put on his Inverness and stood at the door, meditatively drawing on his gloves. "I think I shall have the very devil of a time getting my hands on the man – or men, behind this thing."

"Come, you are making too much of the matter," I protested.

"Let us hope so." The door closed behind him.

It was a considerable time after lunch that Pons returned. He came slowly into the room, on his face an expression that boded no good.

"Something has gone wrong?" I hazarded.

"On the contrary," said Pons shortly, "everything is working out too well."

He threw off his Inverness and sat down opposite me. I looked at him questioningly.

"As I told you," he began, "I left for Hyde Park. There are certain sections of the park where I can always find what the American press calls 'stool-pigeons'. I am acquainted with some of them, and at times they come in very useful, since most of them are from the better classes, and they serve me quite as well in their circles as Frick does in Limehouse and Wapping. One of them knows Mr. Evan St. John quite well.

I learned from him that St. John has for some time past been intimate with a certain social figure of prominence."

"And this figure?"

"Is, I am sure, the man I should like to trap. If I am not in error, it is he who is behind this thing. We are quite familiar with him through the press – the Baron Ennesfred Kroll."

"Impossible!" I exclaimed.

Pons shrugged his shoulders. "Slowly, Parker! You will remember the German Embassy ball last December and you will recall that I was much interested in Baron Kroll."

"I recall it perfectly."

"Aside from a purely personal interest, I acted on advice from the C. I. D. The Baron has been engaged in several rather dubious matters on the Continent; understand, nothing definite has ever been proved against him, but it remains that more than once someone in his household has been arrested for a serious crime. Strangely enough, the criminal, after pleading guilty and being sent to prison, has in most cases been released. Some power has been at work, and no one who knows him has much hesitation in designating that power as Baron Kroll.

"I took the liberty this afternoon of forcing myself into the presence of the Prime Minister, whose initials you might have seen had you turned over St. John's card this morning when you examined it. I enquired about St. John. It appeared that not much was known of him; he had been suggested for the position he holds by no less a person than the Earl of Dolchester. He comes of a very good family, but of his capabilities, the Prime Minister knew nothing except what the Earl had written him. I got the Earl on the wire. He was somewhat embarrassed; it had been suggested to him that St. John would be highly capable in this government position. Might I know who had suggested it – I might, providing I was discreet. It was Lady Djuna Howard, the Earl's attractive niece.

"To come to the point, I learned that St. John's capabilities had been suggested to Lady Howard by Baron Kroll."

"You *have* got into the thick of it."

"Not a doubt of it. But I have had extraordinary luck; let up hope that it continues. My first step, of course, was to urge the Prime Minister to keep all important matters from St. John."

"You think him an accomplice, then?"

"He is certainly responsible for the leak. But I doubt very much that he is consciously an accomplice. I daresay he is unwittingly the tool of Baron Kroll. In all probability, St. John relates minor state secrets to Baron Kroll never suspecting that the Baron is other than the soul of honesty."

"Do you suggest, then, that St. John's traveling companion was the Baron?"

"No, certainly not. You underrate the Baron, Parker. But I have no doubt that it was one of his agents. I daresay the Baron was many miles removed from the scene of the theft, even though he may now have the papers in his possession."

"Is there no way of verifying that?"

"Yes," replied Pons. "With the assistance of a most gracious lady, the Yard has been in constant touch with the movements of the Baron."

"Why not call Jamison, then?"

"I fancy he will only confirm my assumption." He reached for the telephone and called the Yard, asking for Inspector Jamison, whose voice presently sounded on the wire. There was a brief conversation, after which Pons turned from the instrument with lips tight in anger. "As I thought – the Baron spent the entire week at the Earl of Dolchester's country house; he is expected to return to the city some time today."

"You are planning to watch him?"

"Jamison kindly lent me Constable Mecker, who has been keeping the Baron's house in Park Lane under eye since early this afternoon."

"Why that glumness, then?"

"Baron Kroll is wilier than you think, Parker. I fear very much I shall not be able to bag him."

"And the Conference papers?"

"I daresay I shall manage them. I shall deliver them to St. John within the time I promised. It is already obvious that the Baron, though the author of the daring and successful plan to get the papers, has no intention whatsoever of appearing personally in the matter. Therefore, the papers, which were stolen by one of Baron Kroll's men, must be delivered to another German agent, who will in turn send them to Berlin. I daresay I can name the fellow who will clear them."

"And who is he?"

"He goes by the name of Hilary Blount, and he lives at Seventeen, St. Anne's Court, Soho. He is better known to the C. I. D. as Stefan Braun, one of the most capable German espionage agents with whom the Yard has had to contend."

"If you know him, surely he could be arrested on some pretext or other?"

"And so ruin the only immediate chance of getting back the papers? No, my dear Parker, it won't do. Braun must have a free hand for the time being. We shall not have long to wait. Unless I am very much mistaken, Kroll's agent will attempt to dispose of the papers as quickly as possible; they are wanted badly by the Home Office, and Braun knows that they will be brought to him. I have no doubt the arrangement has been made by Baron Kroll, who will send to Braun the man who managed to make off with the papers this morning. The pattern is only too painfully clear. If the thief himself is caught, he will no doubt plead guilty, without a breath of suspicion to touch Baron Kroll, who will then immediately turn about and set the wheels moving in the prisoner's behalf. It's a sorry business, but I can do nothing in the face of diplomatic maneuvers such as those of which Baron Kroll is capable. Nor can we wait on the chance that Baron Kroll may get in touch with Braun; for the papers must be returned before Braun gets a good look at them. If that were not so, perhaps I might have sufficient time to play the game long enough so that in the end I could bag the Baron."

"What if Braun meets the Baron's accomplice somewhere?"

"He will be followed if he leaves his house."

"And the Baron?"

"Anyone leaving his house will also be traced. Mecker has enough men at his disposal; I saw to that. Mecker himself has instructions to follow anyone answering to the rather vague description of St. John's strange traveling companion. No one can get into the Baron's house today without going to considerable trouble, apart from Baron Kroll himself. I daresay we are safe in that; but I am equally certain that the Baron will take no chance whatever; the arrangements have already been made and need only to be carried out. Kroll's agent has the papers; Braun is to have them. We are wasting time covering Kroll's Park Lane house; it is the house in St. Anne's Court we must watch.

"Braun lives alone, as most men of his occupation do. He has a charwoman by day, sometimes a butler; at night he is always quite alone. Moreover, there is an off chance that the Baron may have the papers sent to another agent in the employment of Berlin – even so, all known agents are being watched. But come, let us have dinner, and then join the men who are watching the house in St. Anne's Court."

Number Seventeen, St. Anne's Court, was a small house of one storey, set quite close to the street. It had an innocuous appearance, and was not a new building; so much was evident despite the early darkness. One of Jamison's men was in evidence some distance down the court, and another at the corner of Wardour Street not far away. Pons and I took up our position across the court in the shadow of a protecting doorway, and from this position it was easy to see beyond the partly-drawn shade, a solitary figure occasionally cross the single lit window. We had not been in hiding for many minutes, when the door of the house opposite opened, and a short, rather heavy man stood framed in a faint light from behind. This was undoubtedly the German agent, Braun. He stood there briefly, and had just turned to re-enter the house when a taxicab careened around the corner from Wardour Street and screeched to a halt before number seventeen.

Braun remained on the threshold, one hand on the door-jamb, as if hesitating to close the door. A tall, cloaked figure left the taxi-cab, said a few words to the driver, and ran rapidly up into the house, past Braun. The door closed; the taxi cab drove forward and took its stand at the farther end of the court.

Pons immediately led the way across the court, where we were joined by Mecker, who had left his car in the adjoining street. Mecker and Pons held a whispered conversation, after which Pons crouched before the door of Braun's house and looked through the keyhole.

"Locked?" asked Mecker.

Pons shook his head. He reached silently to the knob, turned it, and the door opened for us. The sound of voices came into the hall from an inner room, from under the door of which light shone in a bright line. This door, too, was unlocked, and in a moment Pons had thrown it back.

The three of us, Mecker and myself with weapons drawn, sprang into the room.

"Up hands, Gentlemen!" cried Mecker.

The two men in the room presented a picture of contrasts, for, while Braun showed his consternation in the fear and convulsive working of his face, the tall man who had come with the papers remained impassive; if anything, he seemed to regard the three of us with scorn.

Pons went directly to the table. "Ah, I fancy these are the papers we want, Gentlemen." He gathered up three packets, examined them briefly, and stuffed them into his inner coat pocket. Indicating Braun casually, he said to Mecker, "Your man. Espionage." Then he turned to the other. "Your name?"

"John Hirsch," snapped our prisoner.

"Employed by Baron Kroll?"

"Say, rather, a freelance, Mr. Solar Pons.'

"You prefer to deny your relationship with the man Kroll?"

"I do not know him."

Pons shrugged. "Hirsch, you are guilty of high treason, but there is an opportunity to grant you a kind of immunity. What part did Baron Kroll play in your well-executed plan? A statement implicating the scoundrel behind you – and perhaps, who knows – we may be able to overlook your part in this little plan. Come, man, what do you say?"

"I say, sir, go to the devil!"

"Ah, very well, then. We shall see to it that Baron Kroll can manage nothing in your behalf. Your man, Mecker."

Outside once more, Pons strode along in deep and silent thought.

"At least," I broke in presently, "you have recovered the papers."

"Ha! That is all you see, Parker?"

"But surely – you have explained everything else?"

"Ah, indeed! It does not occur to you that I was meant to recover the papers?"

"Candidly, no; the motive for that would be beyond me."

"And that we were *meant* to arrest Braun and get him out of the way? The German government has that way of disposing of men whose services are no longer welcome since they are too well-known to the police. I fear it is all very elementary; we have served as we intended to serve; neither Braun nor Hirsch will find a finger lifted in his behalf; and in the meantime,

Baron Kroll will plan and execute coups of more significance to the rising desire for vengeance within Germany.

"But, if not this time, there will always be another time for Baron Kroll, and still another, no doubt, and so on, until it is our turn. Let us just be patient and wait upon time."

XI

THE ADVENTURE OF THE LOST HOLIDAY

As I came from my bath that evening, I saw my friend Solar Pons bent attentively at the wireless. He had evidently just come in, and gone directly over to listen to the news, for he had not yet removed his Inverness. He turned, saw me, and smiled, with a glint of uncommon concentration in his eyes.

The broadcast of the news was just ending. I heard only a reference to Lord Penryn and a cancelled holiday in the south of France before Pons turned the wireless off, slipped from his Inverness and his coat, and got into his smoking-jacket. He came over and sat down beside the table, where he had left his notes when he went out that afternoon.

"Ah, you look fresh and scrubbed, Parker. You did not hear the broadcast, then?"

"No."

"Lord Penryn's holiday in the south of France has been cancelled."

"That is probably not the first time such a thing has happened."

"Very likely not. Yet, it is interesting to reflect that only three days ago, when Lord Penryn's holiday was first announced, it was given out that this was his first holiday in two years. Now suddenly we find it cancelled. It does not seem strange to you that it is so?"

"Not at all."

"Let me put it another way: it does not seem strange to you that the holiday of the Secretary for European Affairs should be cancelled at a time when there are going forward negotiations of great importance between the governments of England and France? A holiday, moreover, in a country which is a party to these negotiations – the party of the second part."

"Apart from involving it a little, it does not seem to change the aspect of the matter."

"Ah, Parker – and after ten years here, – more than ten years!" He shook his head with a faint smile.

I was nettled. "Suppose you interpret it for me!"

"I submit that Lord Penryn's trip to France was not to be a holiday at all, but a journey of state; I submit, moreover, that the negotiations currently going on between emissaries of the two governments have struck some kind of snag which makes the proposed journey by the Secretary for European Affairs unnecessary or futile."

"My dear Pons!"

"No, it is nothing so simple as a mere guess, believe me, Parker. It is widely enough known that the Secretary for European Affairs takes the shooting every year in Scotland, that his sole holiday outside of England took place seven years ago when he had a fortnight in the Alps. This fanfare about his holiday in France has more behind it than it would appear to have."

"Well, I shall have to take your word for it – unless the Foreign Office might perhaps be good enough to settle the matter, which is hardly likely."

"We shall see," retorted Pons, and bent to his notes.

It was then nine in the evening. Within half an hour the matter of Lord Penryn's lost holiday was destined to be brought once more to our attention by one of the most august personages ever to enter our modest lodgings. He did not ring the bell; he entered the building, mounted the stairs directly to our quarters, as if he were personally familiar with our habits, and knocked on the door, a subdued, but nevertheless staccato knock without a note of hesitation in it.

Pons had heard the outer door open, and had listened to the steps on the stairs. "A portly gentleman, carrying a cane, on a mission of secrecy," he observed tranquilly. "Do open the door to him, Parker."

I rose and opened the door to admit our visitor.

Pons came to his feet behind me. "The Right Honorable Sackville Somerset!" he exclaimed. "You have come about Lord Penryn."

The Prime Minister started. "You know?"

"Pray do not be alarmed. I am merely making an exercise in deduction. Will you be seated, sir?"

"Mr. Pons, we have little time to waste. If you are free to come with me, my car is outside, I can explain the matter on the way to Park Lane."

The Prime Minister was agitated; his heavy, jowled face twitched now and then, his lips were pressed together in an expression of the utmost grimness; his eyes were haunted, and a faint dew of perspiration was evident on his brow. Yet his natural austerity was not diminished by the grave concern which troubled him. He paced back and forth, careful to be well away from the windows, while Pons and I made ready to accompany him, and, when we set forth, it was he who led the way in that same silent manner in which he had come, as if he were trying unconsciously to avoid surveillance.

His car, a long, closed Daimler, stood at the kerb. He himself opened the door for Pons and me, nodded to his chauffeur, and followed us into the dark interior.

"Now then," he said nervously, making certain that all communication with the chauffeur was shut away by the glass closing off the *tonneau*, "it is a most painful and grave matter, Mr. Pons, – a matter, I may say, which may well bring about a rupture of relations with one of the Continental countries – if, indeed, not war!" He lifted his hat and touched his brow with his handkerchief. "A certain document intended for a trio of the highest officials of France has been stolen from the study of the Secretary for European Affairs."

"You have notified the police?"

"By no means! The matter is of such delicacy that we cannot risk any kind of publication, and it is not possible to close off beyond question the ranks of the police; some word of the matter could all too easily leak out, and it might be disastrous, Mr. Pons – a national calamity costing not only untold thousands – perhaps millions – of pounds, but also many lives. No, after consultation with those officers of our government who knew of the existence of this document, it was decided to employ your well-known talents in an effort to recover it with as much dispatch as possible. Once it is delivered into the hands of a certain foreign government – God help us in our present state of military unpreparedness!"

"Let us be frank, Mr. Somerset. The power to which you refer is Germany?"

"Let us imagine that I have admitted nothing. It is Germany."

"Very well. You speak of military preparedness – so, presumably, the document in question had to do with joint plans of England and France to arm secretly in order to be prepared for the culmination of that secret re-armament of Germany which is going on under camouflage with the tacit approval of certain American and British industrialists with rich holdings in that country."

The Prime Minister caught his breath. Then, in a spate of words he said, "Mr. Pons, you are more informed than I dared hope you might be. You have hit upon it; the document in question contains to the last detail plans which have been worked out here by a commission of French and English experts for the secret re-armament of our two allied nations. It is well known, there is no need denying it, that Germany rankles under the terms of the Versailles Treaty, and the wounds of that country have been little salved by the Hoover Moratorium or the Dawes Plan which have come out of America. She has begun to re-arm; we are not blind to the fact. However, our people are not prepared to see us enforce the terms of the Treaty by force of arms; they have fallen victim to our own lassitude and to pacifist propaganda, which, however noble in intention, fails always to take into consideration the unknown human element in our sister nations. Moreover, there is no certainty whatsoever that France would support our force of arms, and our own Government is unfortunately sadly divided. In fact, Mr. Pons, I will not be telling you anything you could not learn from another source, but there are in our country an influential group of diplomats and industrialists who would collaborate with Germany at any price, and they have gone so far as to instill grave doubts about His Majsety's Government's official line in the mind of no less a person than the Crown Prince!"

"And the re-armament plan?"

"Ah, yes, the Strong-Cressington Plans. Lord Penryn was to present these plans to the French government tomorrow; that was the purpose of his holiday, as by this time surely you will have guessed. He carried them home with him this afternoon, as arranged, since he had planned to take the night train for Dover just before midnight. He did not leave the papers out of his sight save for a brief period of less than ten minutes, and then they were in his study. He had taken them out to go over them in an effort to settle his doubts about certain clauses; he had laid them on the table in his study; he had gone upstairs after a stronger pair of glasses; when he came back, the papers were gone. The house, moreover was locked, but he discovered on his return that a French window of the study stood slightly open; it had been broken; apparently the thief had made his entry there, and escaped with the papers in that interval."

"Presupposing that Lord Penryn had been watched, and that therefore it was known that such papers were or might be in his possession."

"Exactly, Mr. Pons." The Prime Minister sighed. "Of course, it is impossible to prevent foreign agents in espionage from coming to the correct conclusions when four of the leading exponents of re-armament in France arrive in this country and immediately vanish from public sight together with members of our own re-armament commission and certain ministers of His Majesty's Government. But here we are, and you may talk to Lord Penryn yourself. I assure you he has not left his house; no one has either left or entered the house since he telephoned me; we have issued orders to have the house watched."

"And this took place at what hour?"

"Just an hour ago, Mr. Pons – at eight-thirty o'clock. Lord Penryn was at first badly rattled, and he made the mistake of informing the British Broadcasting Corporation that his visit to the Continent had been cancelled, but when he regained his composure, he recognized that absolute secrecy must be maintained in regard to every phase of his activities."

Lord Penryn's house rose in a spacious square of ground behind a hawthorn hedge, shrouded in trees, and, while not easily accessible from the street, clearly afforded refuge to anyone who succeeded in penetrating the hedge. The Prime Minister slipped from the car; Pons and I followed. Mr. Somerset led the way into the house, and went directly to the study, where we encountered Lord Penryn, the austere, be-monocled Secretary for European Affairs, pacing the floor.

Lord Penryn, a man fully six feet tall, with long, almost haughtily equine features, was haggard and distraught; his monocle swung on its ribbon against his waistcoat; his smoking jacket hung open. His keen eyes turned on us as we crossed the threshold; he ceased his pacing and sighed with some relief.

"Somerset! And these gentlemen... ?" Then he recognized Pons. "Mr. Solar Pons! My dear fellow, forgive me! I am naturally upset. The Prime Minister has told you?" He looked questioningly at Somerset.

"I should like to hear your story, if you please, Lord Penryn."

"Certainly, certainly. Please be seated, gentlemen. I trust you will not mind if I remain standing. I am restless and disturbed. I brought the plans home with me, and shortly after dinner I retired to this room to look them over. I sat down at that table there – yes, Mr. Pons, the one at which the Prime Minister is sitting – at that precise spot..."

"If the Prime Minister will be so kind as to take another seat," suggested Pons, "I should like the scene of the crime to be as little changed as possible."

With admirable aplomb the Prime Minister changed seats.

"Pray forgive my interruption. Continue, My Lord," said Pons, as if he had not just witnessed the silent obedience of the Prime Minister of England to his whim.

"In the course of my examination, my eyes began to ache, and I left the study to go to my room for my reading glasses. I was gone less than ten minutes, possibly closer to five; I could not immediately find my glasses, but I assure you I could not have been gone more than seven minutes. When I returned, I was dismayed to discover that the plans were gone. When I looked around, I saw that that French window stood open, just as you see it, and that a portion of one pane had been broken in. Since then, I have not set foot out of this room."

"You did not consider it indiscreet to leave the plans unguarded, My Lord?" asked Pons.

"I had personally seen to it that every door and window in the house was locked."

"You are alone here?"

"No, Mr. Pons, I am not. The room above is occupied by Lady Sybil Wector, my niece, who has been acting as my hostess in the absence of my wife, now visiting relatives in America. She has been upset by preparations for her marriage to Eric Horrell, Viscount Pellman, and has been indisposed most of the day, though she took dinner with me this evening. Apart from her, there is my brother Cadogan. Both are upstairs. Then there are the servants, of course. But surely you do not suspect anyone in the house, Mr. Pons; I assure you my servants have been with me for ten years and more; they are absolutely above suspicion."

"Those people who are above suspicion are rarely found, My Lord. Let us now consider the possibility of how knowledge of these papers escaped, for obviously it must be so if someone broke into your study and abstracted them. How many people knew of your having the papers here tonight?"

"Apart from my personal staff and the Prime Minister, no one."

"And in Mr. Somerset's office?" inquired Pons, turning to him.

"Myself, my chief clerks, and my secretary. All are unimpeachable, Mr. Pons."

"Manifestly, however, someone let the news slip. How else could anyone have known sufficiently in advance to be watching and waiting for the opportunity to snatch the Strong-Cressington Plans? You are assuming that someone stood on the terrace outside and watched Lord Penryn at his papers; the fortuitous moment arrived, he broke in, he snatched the papers and vanished. That presupposes informed knowledge. What manner of papers were they, by the way?"

"Like these." Lord Penryn took up three loose sheets of legal foolscap and handed them to Pons, who examined them gravely.

"These, too, seem to be plans."

"Of no account. They are public knowledge."

Pons put them absently into his pocket and got up to walk around the table, at which Lord Penryn had been sitting. Then he walked over to the partly open French window. I walked after him and stood looking over his shoulder to where he knelt examining the fragments of glass on the stone sill beyond the door. He touched nothing, however, until he came to examine the broken pane itself; then he detached from one edge of the broken glass a thin strand of some white material, which he handed to me with a quixotic smile.

"What do you make of this, Parker?"

"It is evidently silk. If I were to make a guess, I should say it was torn from a gentleman's silk scarf."

"It appears to be somewhat soft and light in texture for that purpose. But let us see."

He returned to the table and bent above it. Lord Penryn and the Prime Minister watched him with nervous interest, growing steadily more impatient at the thought that even now the precious plans might be on the way to alien hands. The table was plainly that of an orderly and precise man, for everything was in its place; on one side stood ink-wells and pens, together with an antique box of yew containing various clips, pencils, erasers, and similar appurtenances. Beside this lay a letter-opener, and a pen which Lord Penryn had obviously been using earlier in the evening, for one of the inkwells still stood open. On the other side of the table, that closest to the open French window, lay a stack of papers neatly piled together and held down by a heavy glass ball on a flat base; this had at one time sustained several chips, and as my eye fell upon it, I observed that Pons was examining it with interest.

"Ah, you have seen it, Parker? What do you make of it?"

Adhering to one of the chipped places on the paper-weight were two more silk fibres, of a piece with that found on the broken pane.

"Clearly the fellow leaned over here – he would be coming from the windows – he caught his scarf again here, and left his calling-card, so to speak," I ventured.

"That is a most ingenious solution. And how would you account for the strand we discovered on the window-pane?"

The explanation struck me even as Pons asked. "Obviously the scarf was used to muffle the sound of the glass being broken."

Pons looked across to the Secretary for European Affairs.

"Did My Lord hear the sound of breaking glass at any time?"

"No, Mr. Pons. I heard nothing."

"Where is your room, My Lord?"

"At the far end of the upper hall."

"So that it would not be at all strange if you failed to hear such a sound?"

"No, it would not."

"I daresay we have arrived at the correct explanation in regard to the glass. Where are the servants?"

"In their quarters."

"Their quarters are at the rear of the house?"

"Yes."

"They were there at the time of the burglary?"

"Yes."

"I think I should like to question Lady Wector and your brother Cadogan. Do you think you might summon them to the study?"

"Certainly, Mr. Pons, if you wish it."

"I do. Meanwhile, I shall just look about the rest of the house a bit. No, thank you, I will go alone. I trust you will have Lady Wector and your brother here at my return."

"I will get them myself."

The Prime Minister's agitation broke forth. "Mr. Pons, I beg of you! Think – the papers may even now be escaping us! Are these questions necessary?"

"That is impossible to say at this point. They may yield nothing. Nevertheless, I am bound to ask them. Pray trust to my methods, Mr. Somerset."

Thus admonished, the Prime Minister settled back once more, though with obvious reluctance, while Pons slipped from the room, and Lord Penryn followed, on his way to summon his brother and his niece.

When Pons returned almost a quarter of an hour later, Lady Sybil Wector and her uncle Cadogan were waiting in the study. Lady Sybil was a dark-eyed, dark-haired young woman in her late twenties; she was most attractive, but manifestly at the moment uncertain of her role, as was her uncle, also. He was a man somewhat younger than his famous brother, and of a different stamp, rather careless of his appearance, with far less dignity than his brother naturally possessed. He regarded Pons, at his entrance, with openly-shown suspicion, put out the cigarette he had been smoking, and tightened himself up, narrowing his eyes. Solar Pons made an impressive figure standing before them; he had not removed his Inverness, and the flowing folds of his cape seemed to give added emphasis to his lean, hawk-like face.

"Ah, Lady Sybil Wector – I am sorry to inconvenience you," began Pons without the formality of an introduction, "but an attempt has been made to break into My Lord's study," – he gestured casually toward the French windows – "and we are most anxious to ascertain whether or not you heard the sound of breaking glass."

"I was lying down."

"You heard nothing?"

"Nothing but my uncle ascending the stairs, Mr. Pons."

"I see. And you, sir?" He turned to Lord Penryn's brother.

"I heard nothing."

Pons looked at him searchingly. "You have been playing billiards within the past twelve hours?"

The fellow started, and then smiled. "I've heard of your methods, Mr. Solar Pons. I have."

"Yes, there is chalk on your clothes. Did I not see you at the races yesterday week?"

"Quite possible."

Lord Penryn interrupted angrily. "I told you to keep away, Cadogan."

"Yes, I believe you did, My Lord," said Cadogan with an ill-concealed disrespect.

"You were in your room all evening?" pressed Pons.

"Yes, I was."

"And you, Lady Sybil?"

"Certainly, Mr. Pons. I was lying down, as I said. I retired to my room directly after dinner."

The Prime Minister covered his eyes with one hand and sighed. Lord Penryn fidgeted with his monocle. Both gentlemen were manifestly burning with impatience to be up and about doing something more active to recover the stolen papers.

Pons excused Lady Sybil Wector, and stood facing Cadogan. "I fancy it is not a shot in the dark to suggest to you, sir, that you have been gambling."

"Not at all. My brother could have told you."

"He did not."

"How deeply are you in?"

Cadogan got up leisurely and insolently. "I do not believe I am required to answer that question. Good night, Mr. Pons."

"Good night. Try the third horse in the second tomorrow." Cadogan turned on the threshold and gave Pons a rather amazed grin; then he was gone.

"I must apologize for my brother's rudeness," said Lord Penryn in some concern.

"Ah, not at all, My Lord. He was within his rights. I take it his gambling scrapes are a source of some difficulty."

"He has no respect for my position," said Lord Penryn with manifest pain. "He does not seem to realize that there are people who are only too ready to discredit me for what my brother is and does."

"But the papers, Mr. Pons!" cried the Prime Minister in a despairing voice.

"If you gentlemen will put yourself in my hands, I fancy I shall be able to produce them before the night is over."

Both the Prime Minister and the Secretary for European Affairs gazed at Pons in astonishment. It was Lord Penryn who broke the awkward silence.

"Forgive me. You startled me. Whatever you say, Mr. Pons."

"Very well then. There is not much time. Do you possess fire-arms, My Lord?"

"I have a brace of revolvers."

"We shall want them. We shall want the Prime Minister's car."

"It is at your disposal," said Mr. Somerset. Lord Penryn left the room.

"You may call off anyone guarding the house. Now." The Prime Minister looked uncertainly at Pons, but, after only a moment of reluctance, he went to the telephone, called a number, and gave the necessary directives. Then he returned to face Pons.

"If there is danger, Mr. Pons, perhaps we had better notify the police?"

"No, I believe that unnecessary."

Lord Penryn came back into the room, carrying his revolvers.

"They are loaded?"

"Ready for use, Mr. Pons."

"Good. We are going out. I fancy the four of us can deal with the matter. Has My Lord cancelled his reservations on the Dover train?"

"No, Mr. Pons, I forgot to do so."

"Capital! You may yet have use for them. Let us have faith. Now then, if Mr. Somerset will be so good as to instruct his chauffeur to follow my directions without deviation..."

"Certainly, Mr. Pons. We have come this far; we must go all the way."

"I fancy that is politically sound," said Pons dryly.

We left the house and got into the Prime Minister's car. Pons followed us into the *tonneau* after he had given instructions to the chauffeur. After the door closed behind him, the car pulled smoothly away.

"If I may ask – where are we going?" inquired Lord Penryn.

"My Lord, we are going only a very short distance. You shall see."

The car rolled up to a corner, turned, went up a city block, turned again, and continued until we were once more back on Park Lane; the head-lamps went out, the car glided smoothly to a stop. Lord Penryn looked out.

"Why, sir, we are only a few doors removed from my home!"

"Six doors, I believe."

"What are we doing here?"

"Waiting."

"Great Heaven! Upon what or whom are we waiting now?" burst out the Prime Minister.

"Why, we are waiting for a car which will drive out into Park Lane from one of these houses within the next half hour, unless I am sadly mistaken. When it does, we are going to follow it."

Lord Penryn and the Prime Minister exchanged shaken glances. I was myself beginning to feel a little shaken, confident as I was of Pons' methods. I took out a cigarette and would have lit it, but Pons stopped me.

"No smoking, Parker. Someone may see the glow of your cigarette."

The minutes ticked slowly past. Outside the clear sky vanished as a light fog began to form along the street. The Prime Minister and the Secretary for European Affairs could not conceal their uneasiness. Big Ben boomed out the hour of ten; it seemed incredible that everything; which had so far taken place since the Prime Minister called at our lodgings, had occurred within forty minutes.

We had not as long to wait, however, as Pons had supposed. Within a quarter of an hour of the time we had rolled to a stop along the kerb, a car swung out into Park Lane some distance ahead of us; Pons rapped smartly on the glass, and our car started up, almost noiselessly, and went for several blocks without turning up the head-lamps, for there was little traffic at this hour, and the fog was not yet thick. Then the dimmed lights were put cautiously on; our quarry was within easy sight ahead of us. Indeed, we had gone less than two miles before we came to a stop once more. Before us by seven or eight doors, stood the object of our pursuit.

"Here we go, Parker," said Pons. He pressed one of Lord Penryn's revolvers upon him. "My Lord, you will be driven up closer to the other car, which is standing just before the house we want. Parker and I are going around to the back; you gentlemen will oblige me by keeping the front of the house under reasonable surveillance. That is – if a man comes out of the front door, stop him; use the pistol if necessary. If a woman – make no effort to stop her. Stay in the car until Parker comes for you. Now, then, Parker – a clever game is afoot."

We slipped out of the car and ran down along a row of houses there before we darted down a little lane, made our way somewhat incautiously through a yew hedge, and emerged into an attractively planned garden. Pons pushed forward. By this time the fog had increased in density to such a degree that it required care to prevent one from blundering into shrubs or falling over statuary in the garden. Pons went directly up to the French windows opening from the house to the garden; behind them, a subdued light glowed, and, as I came up behind him and pressed my face, too, to the glass, I saw in that room the back of a heavily veiled woman, and across the table from her, a familiar, most sinister figure – that of the arch-criminal, Baron Ennesfred Kroll! At the moment of our coming, the woman had evidently just handed the Baron an envelope which he held in his hands, the contents of which he was just about to examine.

With adroit rapidity, Solar Pons kicked in the French windows and leveled his pistol at the man behind the table. "Baron Kroll, I believe."

An expression of baffled rage made the Baron's sinister features livid. His eyes darted from one to the other of us, to the open doors behind us, across the room to the door into the hall, through which his visitor had come.

"I assure you, my dear fellow, I would enjoy pulling the trigger. I advise you to be more circumspect."

At this instant the woman turned silently and fled.

"Let her go, Parker."

"You are not a police agent, Mr. Solar Pons."

"Sir, I am but a lowly house-breaker," retorted Pons. "I concede that that is considerably below the status of an extraordinary espionage agent and blackmailer, who is not above stooping to any kind of indecency to gain his ends. Parker, you may now summon the gentlemen in the car outside. Pray contain yourself, Baron – one false move, and Berlin will have the opportunity to give you a state funeral."

"You will regret this, Mr. Solar Pons."

Neither Pons nor Kroll had changed his position when I returned with Lord Penryn and the Prime Minister, both of whom preceded me into the room, so that I saw the astonishment and chagrin on their faces, for both had met Baron Kroll socially.

"I think you gentlemen know one another," said Pons suavely. "If My Lord will be so good as to take that envelope from Baron Kroll's hands – pray keep out of range, My Lord."

The Secretary for European Affairs, white with anger, stepped across the room and snatched the envelope from Baron Kroll.

"Pray examine it, Gentlemen. I fancy you will find in it state papers of such importance as to make it necessary to hold Baron Kroll as a foreign espionage agent."

Lord Penryn tore open the envelope with shaking fingers; he took out the folded foolscap within, unfolded it – and let out a low, inarticulate cry, while his features expressed the uttermost horror.

"Mr. Pons!" he cried in a trembling voice. "These are not the Strong-Cressington Plans!"

Pons flashed an urgent glance at the Prime Minister. "I believe Mr. Somerset will identify them as important state papers whose possession by Baron Kroll subjects him to appropriate prosecution under the Military Secrets Act."

The Prime Minister took the papers from Lord Penryn's trembling fingers, glanced at them, nodded, and stepped to Baron Kroll's telephone to call in members of the C. I. D. and order Baron Kroll under arrest. But, clearly, something had gone wrong, though Pons continued to talk and act as if Lord Penryn had made the error and not he, much to my perplexity. Was he then so determined to win the battle of wits with the Baron that he would willingly prosecute him for a theft of which he had not been guilty? But if Baron Kroll had not held in his hands the Strong-Cressington Plans, what papers had he held? He had not had time himself to examine them, for the envelope had not yet been fully opened when it had been passed into Lord Penryn's possession.

"I have met this man in my own house," said Lord Penryn at last in a voice heavy with accusation.

"Baron Kroll does not uphold the same standards as English gentlemen do," said Pons. "He carries on a secondary existence as a particularly obnoxious kind of leech who preys upon human failings by blackmailing his poor victims – not for money, for he has no need of that; I fancy Berlin makes him a generous allowance – but for anything in the way of state secrets which may be of value to his superiors. We shall discover his dupes in good time."

Baron Kroll bared his teeth in a kind of feral grimace. "I demand the right to communicate with my legal advisers."

"No, Baron, I think not," said Pons.

"At least let me be assured that my possessions will not be molested."

"Sir, I am no common house-breaker," answered Pons. "I assure you that *your* possessions will be left strictly alone."

Baron Kroll fenced with his eyes; a fine beading of perspiration became evident on his forehead. But he said nothing more until a Commissioner of New Scotland Yard and two Inspectors, one of them our old friend, Jamison, came to take Baron Kroll away.

They had hardly departed before both Lord Penryn and the Prime Minister crowded upon my friend.

"The Strong-Cressington Plans!" exclaimed the Secretary for European Affairs. "Where are they?"

"Pray be patient, Gentlemen," replied Pons, gravely looking at his watch. "It is not yet eleven. There is plenty of time to make the Dover train." He turned to me. "Now then, Parker, we have work to do. We shall look for letters, photographs, and the usual debris of blackmail."

Forthwith we began to turn the study upside down, but it was Pons who found, behind a large portrait on the wall, the receptacle which contained the things he sought. He took out packet after packet of letters, stuffing them into his pockets, occasionally calling out a name, until at last he had an answer.

"David Regan!" cried the Prime Minister. "He is my secretary."

"Then it was he who informed Baron Kroll that Lord Penryn had taken the Strong-Cressington Plans home with him!"

"Impossible!"

"Not at all. Here are his letters. I fancy the Baron paid handsomely for them, that he felt his indiscretions of more importance than state secrets. He telephoned the Baron, and the Baron telephoned another of his victims whose circumstances were even more pressing. She brought him the papers."

"But no!" cried Lord Penryn, agonized now. "Mr. Pons, you are playing with us."

"Not at all, My Lord. Come, we are finished here. We shall return to our lodgings if the Prime Minister will be so kind."

We drove rapidly to number seven, Praed Street, Pons discoursing all the way in the most agonizingly leisurely fashion on the foibles of men and women, and the ways of blackmailers, who invade the defenseless and put spiritual pressure upon even the strongest men and women with disastrous results.

"Come in, Gentlemen," invited Pons as the car drew up before number seven.

The Prime Minister and the Secretary for European Affairs had no recourse but to follow Pons. Once more inside our rooms, from which we had taken our leave less than two hours before, Pons divested himself of his Inverness and stood next to the fire, rubbing his hands and gazing at the clock.

"There is still time to make the Dover train, My Lord." He smiled and turned to the Prime Minister. "Mr. Somerset, be advised to do all in your power to see to it that Baron Kroll cannot operate any longer in England. I know that powerful pressure will be brought to bear, both by his government, and by his friends within our borders. Regan must be dismissed; but do not be too harsh with him; God knows what torture was applied by that scoundrel." He turned to Lord Penryn. "My Lord, do you know who stole the Strong-Cressington Plans?"

"Mr. Pons, I do not. I cannot think."

"It is of little moment, in the circumstances. You will come to it in good time; pray do not forget to be merciful. Here are the papers."

So saying, Pons reached into the inner pocket of his coat and gave the Strong-Cressington Plans into Lord Penryn's hands. Lord Penryn allowed them to fall open so that he could identify them.

"Thank God!" he cried.

The Prime Minister looked at Pons with a dark frown. "By what legerdemain did you accomplish that, Mr. Pons?"

"Remarkable! Astounding!" babbled Lord Penryn.

"You over-estimate my modest powers, Gentlemen. The Strong-Cressington Plans were not for one moment out of Lord Penryn's house until I carried them out myself."

"You!" exclaimed the Secretary for European Affairs.

"Ah, yes, My Lord. Surely it was obvious that no one had entered by the window? Even my friend Parker came close to seeing that. You will reflect that the broken glass from the pane of the French window lay on the stone sill, which is on the outside, not on the floor inside, thus indicating that the glass had been broken from the inside. Moreover, the strand of silk I picked from the jagged pane was taken from the inside. And, finally, the paper weight had been wrapped in the silk cloth for the purpose of breaking the window, thus accounting for the silk fibres adhering to it. Observing this, having the assurance of the Prime Minister that no one had entered or left the house since Lord Penryn's discovery of his loss, I had no alternative but to realize that the papers had not been delivered; therefore it followed that they were still in the house; and I had only to look in the most likely place, find them, and substitute the old papers which you, My Lord, had so kindly shown me but a few minutes before. At once I felt that the Strong-Cressington Plans might lead me to Baron Kroll, with whom I have had several encounters, ending less happily, ere this."

"Mr. Pons, allow me to congratulate you," said the Prime Minister.

"Thank you. But now, as you see, it is past eleven. I fancy there is still time for Lord Penryn to change his mind and take his holiday in the south of France, after all. Good night, Gentlemen."

After he had shown our distinguished clients from our lodgings, Pons returned to the packets of letters he had taken from Baron Kroll's study. He sought through them until he came to a small packet on cream stationery.

"Ah, here are Lady Sybil Wector's most indiscreet letters to young Alison Scott. Dear me! I fear Viscount Pellman would never have appreciated them; he is rather stodgy, and doubtless the Baron is well aware of it. Let us just slip them into an envelope and mail them back to Lady Sybil tonight. We shall see to it that the other letters reach their rightful owners tomorrow."

"It must elate you to have cornered Baron Kroll at last, Pons."

"Ah, how sanguine you are, Parker! You know the ways of the world. I have cornered him tonight – tomorrow, who knows? Diplomacy is not your field. But at least, I fancy England will be free of him for a time. There are darker days coming. I had rather he were permanently disposed of, but an alert opponent adds zest to the game, and, though he is a scoundrel, he is an opponent worthy of my mettle."

Nor was Pons wrong in his final deduction in the matter of Lord Penryn's lost holiday. Within a fortnight the Right Honorable Sackville Somerset did him the courtesy of sending word that Baron Ennesfred Kroll, claiming diplomatic immunity, had been given the support of the German embassy and had so escaped punishment under the Military Secrets Act. The Prime Minister, however, succeeded in having Baron Kroll stigmatized as *persona non grata* to His Majesty's Government, and thus forced his recall to Berlin, just as Solar Pons had foreseen.

XII

THE ADVENTURE OF THE MAN WITH THE BROKEN FACE

Early one evening in mid-September, on my return from an obstetrical case, I found my friend, Solar Pons, waiting upon the door with a pronounced air of expectation.

"I fancy we shall soon have a visitor, Parker," he said, "and I trust you are not too tired, for, unless I am much mistaken, we have before us a trip into the country."

"A client?"

"I believe so. For the past hour a young lady has been trying to make up her mind to call. Twice she has actually stopped her trap before the house, and once even got out of it with the evident intention of mounting to our lodgings. Each time she has gone away. On a third occasion she drove slowly past, eyeing these windows with considerable speculation. She paused at the corner and went into the chemist's shop there; since she carried nothing out with her and was gone for some time, I fancy that she was at the telephone, and, unless I err grievously, she was putting through a trunk call. No doubt it was she who telephoned early this afternoon and asked whether I would be at home this evening."

"Who is she?"

"She failed to give her name. Nevertheless, from what I have seen of her, she is obviously a young lady close to thirty years of age, of genteel breeding, to whom the making of decisions is rather new and comes with patent difficulty. She is somewhat nervous, and at this time much agitated. Clearly, something has taken place for which she cannot account; she does not want to go to the police, but she does not really want to take anyone at all into her confidence; yet she appears to have no alternative, for here she comes once again. And yes, this time I fancy she has made up her mind. She has stopped; she is getting out; there is a marked air of determination about her... Now then!"

He turned from the windows, rubbing his hands together in expectation, and gazed, as was his habit, toward the bell, which, quite as if it were a living entity in a little drama and had been given its cue by Pons' glance, rang immediately. And, in a very little while, Mrs. Johnson had shown into the room a young woman whose appearance did indeed suggest many of the descriptive facets Pons had voiced.

She was in her late twenties, and clearly a spirited young woman, though at the moment in manifest distress. Her hair was worn long, and it was ash-blonde in color; she had good reason to shun the use of cosmetics, for her color was good, her cheeks and lips naturally red, and her blue eyes strong and direct, with heavy dark lashes. She was dressed for riding, in rather masculine apparel which did not however for an instant conceal her femininity. She had no difficulty choosing between us, and identified Pons without hesitation.

"Please forgive this delay, Mr. Pons. I telephoned you this afternoon. I am Sylvia Norton."

"Pray sit down, Miss Norton. Clearly, the problem which impelled you to come to me has not in any way improved since you reached London, as you hoped it might have done when you telephoned home a little while ago."

Miss Norton smiled. "I am sure that even my father could not have taken exception to my seeking your assistance, Mr. Pons."

"Ah, so your father is missing, Miss Norton. I seem to think your features familiar. Are you, by any chance, the daughter of Captain Hyatt Norton?"

"I am."

Hyatt Norton was known as one of the minor heroes of Britain for his valiance in attempting to save a valuable cargo of diamonds when the ship of which he was the skipper, went down in a storm off the Cape of Good Hope three years before. He had, indeed, brought back to Britain a part of that cargo, at great risk to his life, the sole survivor of his crew, managing after almost incredible hardships to make his way back to his native country after a period of being marooned on an island where he had had time to repair his damaged boat. He had retired to his home somewhere on the coast north of London, and had sought only to live down the public acclaim which had followed his homecoming with one of the chests of diamonds.

"Perhaps you had better tell us your story as you see fit, Miss Norton. Obviously, it does not begin with your father's disappearance, for something must have taken place prior to that, since you suggest you talked over calling someone in."

"Yes, that is right, Mr. Pons. It begins four days ago, to be exact. As you know, we live between Maldon and Tollesbury, on the coast road north of London; our house is modest, one storey in height, but somewhat rambling. It is set round with trees, except for a small garden in the rear. My father, my aunt – my mother's sister – and I live there alone. We had a servant at one time, but had to let him go, for he was surly and ill-tempered; since that time we have managed very well by ourselves. We have always lived a quiet life. My father never liked the publicity which attended his homecoming three years ago. He has always been a genuine country type, and seemed to be happy just idling in the villages or hunting on occasion, or keeping the garden. He did not read very much, though we subscribe to the *Times*, and he read this faithfully, now and then writing letters for its columns. Our existence there has been uneventful, save for a single instance, which I regret to say was caused by my father's objection to my fiancé, an objection to which naturally I paid no attention.

"On the fourth of this month, I could not help noticing that my father was preoccupied and restless ever since receiving the morning post. I guessed that he had had a letter disturbing him, but he had received only two letters, and both were obviously from tradesmen, one in London, and the other in Maldon. He ate very little that day, and by nightfall he was nervous to such a degree that he put us all a little on edge. My aunt went to bed quite early, as is her custom, but my father and I stayed up. We both sat in the study, which is a long, low and very pleasant room facing the sea, he at the table, and I beside the fireplace, reading.

"I think it must have been about mid-evening when I was aware, with that intuition most women have, of something wrong; perhaps it was the absolute stillness of my father that made me look up. But I did look up, I looked over at him, and Mr. Pons, I saw my father staring at the windows with an expression of such abject terror on his face, so startling and fearful an expression that I could not even yield to impulse and cry out; his eyes seemed to be starting from his head, his mouth was agape, and his forehead was beaded with perspiration; at the same time his hands were clenched white upon the table before him. I forced myself to look cautiously over the back of the chair, and so I too had a glimpse of that horrible thing my father had seen. It was – or perhaps I had better say I think it was a man's face, but Mr. Pons, what a face! It was a ghastly travesty of a face; it looked like only part of a face – I would describe it as a *broken* face, for part of it seemed broken in. It was horrible, and if it had not vanished, I do not know what would have happened to me. But it did; it seemed to dissolve even as I looked at it. Then I found my voice and called to my father.

"To my surprise, he said only that he was not feeling well; apparently he had eaten something which did not agree with him. He said not a word about that horrible face at the window, with the result that I did not mention it, either. I thought this most peculiar, but I felt that in good time he would speak what was on his mind.

"But he did not. I saw that he was not himself in the morning. I had heard him up and about during the night. I myself finally broached the subject to him, and suggested that if something were wrong, it might not be amiss to report the matter to the police. He was surprisingly gruff.

"'Nothing's wrong,' he said shortly. 'And let me hear nothing further of the police – they are worse than inefficient.'

"'A private investigation, then,' I said.

"'Nonsense. You are growing into an hysterical young woman.'

"That was all he said. Nothing further happened that day, and on the following day, that is, yesterday, the sixth, I was hostess to a little garden party for some of the ladies from Tollesbury. As a result, I was very tired last night, and so was my aunt; both of us went to bed early. I left my father in the study, reading the *Times*.

"Mr. Pons, that was the last time I saw him.

"When I came into the study this morning, I found the light still burning, and the paper open, just as my father had left it. Across the room, one of the French windows stood partly ajar. I went over and closed it, for the September morning air is not warm. Then I folded the paper and turned out the light, thinking at first that my father had forgotten to return to the study, though he had not done such a thing before. About quarter of an hour later, it occurred to me that my father was not likely to be so remiss, and I became alarmed; I went to his room and discovered that his bed had not been slept in. I then began a systematic examination of his clothes, to discover if possible whether or not any of his clothing was missing. Nothing was gone, nothing but what he had been wearing when last I had seen him – that is, his trousers, bedroom slippers, a white shirt, and a smoking jacket. And, I suppose, his underclothing.

"I hesitated to take any immediate action, but by noon, both my aunt and I were convinced that something had happened to my father. This was made all the more pointed when we discovered that someone had pulled open drawers of my father's study table during the night, and, though nothing seemed to have been taken, still, it could not have been done by my father, for he would not have left such disorder. Shortly after this discovery, I telephoned you. I waited then for some time, lest my father return; when he did not, I came to London. Even then I hesitated, knowing his antipathy to my course; but, after telephoning my aunt, and ascertaining that he had not yet returned, I hesitated no longer."

Pons sat for a few moments in contemplative silence. "This face you saw," he said presently, "impressed you as being broken. Could you elucidate that, Miss Norton?"

"I don't know, Mr. Pons. It was just – well, horribly smashed. As I remember it, it looked as if one side of his face had been just – well, caved in, and never attended to; it was something like that."

"Its effect on your father was fully as frightening as it was on you. Yet he made no mention of it. How do you interpret that?"

"Knowing him, I should say it was because he did not want to frighten me; he did not know I had seen it."

"I see. What do you expect of me?"

"I want you to find him, Mr. Pons. If possible, I want you to come with me now and solve this horrible mystery – find my father and solve the riddle of that terrible broken face."

Pons gazed at her thoughtfully. "Very well, Miss Norton. Your problem intrigues me, though I cannot make promises. Let us just lose no time getting to the scene, for, unless I am very much mistaken, your visitor may return."

"Oh, I hope not!"

"I have a fancy to encounter him," said Pons.

It was well past mid-evening when we arrived at the house on the coast road above Maldon, and, since the night was dark, save for a few stars and a sickle moon low in the western heavens, it was not possible to see much of the place. Miss Norton's aunt, an austere woman with a forbidding countenance, welcomed us; she wore black hair drawn back from a parting in the middle to be knotted behind her head, and gold-rimmed spectacles; she had been waiting up for us. Miss Norton put her horse and trap away, and came around into the house from the opposite side; she had introduced us to her aunt, and the older woman, now that her niece was once again at home, withdrew, leaving us to be taken to the study at Pons' request.

"You may leave us now, if you like, Miss Norton," said Pons.

"I have a duty to perform, Mr. Pons. I have brought you gentlemen all the way from London without dinner. At least let me make you some tea."

"Ah, that will be welcome indeed."

When she had left the room, I turned to Pons eagerly and asked, "What do you make of it?"

Pons did not look up from his task of examining the table and chair where Norton had been sitting when last seen. He shook his head grimly and muttered, "Dark waters, Parker; dark waters."

I was nettled at this ambiguous reply. "But surely there are some aspects of it which present no problem to you?" I cried.

"There is no aspect of the problem which gives me cause for second thought, unless it is the present whereabouts of Hyatt Norton; and I believe I could make a good guess at that, too.

No, there is not much opportunity given us for speculation, Parker."

"You know all, then?"

"Not quite all," said Pons modestly. "Surely it is obvious, Parker?"

"I confess that nothing at all is obvious."

"Very well then. Let us re-examine the matter as Miss Norton related it to us. Let us take the man with the broken face. It is certainly not to be doubted that Norton knew who it was looking into his study, for if he had not known, why then his hesitation to confide in his daughter? I fear the theory that he might frighten her does not hold water. Accepting that, then, we must also accept the fact that Norton had good reason for not confiding in his daughter or in anyone, and he had the same reason for not calling in the police."

"Presumably then, the man with the broken face meant him no harm."

"That is a *non sequitur*, Parker. Think again."

"I don't follow you."

"If he meant Norton harm, there was clearly greater harm threatening from another direction. So much we can safely assume. Now, Miss Norton said that the French doors were ajar. Very well. Norton opened them. The September night was chill; he did not open the doors for fresh air. He opened them for a visitor. Let us just step outside and see what evidence we can find."

He suited his actions to his words, and I followed him. Immediately beyond a flagstone terrace there, Pons turned his flash upon a narrow lane between two flower-beds, where footprints were clearly manifest. He read these footprints with a facility that was beyond my own slowness.

"Ah! Our fellow with the broken face limps. He has a leg injury then. Or no, I retract that, Parker. He has a wooden foot or leg – see, the difference between the prints is clear and unmistakable in its implications; this foot has not bent; the other has."

"There are other footprints," I pointed out.

"Norton's," answered Pons shortly. "He walked away with him. Let us assume they had something to talk about, and Norton wished to talk out of hearing of the house."

"You suggest that Norton let the fellow in?"

"Or went out to him. It is all the same. He left the study willingly. Afterward, the other fellow came back alone. What does that suggest to you?"

"Foul play."

"Apart from sounding like a cinema melodrama, I daresay you are right."

We returned to the study, where Pons' keen eyes soon lighted upon a number of copies of the *Times*, neatly stacked on a half-filled book-shelf. These he took over to the table, and commenced to look through them, while he continued to speculate about the problem.

"As for the nocturnal visitor who so badly frightened the Nortons," he said, "what does his description suggest to your medical mind?"

"The victim of an accident."

"Ah, yes, but in what circumstances?"

"Presumably in a place removed from proper care. I submit he did not have the medical attention necessary to prevent the malformation of his facial wounds."

"Capital, Parker! You improve with time and experience. I commend that fact to you for further study."

At this moment, Miss Norton returned to the study with tea and sandwiches she had made up, profusely apologizing again for having so thoughtlessly deprived us of our evening meal. We fell to without delay, Pons, however, carrying on an oblique conversation about Norton's ill-fated ship, which was the *Monsoon*, a small, privately-owned merchant ship not usually carrying such valuable cargo as she had carried on her last trip. She had foundered and been fired during a storm off the African coast, and the small crew had taken to the boats. Norton and two of the men had gone last, Norton carrying with him two small chests containing the diamond shipment. One of the men had died on the second day out, and the other three days later; during a squall, Norton had lost one of the chests. He had clung to the other for dear life and, after being cast upon an island, where he had time to repair his boat, he had set out for England, faithfully discharging as much of his duty as possible by delivering the partial shipment of diamonds to its consignee. So he had been acclaimed as one of England's heroes of the sea.

It was an old story to both of us, but Pons listened with unfeigned interest to Miss Norton's telling of it, asking questions from time to time, and generally putting our charming hostess at her ease, despite her natural concern for her father's welfare. I sat pondering Pons' cryptic charge, but could not find it possible to pursue that trend of thought beyond the boundaries I had already achieved, and these were, manifestly, such as any medical man would naturally reach.

After Miss Norton removed the remains of the meal, Pons turned again to the *Times*, and, after glancing through an issue, tossed it, with a smile of satisfaction, to me. "Now, then, Parker, exercise your ingenuity."

I saw that the paper was the issue of September fourth. "You assume that because Norton was not agitated by letters, he saw something in the *Times* that troubled him?"

"Surely that is obvious?"

I went through the *Times* with care, and found nothing significant.

Pons was impatient. "There is one item which ought to be of interest to a retired seaman."

"Oh, that!" I cried. I read it aloud, having found it again. "'James Smith, seaman, was released from Seaman's Hospital yesterday after treatment for exposure and malnutrition. Mr. Smith, the victim of an accident at sea, and suffering from amnesia, was rescued from a raft near Dakar last month.'"

"I submit it was that which agitated Norton."

"I make nothing of it."

"'James Smith' is surely as good as no name at all."

"The man is admittedly an amnesiac," I protested.

"I do not recall that the account speaks of his amnesia as in the present tense. He was suffering from amnesia at the time he was picked up. He would not be released if he were still an amnesiac. Or would he?"

"No, of course not."

"Very well then. I submit that James Smith is very probably not his name. He is described as a 'seaman.' Now that is ambiguous, to say the very least. If a seaman and the victim of an accident at sea, why is his ship not named? It is not too much to assume that the failure to do so lies in the twin facts that Mr. Smith cannot remember, and that James Smith cannot be identified by any registry. Assuming then, that our Mr. Smith is no longer an amnesiac, he must surely have had a very good reason for clinging to his common name and for making full use of his previous amnesia. In short, it is not too much to suppose that it was not desired by Mr. Smith that his ship be made known. I put it to you that Norton's reading of that paragraph was fully as cognizant as mine."

"But it fails to hang together."

"Does it, indeed? I wonder."

"Your inference is plain – but I fail to see any kind of motive."

"Suppose you start over, Parker, and take nothing for granted. You may quite possibly have a different light on the matter."

On this note we retired for the night.

In the morning Pons roused me before the rest of the household was up. He led the way back to the study and out through the French windows, where he picked up the trail of the two men and followed it until it was lost in the lawn beyond the flower-beds, then discovered it again leading in the direction of the seacoast, and continued to follow it until it was once again lost. However, it was plain that the route taken by the two men was north along the coast in the direction of Tollesbury. The coast at this point, which was not far above the Blackwater River estuary, was singularly broken, and, as he went along, Pons scrutinized the shore sharply, often weaving in and out from the coast-line, until he came to a point of high ground about half a mile from Norton's house; there he paused and examined the ground with close attention.

The clear evidence of some kind of struggle showed there.

The edge of the high ground had been broken away, and it appeared that a heavy object had gone over into the sea there. "I fancy this is where Norton met his end." said Pons grimly.

"Dead?"

"I think no other alternative presents itself."

"But for what motive?"

"That should not be difficult to arrive at."

"If he went in here, then surely we'll not find him. The sea will have taken him."

"Not necessarily. The chance is equally good that his body is lodged somewhere among the rocks along the coast here. Let us just look carefully about."

So saying, he took from his pocket a small pair of binoculars and, lying down on the ground, began to examine the sea's edge. I looked around and decided that the man with the broken face, if indeed it were he who had brought Norton to this spot, had chosen the spot well; for it was lonely, and little traveled; the gulls screamed here without interruption, and shore birds nested under the overhanging crags. If any outcry had sounded, surely no human ear but that of the murderer had heard it.

An exclamation from Pons interrupted my reverie. “Look there!” said he, handing me the glasses and indicating a rocky cove some distance up the coast. “I daresay that is our quarry.”

“It certainly appears to be a body,” I agreed.

“Come.”

Nor was Pons mistaken, for there, when we came to the rocks in that cove, was the body of the late Captain Hyatt Norton; the tide had doubtless wedged it where we found it. It was that of a portly gentleman of well past middle-age; he was grizzled and square-jawed, with a white moustache and iron-grey hair, and his dress fitted Miss Norton’s description of that worn by her father when last seen.

“Your show, I think, Parker.”

“Bruise on the head,” I said. “Possible fracture. Not fatal.”

“Drowned, then?”

“In all probability. Pushed off the shore while unconscious.”

“Evidence of murder?”

“Difficult.”

Pons took his place beside the body. “His shirt has been opened.” He drew away the shirt as he spoke. Norton’s trousers, too, had slipped down a little, exposing a portion of his waist. Pons’ action disclosed a slightly discolored band of flesh which apparently ran around Norton’s body. “Ah, what do you make of that, Parker?”

“A belt mark, I should say.”

“But he is plainly wearing his belt, which is much narrower than this band. What he wore there was surely worn next to his skin.”

“Certainly.”

“That suggests one of those belts in which one carries valuables, eh? What do you say, Parker?”

“I agree.”

"So, then, it is gone. The fellow got it. Yet he did not get everything he sought, or he would not have returned to the house."

"Elementary," I said.

"And unless I am in grievous error, he is still skulking in the vicinity and will pay another visit to the house. We must plan to be there. But for the present, we shall have to convey news of this melancholy discovery to Miss Norton and her aunt, and, if possible, to prevail upon them to have the body removed into Maldon, with themselves in attendance."

The final act of this curious drama took place in the Norton house that evening. Both Miss Norton and her aunt had yielded to Pons' importunings that they spend the night in Maldon, which was neither too far away nor too close to the house. Pons assumed that the murderer of Captain Norton was in hiding somewhere along the coast, but not far from the house; certainly he might be expected to be ensconced somewhere close enough to enable him to keep the Norton house under surveillance from time to time.

I confessed that I could not follow Pons. Miss Norton, despite her grief at news of her father's death, had steadfastly submitted to questions, and had divulged the fact that her father kept a modest account in the Maldon bank; she had no knowledge of anything of value kept in the house itself, apart from certain antiques which had more intrinsic than actual value. Nor were there any papers, to the best of her knowledge, which could be of any worth to anyone apart from members of the family. She could not explain what thing of value in the house might attract the attention of a burglar for the ladies, as well as the constabulary, had been given the suggestion by Pons that Captain Norton had taken out after a burglar and had met his death in some manner along the coast. He had been extremely careful, I observed in some perplexity, to avoid any direct suggestion of murder.

No sooner were the ladies gone, however, than Pons was in the late Captain Norton's bedroom. "This, it would seem to me, is the proper hiding-place for anything of value Norton might have."

"All the evidence is that he wore his valuables in his money-belt."

"Presumptive evidence, only. His murderer came back to the house, remember. At least he has reason to think there is something more. So let us begin."

Almost the first thing we discovered was a loaded revolver.

"So our friend, the late Captain, was not entirely unprepared," observed Pons. "He kept his weapon ready and in good condition."

"A not necessarily indicative precaution."

"In the light of events, most significant. Yet he did not have it with him when the end came."

"Apparently not."

Pons went on searching, going through the bed, the bureau, even examining the chairs and taking up the rug in the hope of finding some receptacle in the floor. But there was nothing; there was nothing in floor, furniture, or walls.

"What the devil are you looking for?" I asked finally, in some exasperation.

"Treasure," answered Pons without a smile.

"Treasure, indeed!" I protested. "If we had some idea of what to look for...."

"Well, be patient, Parker. It is not money; it may be gold, silver, jewels. Let us persevere."

He sat down on the late Captain's bed and looked soberly around him. We had examined everything in the room with one exception; that was a large, framed print of a merchant ship which was apparently that of the *Monsoon*; and it was upon this that Pons' eye lighted at last, at first in speculation, and then with a gleaming light of calculation. Abruptly he sprang up, strode across the room, and took down the picture.

"If it is here at all, it is in this."

He turned it over, and disclosed that the back of the picture was unlike that of any other picture we had ever seen. It was not only tacked shut, but also taped quite heavily. Pons gave the back of the picture a sharp blow, and then shook it; a faint rattling was his only answer.

"Now, then," said Pons. "Let us just take this with us."

We retired to the study, where Pons carefully deposited the picture on one of the book-shelves, setting it upright, so that it might readily be seen by anyone entering the room from outside.

It was now that last hour of dusk in which darkness comes upon the country, and already the study was murky with twilight. I would have lit the lamp, but Pons stopped me.

"No light, Parker. Let him assume that the house has been deserted." He took from his pocket the late Captain Norton's revolver and thrust it at me. "I suggest you take this. I'll arm myself with the fireplace poker."

"Am I to use it?"

"Since our man has already killed once, he will in all probability not hesitate to do so again. If it becomes necessary, fire. Now, then, dispose yourself. I suggest you take that seat beside the hearth; I will sit opposite you in the farther corner, facing the French windows."

"You expect him to come in at that point?"

"That is the familiar entrance for him. And so far, he has not gone beyond the study. So he will in all likelihood enter by the windows to continue his search where he left off the other night."

It was after midnight before there was any sound to reward our patience. Then it was a startling one – the blow of some hard object against glass, and the tinkling breaking of glass. I felt, even if I could not see, a hand reaching in through the broken pane to unlock the French doors. The doors opened and closed; then there was that infinitesimal sound of footsteps moving carefully across the floor. I turned my head slowly in an effort to look in the direction of the sound.

At that moment a match was struck, and I got a full view of a hideous travesty of a human face – of ghastly, broken features incredibly pitiful and terrible at once – before the fellow's hand came up and shielded his eyes from the little flame. He walked across to the desk, unaware of Pons or me, and calmly lit the lamp there, certain that no one occupied the house at the moment, and sure that no one passing on the coast road would become suspicious at sight of lamplight in the house.

No sooner had the light gone up, I was sure, than he would see Pons. But not so; what he saw instead was that picture of the *Monsoon* Pons had cleverly put up where anyone standing where the intruder now stood would be certain to see it. With an oath, the man with the broken face darted around the desk, seized the picture, and turned.

Thus he saw Pons.

"Stand where you are," said Pons.

But he had already observed that Pons was armed only with a poker; dropping his find, he whipped out a knife, bent his arm back, and let fly. Alarmed at Pons' danger, and sickened anew at sight of the fury mounting in that bestial travesty of a human face, I lost my head and fired twice.

I heard Pons' exclamation of dismay, for he had parried the knife with the poker easily enough; then, simultaneously, he and I sprang toward him just as the man with the broken face toppled forward with a little moan.

Pons caught him and lowered him to the rug, whipping out his handkerchief to stanch his wound, which was, I saw at a glance, close to being mortal. One bullet had apparently failed to hit the destined target, but had instead passed through the picture of the *Monsoon*, with a result as startling as it was unexpected, for through the rent in the picture had come a stream of rough, uncut stones that gleamed and shone in the light of the lamp!

"Lend a hand, Parker," cried Pons. "We may save him."

I was brought to earth instantly by Pons' irritated commands, and came to my knees beside the man with the broken face. I tore open his shirt and carried on from where Pons had left off, for Pons was now engaged in encouraging the victim of my shot to speak.

"Come, man – you may be dying. Your name?"

"Farway – Herbert Farway."

"Of the ship *Monsoon*, sailing under Norton with a cargo of diamonds?"

"Aye, ye know it, then. Ye know 'im for what 'e was – as black a scoundrel as ever sailed the seas! 'E's done for now, and I'm glad I did it. I'd do it again – and again – and again for what 'e done to me."

He was breathing somewhat easier now, and was in no immediate danger of lapsing into unconsciousness. Watching me, he was reassured by my attitude, and he began to talk, rapidly, as if he must tell everything before he died.

And the story he told was as horrible as his tortured features, a tale of deceit and murder, of theft and hypocrisy. For the late Captain Hyatt Norton, far from being a hero of the sea, was exactly the opposite. His ship had gone down much as he had told of it; but he had departed from truth thereafter. He and his two companions, of whom Farway was one, had arrived safely enough on an island off the coast of Africa, and had set about to repair the boat. Moreover, both little trunks of diamonds were with them, and safe; neither had fallen into the sea. When they were ready to set forth again, Norton had set upon his companions, killed the other, and left Farway for dead, horribly beaten. But Farway had not died; he had been discovered by a party of blacks from the mainland, blown off their course by a gale, taken off the island into the African forests, and brought back to a semblance of health. He had finally set out from that country in one of the blacks' canoes, but this had given out, and he had set to work to build a raft, from which he was rescued. It had taken three years to get back to England, and he lost no time thereafter in finding out where Norton lived, hoping he still lived so that he could avenge himself, for he knew Norton meant to take part of the diamonds. And so he had; he had come in along the coast in the night, hidden one of the little cases of diamonds, and then made a show of loyalty and duty by delivering the other and all these years taking the acclaim of his country as a hero and living safely on his gains, while marketing his diamonds in Ostend and Amsterdam by boat directly across the channel. So much he had learned from Norton on that fatal walk, when Norton, hoping to rid himself of Farway, had offered him part of those ill-gotten diamonds, and rebelled when Farway wanted them all. It was Farway who was that James Smith whose discharge from that London hospital had filled Captain Hyatt Norton with that intuitive uneasiness which heralded the long-delayed payment for his crime, for, though he had believed in Farway's death, he had never been certain, and Farway's appearance that first night, with his horribly broken face the plain evidence of Norton's homicidal attack had with every reason frightened and terrified him. And Farway had got the diamonds in Norton's belt, and some of his money, too. The rest of the stones lay there gleaming in the light beside the dying man.

There was nothing more to be said. Farway died within an hour; nothing could be done to save him, and he seemed to have lost the will to live.

"Dark waters," murmured Pons again. "And they must remain undisturbed – for the sake of that poor girl, Norton's daughter. We shall manage to restore the diamonds to their rightful owners and persuade them and the insurance company to keep silent without telling the true details of the matter. A burglar shot – Captain Norton's accidental fall from the shore to the rocks below. Yes, I fancy that interpretation will do as well as any. Surely nothing can be gained by bringing any more misery into Miss Norton's life."

For more details and a full list of titles:

visit https://www.hachetteindia.com/home/yellowbacks

WELCOME BACK TO THE GOLDEN AGE

H. Rider
Haggard
MR. MEESON'S WILL

Melville
Davisson Post
MASTER OF MYSTERIES
THE COMPLETE UNCLE ABNER COLLECTION

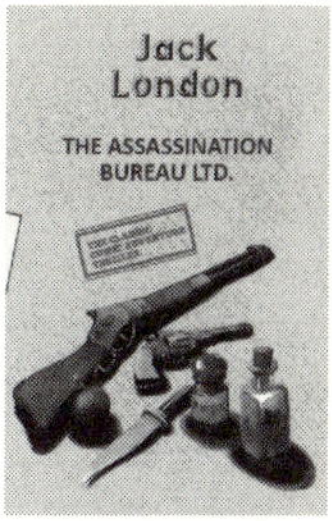
Jack
London
THE ASSASSINATION
BUREAU LTD.

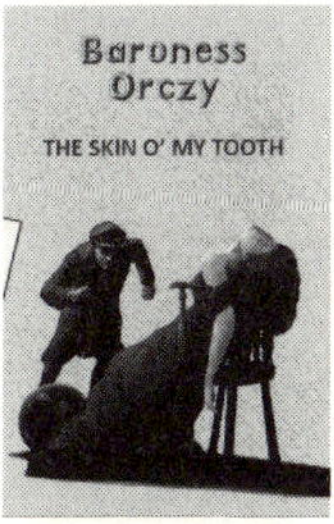
Baroness
Orczy
THE SKIN O' MY TOOTH

Earl Derr
Biggers
SEVEN KEYS TO BALDPATE

Horace
Walpole
THE CASTLE OF OTRANTO

Sexton
Blake
THE SEXTON BLAKE
COLLECTION
VOLUME 1

Francis
Beeding
THE HOUSE OF
DR. EDWARDES

A. E. W.
Mason
AT THE VILLA ROSE

Fergus
Hume
THE MILLIONAIRE
MYSTERY

Donald
Henderson
A VOICE LIKE VELVET

Richard
Hallas
YOU PLAY THE BLACK AND
THE RED COMES UP